Praise for Kay Langdale

'This haunting and beautifully written novel about love will linger in your mind long after you've turned the final, satisfying page'
Lucy Dillon on *Away From You*

'The sympathetic understanding of [Langdale's] characters, the even-handed exposition of different types of mothering and the beauty of her crystal-clear prose all come together to make this a must read'
Red on *Her Giant Octopus Moment*

'Langdale is a wonderful writer, plots beautifully and is brilliant at showing her characters' inner worlds'
Daily Mail

'A compelling exploration of the nature of grief . . . a moving tale of motherhood and morality'
Oxford Times on *Away From You*

'Readable, poignant . . . the author's skill is to woo the reader into empathising with conflicting viewpoints'
The Sunday Times

'Thought-provoking' ★★★★★
Woman's Own on *Her Giant Octopus Moment*

'An endearing child-heroine and a controversial moral question make *Her Giant Octopus Moment* a must-read'
Good Housekeeping

'Langdale's psychological intelligence informs every angle of a thoroughly contemporary tragedy'
The Times on *Away From You*

Also by Kay Langdale

Her Giant Octopus Moment
Choose Me
Away from You
The Comfort of Others

What the Heart Knows (Rowolht, Germany)
Redemption (Transita, published as *If Not Love*
by Thomas Dunne Books, St Martin's Press)

KAY LANGDALE

The Way Back to Us

HODDER

First published in Great Britain in 2017 by Hodder & Stoughton
An Hachette UK company

1

Copyright © Kay Langdale 2017

A CIP catalogue record for this title is available from the British Library

Paperback ISBN 978 1 473 61836 7
Ebook ISBN 978 1 473 61837 4

Typeset in Plantin Light 11.25/16 pt by Palimpsest Book Production Limited,
Falkirk, Stirlingshire

Printed and bound by Clays Ltd, St Ives plc

Hodder & Stoughton policy is to use papers that are natural,
renewable and recyclable products and made from wood grown in
sustainable forests. The logging and manufacturing processes are expected
to conform to the environmental regulations of the country of origin.

Hodder & Stoughton Ltd
Carmelite House
50 Victoria Embankment
London EC4Y 0DZ

www.hodder.co.uk

For Barbara Bradshaw, cara amica.

How does it happen that our lives can drift
far from our selves, while we stay trapped in time . . .
Carol Ann Duffy, *Rapture*

Anna

I wake abruptly with a terrible start, because it feels like I'm holding something very, very precious, and I've dropped it. When I snap my eyes open, heart thumping, it's always just fallen from my arms. It's Teddy I'm dropping, even though I never actually have. In my half-waking, half-sleeping state I see it happen, as if I am both in and out of my thrumming body.

Teddy's still a baby in the dream, and he's wearing a striped red-and-white romper. My right hand is cradling his head, and my left hand is curled up and over his knees. Looking at us – and I can see that my crossed elbows are an additional hammock beneath him – dropping him couldn't feasibly happen, but it's always the sensation I have, my mouth parched, my arms flailing.

The babygro – the red-and-white-striped one – is an accurate memory. I'm confident of that. I must still have it, neatly folded in a cupboard somewhere. We're not by ourselves in the dream. The health visitor who was assigned to Teddy is there too, a woman who yawned constantly, her hand barely covering her mouth, her broad face placid and bovine. Perhaps she was bored, or tired, or maybe in need of more oxygen than the series of rooms provided.

The sequence begins as I put him in the scale pan, and he lies there, soft as butter, wearing a cotton-knit hat shaped like a strawberry. The hat accentuates the colour of his lips, and his tiny Cupid's bow, and I resist stretching across to kiss him because I know it would get in the way of the weighing, the measuring, the calibrating, and the jotting in the red book with her cheap biro that smudges. And so, while the health visitor writes, I am self-contained, sitting with my hands in my lap, my back straight, surreptitiously checking my watch, and with just the beginnings of a sprightly fretfulness that Isaac will shortly finish school and I will not be at the playground gate.

The health visitor looks at her notes and her tick-box charts, and gestures to indicate that I can pick Teddy up again, and as I lean to gather him to me, that's where the accurate recall stops. Instead, there's the chest-punching horror that I've dropped him, my arms flung inexplicably wide, my palms facing ceilingward. When I look down to where he should surely be falling towards my feet, I can't see him there either. There is nothing other than a dizzying blackness that tilts and shifts around me, as if we are in fact both tumbling in free fall, our arms and legs spread wide like stars, with Teddy invisible beyond my reach, cartwheeling down through space.

If I look over my shoulder – and the room is shrinking behind me and is suddenly bleached of all colour – the health visitor is still sitting plumply by her scale pan, her pen poised in mid-air. Her expression doesn't change, however many times I dream it. She is not startled, or concerned. She doesn't even drop her pen. What her face mostly shows is disappointment. She is clearly disappointed in my failure to scoop up Teddy properly.

Tom

Is it Eliza? It takes a moment, looking through the smoked grey glass of the hotel in Geneva, to confirm that it is. Her swimming costume is red; a red so bright she is as vivid as a scarlet poppy when she walks out from the changing room. The colour is unexpected, almost startling. Her work clothes are usually muted – neutrals and greys, and sometimes a blue that is almost black. Occasionally her lips are red; the only clue that would suggest her choice of swimming costume. When they are, I find it hard to look directly at her as she speaks, instead focusing on her temple, or her hairline, or the space beyond her. She wears blouses that are cleverly tailored and which have neat little tucks and seams and move entirely with her. A seamstress would understand the mechanics of that. I do not, but recognise that they are pieces she must have chosen with care and insight.

Eliza walks to the poolside shower, tilts back her head, and momentarily lets the water drench her. She shivers as it touches her skin. The act of observing her, even though in a public place, seems an intrusion. She pauses momentarily by the deep end of the pool and leans to look out of the window at the street below. The snow, which began thawing earlier, has continued to do so, and the pavement is slushy with gritty melt. It is much warmer than yesterday; unseasonably so. She won't need to wear the coat with the high lambskin collar that she wore on the way from the airport.

From her cupped palm Eliza produces goggles, which she

snaps on with a surprisingly practised hand, licking her fingertip and quickly tracing the lens. She blows out through her lips, rises to her tiptoes, lifts her arms above her head and stretches.

Anna and the boys look up at me from my iPhone screen saver. Isaac is standing next to Anna in the garden, his hands held behind him like a soldier standing to attention. I look at the photo fixedly to navigate myself back to them. Anna is smiling, but – seeing her freshly in the clean Swiss light of this calm and neat breakfast room – it occurs to me that it is a grim, stoical smile, which ends at the corners of her lips and is firmly staunched by the clamped press of her jaw. Teddy is on her lap, his head spooled back on her collarbone.

Time for a quick chat?

Her response is instant.

What do you think?

Perhaps I should send an emoji with a downturned mouth and a question mark beside it. Perhaps then she would respond. Likely it is just one of those mornings and she is best left alone. She has said, many times, 'Just let me get on.'

My gaze is drawn again to Eliza, who dips her chin to her chest and dives in. Without pause, she begins to swim an efficient crawl, her hands meeting momentarily at the front of her reach so that she seems to spear effortlessly between strokes. Her body skates through the water.

I should text my assistant and confirm the time of today's flight back from Geneva. The 10 a.m. meeting should not overrun; most of what was required was successfully completed yesterday. Eliza, at the boardroom table, going through the PowerPoint presentation, her grey eyes fixed purposefully on the client. I make the image of her dissolve, as if it is occluded by blotches of snow.

The waitress appears with the breakfast menu which is loaded with waffles, pancakes, Viennoiserie.

'Just an Americano, please.'

Am I only a heartbeat away from sitting here old and unfit, instead of forty-two and in reasonable shape? The other guests at the hotel are mostly the former. Perhaps the pool was built next to the breakfast room as a kind of subliminal taunt.

Eliza is still swimming, completing each length with a neat turn, her hand outstretched to touch the pool wall.

I'm reading a newspaper when she arrives beside me, dressed in a skirt that is possibly blue, possibly grey; it is hard to call it. She has on a jacket cut exactly to the curve of her body, which is somehow clearer to me now that I have seen her in her swimsuit. The waitress appears again.

'A flat white and some bircher muesli, please.'

Eliza's hair looks perfectly dry and is secured into some kind of chignon with a curved pin that has a small flurry of seed pearls at its tip. It's only when she reaches forward to return the menu to the waitress that it becomes visible: one small, damp curl stuck to the palest skin at the side of her neck, just behind and below her ear. I turn away, guilty with the noticing.

Anna

I've lost count of the times I've said, 'Don't text first thing.' It's not that I don't understand the inclination; can't remember perfectly, in fact, the impulse to do so: arriving early for a meeting, grabbing a coffee in a café, or sitting in a bland hotel lobby waiting for a taxi; the reflex to touch base, to check in, to report back.

Not now, though. The possibility of silence, first thing, is something to be safeguarded, like a small rectangle of lustrous matt whiteness snipped from a paint chart and held carefully in my palm. A window of opportunity, even though my use of it is increasingly questionable. Cleaning. Sanitising. Scrubbing at nooks and crannies in the kitchen with my lips pursed before the day has even begun. Who would have guessed that my grip on a mop could be so accustomed, so adroit? I think habits can be tracked back to their source, like long twisty rivers, or birds that have made complex migratory flights. All of this – all of what I begin each weekday with – flows back to a junior doctor, her hair held high in a swinging ponytail, who examined Teddy when he was in hospital for a chest infection last winter. She washed her hands at length, meticulously soaping between her fingers, the mechanised procedure still freshly learned. 'It's amazing quite how much infection can be prevented if people wash their hands regularly and thoroughly. Cleanliness makes a real difference to children like Teddy and their level of exposure to risk.'

Bullseye. Thoughts gain traction and heft, and now I sanitise all the kitchen surfaces, even though I can't rationally say what contamination I think happens during the night. Flies do not drop from the ceiling; cats do not pad in through the letter box; germs surely don't sally forth from the sink.

I repeatedly scrub my hands like the doctor did, so much so that the skin between my fingers is cracked and sore. If I stretch my hands wide it flashes at me like small, cross-hatched ensigns. At the table with Tom I keep my fingers pressed together, as if they are contained in invisible mesh mittens. On my phone I have googled the definition of 'open-handed'; it means *giving freely*, or *generous*. Perhaps now I don't qualify as either of these; instead I am a woman with a masterful grasp of a mop, who wrings it out into a second bucket so that the original water is not sullied with dirt.

Isaac will appear in a moment. For a child of almost ten, he is unusually obedient to his alarm. ('Snooze button? Lose button,' he said once. 'Why would anyone want one of those?') He will tiptoe into the kitchen, trying his best to avoid the patches that are not yet completely dry, and pick up the bowl of cereal I have put out for him on the counter. He will sit on the stool and hold his legs bent at ninety degrees so that I can swoosh past him more easily. He pours the milk carefully and makes sure not to spill it on the clean surface. I should tell him that I am grateful for this; for this gesture of allegiance, of tacit support. *I get it*, his body language seems to say, his elbow suspended at a right angle above the worktop.

Most mornings there is just the sound of him eating his cereal, and the clink of his mug of milk as he puts it down. I worry that his almost-silence is because I give the impression of listening for something else, a sound that will come from just beyond us and which I might miss if I don't give it my full attention. Only yesterday, I shushed him mid-sentence and then waited in the hiatus for the sound of Teddy stirring, while Isaac held the cereal spoon midway to his mouth like someone caught in the shutter of a camera frame. Perhaps this is why we start each weekday in the kitchen in what I'd prefer to think of as companionable silence – my elder son eating, me mopping and wiping, the street lights blinking off outside as the daylight increases.

Even now, as I empty the bucket into the sink, my head is cocked like a gun primed to smoke blue. I knead the side of my neck with my fingertips, aware of a tightness that tracks to my left ear. It is constantly tilted upwards, as if a particular sound will be poured into it abruptly, like water from a jug. Teddy frequently wakes with a coughing fit and can be promptly sick. On these days it is not just the bottom sheet but all the bed linen that needs changing.

Weekends are not like this. The cleaning and sanitising does not happen when Tom is sitting here, reading the papers, a coffee in his hand, filling the kitchen with his solid certainty; the length of his femur, his hand span, making me feel that germs are surely vanquished. If he saw me doing this, he would look at me, baffled. When I used to have a cleaner, I saw her wiping the side with the same cloth she'd just used for the floor. I told her – white-lipped – that from now on I didn't want her to touch the kitchen. She looked at me sideways with a flintiness in her expression that suggested detached, dispassionate evaluation. *See how you'd deal with it*, I wanted to say to her. I fired her shortly afterwards, relieved to be free of another set of eyes scrutinising me, and at the same time wondering how I became a person who might audibly crackle with internally generated bolts of lightning.

I take down Isaac's jacket from the peg in the hallway and put it next to his school bag. At least it isn't raining. The guilt is worse on wet mornings, when he goes off by himself, his feet nimbly hopscotching the puddles. He has walked to school alone for almost a year. I comfort myself with the fact that it's only a short distance and there are no unsupervised roads to cross.

Getting Teddy up and ready to accompany him brought its own kind of chaos: Teddy wailing because he wanted breakfast and there wasn't time to feed it to him; or often a coughing fit that would bring everything to a halt, all the time Isaac standing patiently next to the front door, tapping his book bag against his knees.

One morning, as I knelt on the hallway floor zipping Teddy into his snowsuit, Isaac simply said, 'Why don't I walk by myself? It's no trouble. It's not like I don't know the way.'

No trouble. I could print that on a T-shirt and give it to him to wear; Isaac with his quick, dark, watchful eyes, which I suspect probably see more than most.

Now, he comes down the stairs, tugging his sweatshirt into place, and I step forward to wrap my arms around him in a hug.

'You are such a star.'

Is it surprise that he is registering? He gives a quick smile.

After he has cleaned his teeth, he walks off down the path. I sit on the bottom stair with a cup of coffee on the tread beside me. Perhaps Tom is still wherever he texted from earlier. Half an hour has passed. It's more likely he will have left for a meeting and already be busy. My reply would anyway be stringy and lumpen, and a kind of withholding. I see that clearly.

Teddy has an appointment with the musculoskeletal team this morning. It's better that he sleeps; better that he is his best possible, strongest, straightest self.

The sound of a blackbird filters through from the cherry tree beyond the porch. Last week, there was a robin perilously close to the open casement. When I was a child, a great-aunt told me that a bird coming into the house is a foreteller of a death. This is why I am a woman who flaps her arms, panic-struck, to shoo away bold fledglings that alight on a sill. This is why I crane my neck, now, to make sure the blackbird is tucked in the tree and not actually inside the porch. My great-aunt's superstition is like a sticky cobweb; I would like to brush it away and feel my skin smooth and clean.

And then, there it is: a small, yawny mewl. Teddy. Awake. I scramble to my feet, the coffee untouched where it sits on the tread.

Teddy

My curtains *flap flap flap* like the wings of the Canada geese I watched taking off from the muddy riverbank. I can lift my arm a little, and move my hand in and out of the slice of shadow the curtains make. My window is always just a little bit open because fresh air is good; good in my nose, in my lungs, in my chest, in my blood. This is what Mummy says when she is helping to expectorate me. EX-PEC-TOR-ATE. She says it in time with the tap-claps on my chest. I am not a drummer boy like the one with gold buttons on his jacket in one of my books. I am like an actual drum; a drum that is properly alive and has real skin, pink and soft, rather than dried skin stretched tight. Each time I cough, the fresh air helps to draw the bad stuff up. When I breathe in, Mummy says I am filling my lungs with goodness. I am supposed to think of my lungs like balloons, and blow them up, full as possible.

Big breaths in also means I'm champion at smelling things. I can even smell colours if I think very hard. The air smells of grass on summer afternoons when Daddy has mowed the lawn. It smells emerald green when it goes into my nose. On winter mornings I think I can smell frost, and that if I could just lick the window pane with the very tip of my tongue it would stick to the glass like it does to an ice cube.

My bed smells of things that make me feel safe. Most mornings, when I'm only just awake and beginning to look up at the ceiling through my eyelashes, I sniff – *quick quick* – to check that everything smells just as it should do. Mummy says I'm like a little mouse, starting the day coming out of its hole with its whiskers twitching and wobbling. What I can mostly actually smell is washing powder, because my sheets are changed each day because there are all kinds of spills, and also the warm plastic of the mattress cover, which is sweet and sharp all at the same time.

Next to my bed are my *armies*. This is Mummy's name for them, and it makes me feel like a general with medals and ribbons on his chest rather than someone whose arms are mostly a bit floppy. They're two little red slings that attach to a frame to help me exercise. I hold two tiny cymbals and when I bring my arms together, the cymbals can *ding*. If I can't quite reach, there's no sound and I don't win a point. My points get totted up on the abacus next to my bed. That's another of my exercises – pushing the wooden beads along the length of the wire – but that one is for my fingers. It's important to keep my arms and hands as strong as I can, and also to practise sitting up a lot. Children like me are either sitters or non-sitters, and being a sitter is better, although I'm not quite sure why.

When Mummy comes up the stairs and into my room, the first thing I hear is the rustle of her clothes, which are always *soft soft soft*. Then it's her voice, and she coos like the wood pigeons who sit on the chimney pot. 'Teddy, Teddy, Teddy,' she says, her voice in a sing-song. When she leans down to me, the ropes of her hair always touch me before her hands do. If I were quick and strong I could climb right up them. She wears two silver bracelets that chink as she comes up the stairs.

Her footsteps are always quick and hurried: *busy busy busy*. At home, outside, inside, everywhere. Even if I couldn't smell her (say I had a peg on my nose) or see her (say I had a blindfold tied around my forehead), I'd know it was her footsteps – *swip swip swip* on the landing carpet. Sometimes I can hear her in the bathroom and she calls, 'I'm coming, I'm coming', even though I haven't even called out to her, just maybe hiccupped or have a frog in my throat.

Yesterday she almost ran into my room. Maybe it sounded like I might be sick. She stood by my bed and caught up with her breath, and she laughed and said, the words coming out in a spill, 'Just making sure you're not about to do a runner on me.'

I will do when she's carried me downstairs and put me into my Wizzybug. Isaac says I'm like Lewis Hamilton when I get into that. Mummy got it for me when I was three, and I'm so good at driving it I can zip around everywhere. Now that I'm five, I'm almost too old for it, and Mummy is talking to the physiotherapist and the occupational therapist about what I should have next.

The Wizzybug has a sticker on the side that says: *With my Wizzybug, I'm free to be me.* Mummy has also painted in tiny silver letters: *See me, not the chair.* Mostly people screw up their eyes at that part, so it might be a bit too small to read.

She's coming in now and she bends down to kiss me. I lift my hand and pat at the side of her cheek.

'Morning, my little charmer,' she says. 'Who's my beautiful darling boy?'

Isaac

Tiptoeing across a mopped kitchen floor means damp toes, or at least damp socks first and then damp toes. Do they smell of Flash? Possibly.

There's also the chance that my jumper smells of Dettox where I accidentally leaned against the side, although Dettox is not actually meant to smell of anything at all. It's meant to leave everything not just clean but *hygienically clean*. There must be a difference, but I don't think it's a difference you can see; not in this kitchen anyway. The bottle has an extra label that says it's effective against cold and flu viruses. Mummy gave everything a few extra zaps today as if to make sure.

The whole kitchen, actually, must be hygienically clean, whatever that looks like. Five mornings a week when I come downstairs Mummy is scrubbing, so that means it must be. She uses a toothbrush to clean in between the tiles behind the cooker. She replaces the toothbrush after a week, and there is a neat stack of new ones in the cupboard with the cleaning products. It's like a shop in there, everything in super-neat rows. I wonder if the people who design toothbrushes think they might be used in this way – first horizontally and then vertically. They probably imagine rows of white teeth, not tiles with very clean grouting.

Mummy bought a steamer recently. It gets used on Tuesdays and Thursdays, and then it feels like a rainforest in the kitchen. A parrot would be perfectly at home. The steamer is bright yellow and made in Italy. It has *Ciao!* written in red letters on the side, although this disappears each time Mummy pulls the trigger and a huge cloud of steam comes out. I haven't decided whether socks that smell of Flash are a better start to the day than socks that are properly damp – steam travels further and quicker than you think – but there doesn't seem to be much point in deciding, because none of it looks like it's about to change. Anyway, my socks dry out surprisingly fast. My toes must pump out heat like a radiator, because they always crisp up nicely before morning break.

One of the best things about walking to school is looking in everybody's window. Not in a staring, nosy kind of way, but in a super-speedy one. Walking along and looking through kitchen windows is a good way of learning that people are very different. One lady sits by the window reading the paper in her dressing gown with her hair all over the place and an enormous mug in her hands. She doesn't look like she'd be keen on a stack of fresh toothbrushes for cleaning thoroughly between tiles. An old man two doors along opens the window just a crack and waters his window box carefully with his teapot. I don't know if it contains leftover tea, or just the water he's rinsing it out with. Either way, it doesn't seem to be bringing anything in the window box to life. There are no shoots, no stalks, nothing. *Nada.* That's my new word. And *niente.* Both mean *nothing.* I've taught them to Teddy. We call out *nada, nothing, niente* when Mummy shouts up the stairs to ask what we're up to, and then fall about laughing when she suddenly appears and says, 'Really?' her head poking around the bedroom door.

It's colder today. It's the first morning with my hands properly stuffed in my pockets. Daddy slept in Geneva, which means there will be a present. Judging by this morning, gloves would be good. Not babyish ones that thread through your coat sleeves and are impossible to lose even if you hate them, but cool ones like my friend Harry's, which are special skiing gloves and have fingers made from leather. Those are the kind of gloves that I would be very careful not to lose. They are also the kind of gloves that would be good for helping to push Teddy to school, although it doesn't look like this is going to happen any time soon. Firstly, because Mummy keeps having to go in for meetings about what needs to change – ramps, handrails, a special loo – and that list seems to be getting longer, and secondly because arrangements need to be made for a teaching assistant to help Teddy all the time, someone who will sit right next to him, which Mummy says is 'an issue for the finance committee and the governing body'.

It's not that Teddy won't understand what the reception class teacher says – he'll be onto that in a whizz – but because there will be a lot of picking up required. I could have told them that before all the meetings. Mostly paper, pens and scissors, which will rain to the floor when Teddy's hands get tired. Also, someone to help at lunchtime, what with Tupperwares to be opened, and buttons and zips after going to the loo, and also the caps to pop up on the water bottles. It would have been a good idea if they had asked me what help Teddy might need, seeing as I am the only person who lives in the same house *and* goes to the school so probably count as an expert. Nobody has, though. I'll give Teddy some top tips anyway, and Teddy will store them up. He can be counted on for that. He might look as if he's just lolling about in his wheelchair, but he's not. Ever.

Problem is, adults mostly don't listen to your advice when you're almost ten. The occupational therapist could do with some listening-up for a start off. The activities she tries to get Teddy to do are mostly lame. Last week she tried to teach him to play cat's cradle with a loop of pale blue wool. 'It's fabulous for manual dexterity,' she said to Mummy, who looked across at us with her eyes a little bit extra wide in the hope that Teddy might be up for a stab at it. He made a total hash of it, the wool in a crisscross cobweb around his fingers. He thought it was boring – it was easy to see. Sometimes he makes his hands go extra limp on purpose, especially if it's something stupid that he's been asked to do. I could have told the therapist – if she'd even bothered to notice me – that shuffling cards is far better muscle exercise. I do that with him sometimes, and I've made a small sign saying *Viva Las Vegas* in red and purple to put beside him as he does it. Next time we practise, I'm going to sneak a bow tie from Daddy's wardrobe so that Teddy looks like a proper dealer at a casino table. I'll pretend to smoke a cigar and drink a cocktail while waiting for my fan of cards, and Teddy's heart will practically beat out of his chest with the trying. Cat's cradle is never going to ace that.

In the playground, Mrs Jackson is trying to get everyone into a neat line before the bell rings.

'Boys, boys, stand nicely and stop whirling about like seeds from the sycamore tree.' She makes a helicopter motion with her index finger just to be extra clear. You can always rely on Mrs Jackson for a seasonal simile. The girls don't look that neat and tidy either but she never seems to notice that. The playground is, anyway, all of a muddle. Maybe she could also do with a steamer with *Ciao!* written on the side. One burst of that and the whole class would be lined up straight as a ruler.

Teddy has an appointment at the muscle clinic today. It was written up on the whiteboard in the kitchen. If it is on time and they're out just before school finishes, Mummy will drive back past school and park on the road next to the playground and pick me up. She might bring some banana cake or a cookie from the Pret that's opened on the ground floor of the hospital. Before Pret, the best to be hoped for was a tuna and cucumber sandwich from the League of Friends café.

Mummy's not usually in the best of moods after hospital appointments. What she often says is 'I'm spitting feathers', and then she quickly changes the subject. When she says that, I can feel actual feathers, dry and scratchy, on the back of my throat. It makes swallowing difficult, which spoils the banana cake or the cookie, which I know isn't what Mummy means to happen.

There's a small shred of skin next to my thumbnail. When I tug at it with my teeth, it peels off, and the skin underneath is red-raw and shiny but not quite bleeding. It's as if my blood is determined not to come out.

In the summer, at the seaside, I went in a double kayak with Mummy while Daddy looked after Teddy on the beach. Mummy paddled straight out in a direct line over the waves. The paddle quickly gave her a blister on the side of her thumb. It was small and dark and the colour of a beetroot. Later, when she noticed it, she popped it with the tip of a kitchen knife and the blood shot out onto the splashback of the sink. I wiped it away when she carried Teddy upstairs for his bath. It's funny that I should think about that now, waiting in line for my head to be tapped lightly because Mrs Jackson always likes to do a quick count-up before we go into the classroom.

My thumb's quite sore, and it's hard not to keep stroking it with my finger, which isn't helping at all. The skin's gone all oozy.

The memory's still a shocker; Mummy's blood was so bright red and fast and then became brown and dry so quickly, like it had never been alive at all.

Anna

Teddy's laughing as I cradle his head and swoosh the water gently across his face. The water dribbles down his jaw and into my palm.

'Stop wriggling, you little monkey. Look, it's going in your ears. How have we managed to get Weetabix in your ears? If the doctor takes your temperature, his thermometer will come out with half your breakfast on it.'

I wipe carefully beneath Teddy's chin. The skin is softest there, and if left damp will chafe against the collar of his shirt and bloom red and sore. I dab, dab, dab with the muslin cloth.

'Look, you're my dab chick.'

'What's a dab chick?'

'A little duck, I think. A dumpy little duck with a fluffy bottom. Here's your shirt; we can do five buttons each.'

'No buttons, no buttons. Plee-ase a sweatshirt today.'

'Nope. You'll be the smartest boy on the ward, and the one who's had good button-doing-up practice as well. I'll race you; you do this one and I'll do the top one.'

'I hate buttons.' His tone is playful, rather than insistent.

'Tinker, tailor, soldier, sailor, rich man, poor man, beggar man, thief. Tinker, tailor . . . How can you hate buttons? See, you're a tailor this morning! You're not a dab chick, you're the Tailor of Gloucester, sitting cross-legged with a thimble on your finger and sewing tiny stitches.'

'You didn't count all of them, you missed the ones on my trousers. With them, I'd be a sailor.'

'Okay then, a sailor. An admiral, in fact. Let's get your socks on, Admiral of the Fleet. If you do the buttons properly, I'll give you a salute.'

Most days it takes an age; the dressing and the washing and the toileting, the cajoling and the coercing, the encouraging. Now he lies before me on the changing mat, the flat light of the morning spilling down over him through the Velux window.

'You'll have to tell the receptionist you're late because you won a medal for the slowest sock-pulling-on in the world.'

There is always, however, the momentary pleasure of clean skin and fresh clothes. And, parallel to it, the small residual sadness that I am never removing trousers with knees scuffed with mud or grass stains but instead clothes with spilled food: drooled yoghurt, or juice, or porridge.

'Hold your hands out straight for me so that I can clean them properly with the flannel. And now your teeth. Oh my goodness, how wide can you open your mouth? As wide as a goldfish, a bear or a great white whale? How much plankton could you scoop in there?'

I circle my finger around the outline of his lips. A memory comes to me of how we used to wash Isaac on a beach the first time we went on holiday as a family to Greece.

We would walk down to the little pebbled cove in the late afternoon, when the sun had lost its heat but still retained its warmth. Isaac loved the water, and we would hold him and let him float on his back, and swirl him around in swooping crescents like a small, gleeful Poseidon. Afterwards, I would stand on the beach and take him beneath his arms and hold him out from my body while Tom poured fresh water from a bottle over him, and soaped his limbs until they were slick and slippery. He would wriggle and laugh as Tom drenched one limb at a time. I would take the edge of the towel in my teeth, Isaac now pressed to my shoulder, and swaddle him in it and then sit on the smooth pebbles with him damp-haired in my lap. I fed him his supper while Tom shook out our things and packed them ready to go.

We would walk back to our little stone house, Isaac already fast asleep, his cheek rosy where it was pressed to my chest, and Tom and I would sit outside and eat supper on the terrace and watch the sky turn indigo. I thought there was nothing so beautiful, so heart-stoppingly joyful, as washing our sleek, clean child together, drenched in the late-afternoon rose light of the beach, with the salt-kissed taste of him fresh on my mouth.

And now there is this, which is not the same thing at all, and which spikes me, suddenly, on a Tuesday morning at 9.30 a.m., because there will never be, can never be, that simple, unfettered, unencumbered joy. I trace around his mouth again.

'Your teeth are like pearls. See in the mirror how white they are. Who's my Bobby Dazzler? How busy we are today.'

Tom

I always buy the boys something from the airport on the way home from a business trip. I pretend that I've forgotten to think of them and then pull the gift from my coat pocket or bag as if I'm a magician. *Ta-daah!* Isaac always cheers. Now, standing in duty free, my briefcase held carefully on the floor between my feet, I skim past bumper packs of Milka chocolate, the purple-and-white wrappers gaudy on the shelves, and dismiss bright plastic watches, and beanie hats, and a miniature alpine horn that I can see Teddy trying, and failing, to blow. There are battery-operated walkie-talkies, with a drawing of a child crouched by a hedge, saying, in a speech bubble, 'Over and out.' If I buy them, will Isaac do his best to look grateful, but consider them a faff? Will Teddy have the fine motor co-ordination to operate the switches? I can see Anna looking at me with her eyes narrowed and her voice sown with disappointment: *Why would you buy him something that underlines what he cannot do?*

I pick up a stuffed fleece cow with a bell around its neck and give it a shake; it sounds miserable. I'm drawn to the walkie-talkies again: there is always the temptation to aim high, fail big. Perhaps, miraculously, they will be a huge hit; Teddy will sit under the apple tree in his wheelchair and direct Isaac merrily on some kind of intricate scavenger hunt. I will devise clues, hide things; be the kind of father I find it easier conceptually than actually to be. Their childhood bears so little resemblance to mine on the farm. Streams, trees, meadows, sticks, fishing rods, wellingtons, hay bales, chickens; a warm egg held precious in a dirty fist. Scant regard, then, for books, or sitting still, or tears. Edward, my older brother, challenging, 'I dare you, wetter, I dare you,' at the foot of a just-about-climbable tree. Mum coming out on the stoop in a summer twilight and banging a wooden spoon on the colander – 'Bathtime, now!' – flushing the four of us out like rabbits from a warren. There were multiple litters of puppies, a ferret that stank, and once, a leveret found injured in a ditch and kept in a crate until its leg mended, its eyes wild and liquid, our voices hushed, our fingers looped through the chicken wire, knowing we must not touch.

One summer we became secret agents. What we would have given for a pair of proper walkie-talkies. We devised codes, planted clues, spoke in sentences that looped back obliquely on themselves. Mum gave us tomato tins and a large ball of twine, and it is this that comes to me now as I stand, indecisive, in Geneva airport.

I am again under the bridge by the stream, my back pressed to the damp stones, my feet bare in the summer trickle of water, the can smooth in my hand.

'One of us should hide under the bridge and the other in the red dust hollow in Flanagan's meadow,' James shouts.

His footsteps recede as he sprints to Edward in the hollow. I tug on the string as it runs taut away. I press my ear to the opening and listen; it sounds as if I have a shell pressed to my ear – a faint swooshing and whooshing – and beyond me the *plink* of water dripping from a crack in the bridge. I listen again. Nothing. And then William's footsteps, slower because he is the youngest, and then his out-of-breath voice:

'Pull it harder. Edward says stop being a dope. It's your turn to speak and you have to remember to say over and out.'

I push the can to my mouth. The rim is cold and wet.

'Checking in from Bridge Point. Over. Over and Out.'

'And now?' I say to William, who is lying on his front on the bridge so that only his head peers over. The sunlight bounces off his tangled red curls.

'I dunno. Shall I run back and check?'

When I press the can to my ear, there is a ripple of Edward's voice. I touch the twine and can feel the faintest of trembles. What is Edward saying? The words shiver into themselves. I can hear James's actual voice, out in the meadow, calling to William.

'They're too far apart; that's what it'll be. The twine needs to be shorter. They should be closer together.'

I peep over the bridge and see the length of the twine threading its way through the field margin. Far beyond us, the combine puffs up a cloud of chaff. I press the can to my ear again. What is Edward saying? *Can you hear me? Come nearer? Use your ear?* I scramble out from under the bridge and hold the can pressed to my chest. Edward is running towards me, white-faced and furious because his voice has not carried, and the walkie-talkies and the plan have not worked, and his brothers are all idiots and no one listens to instructions properly, and he shouts all this at me, standing holding the twine, which I think is perhaps only suitable for the baler and may not be able to carry voices at all. I silently hand him the can.

'You can't do anything right,' he says, thumping me casually on the upper arm.

Maybe I still can't.

Eliza is talking.

'Did you see? Our flight's been called. It's gate twenty-three. It's on time, thank goodness.'

Since when did I become so indecisive? I put back the walkie-talkies, and pick up a tin of Caran d'Ache crayons. They are not overly slender; Teddy will be able to grip these. Isaac will perhaps draw something intricate and extraordinary. Anna will say they will result in five minutes' peace. I take out my boarding pass and hand it to the assistant, and count out the amount owing from my accumulated coins. As I do so, there is the taste of tin, fresh again in my mouth.

Anna

The doorbell is unexpected.

Teddy and I are playing with his shape sorter; pushing triangles, squares and hexagons into pre-cut holes. He is lining them up and swatting at them with the flat of his hand, and I'm sitting on my palms, because this way it is easier to resist doing it for him, and I've promised him a trip to feed the ducks in the park if he posts all the shapes before the timer beeps. That's why, when the doorbell rings, I cross the kitchen with a red wooden triangle in one hand, which I've picked up from the floor, and a mouse-faced egg-shaped timer in the other. When I open the door – both items now transferred to my left hand – it's Sophie on the doorstep in immaculate work wear, her hair perfectly blow-dried and wearing a shoe with a heel shape that probably has a descriptor but I don't know what it is. I would have known once.

'Hi! Surprise!' Her voice is a little louder than it needs to be; the tone a little brighter, and she makes an exaggerated jazz-hands gesture as if to underline the intended playfulness of what she is saying.

'I'm just on my way back to town from an overnighter in Birmingham. I was going past on the M40 and I thought . . . just on the off chance . . . I'd see if you were in. You are *useless* at answering my texts, and I promised admin that I'd wing by and check you hadn't moved or evaporated. It's quite a thing, you know, knocking on a door with the possibility that a total stranger might answer it and leave me floundering.'

I am not a total stranger – even if it suddenly feels that I may be – but perhaps I am leaving her floundering anyway. The triangle brick falls from my hand and I stoop to pick it up.

Sophie pauses. 'Are you about to go out? Have I caught you at an inconvenient time? I could stop for a coffee if it suits you. It's just none of us have heard from you for ages and so I just, I just . . .'

'Come in, of course. That's really kind of you. And yes, I'm here.' I proffer the brick. 'Advanced geometry this morning.' There is a taste of ash in my mouth. I am a topic of discussion in the office. She will report back to admin. The level of scrutiny I am under laps wider each time I check.

I put on the kettle. Teddy peeps out from the playroom.

'It's no one to see you,' I say, and he chuckles and disappears, pleased to be off the hook. The timer in my hand starts to squeak. I turn back to Sophie. 'If you need to charge your phone, or send a quick email, go ahead. I remember how pit stops always involved multitasking.'

She looks at me intently. 'Thanks, but it's okay. Hell, I don't even need the loo.' She laughs. 'I still cringe at the memory of having to wee at the roadside when we were en route to that distillery in the Highlands. Thank God I'm not working on any luxury brands located in remote places far from service stations.'

I smile, but it is a smile that doesn't reach the edges of my mouth. What a thing for her to give thanks for, in the knowledge that God seems to have very little truck with issues deserving greater gratitude, and roadside wees presumably not featuring on His radar at all. I check myself. How mean and disparaging I am. Sophie's expression is benign and expectant, as if I will now snowball along with a parallel memory of the accounts we worked on together, and affirm that I am as I was, and that I remain intact.

And yet I find it hard to not stare back at her, as if she is something exotic and precious released into unfamiliar territory. Social workers, dieticians and physios do not dress like this. She is lustrous, wearing a blush-coloured jumper with a polo neck that drapes cleverly, and a pair of black trousers that are cut adroitly for her shape. Her make-up is flawless, and her highlights the perfect caramel. Did I look like this when I worked alongside her? It seems inconceivable.

I gesture to her to sit down at the kitchen table and notice, too late, that I did not wipe it properly before whisking Teddy off to the bathroom after breakfast. There is a tiny blob of Weetabix congealing to her left. I register the smallest of movements; first that her hand brushes the seat just as she sits down, wary, I presume, of crumbs that might mark her trousers. And then, with her fingertips, just the smallest of sweeping touches before she places what is a beautiful handbag down on the table. I would like to say, 'Don't worry, it's not sticky, I've cleaned everything this morning already,' but those words are suddenly crushing, and I can't even spout them with a faux jollity or bravado. I *have* cleaned everything this morning, whilst she has met with a client, and in preparation for that, applied make-up with precision, and put on clothes that make mine look beyond shabby. I pass her the coffee in my leggings and sweatshirt and I suddenly can't bear the thought of her going back into the office and reporting all this to admin, and them clucking with the pleasurably convivial nature of collective regret.

'So how are you?' She looks expectantly at me, as if the first thing I will reach for is an honest, direct answer. Instead, I am transfixed by the perception that what she is holding in her hand is a very large magnifying glass, one which will draw into its focus all the available light in the room and then make the skin on my cheek singe.

'Things are . . .' I stretch for some glossy and impermeable words. With perfect timing, Teddy swings past in his Wizzybug.

He's sorted himself an admiral's tricorn hat from the fancy-dress box in the playroom.

'Shipshape and Bristol fashion,' I say lightly. 'The admiral, obviously . . .'

I find I can't take my eyes off the polo neck of her jumper. She touches it fleetingly.

'Detachable. Look.' She tugs at it a little to show me how it attaches. 'Two jumpers in one.' She laughs, and I am reminded of how we used to sit in the Costa opposite the office when I was pregnant with Teddy and howl with laughter about some of our workmates. Although done without malice, it was with a sharp eye, and perhaps she is looking at me now with the same; my hair unkempt, a stain on my top.

She presses her glossy lips together. She has the air of someone trying to navigate herself towards more solid ground.

'I'm arranging a spa day – on a Saturday; we're all going to Cowley Manor. Did you know Maggie's pregnant? It will be her last outing before maternity leave, and Jess is coming, and Kate too. You bailed on the invite to the office summer party, so it would be great if you could make this. I can email you the dates. We're all clubbing together for Maggie's gift – maybe you could give us some advice, seeing as the rest of us are still valiantly batting for the childless.'

I nod, mindful of how even the thought of me probably spooks Maggie. I am the woman who sailed through pregnancy to then crash and burn. My presence at the baby-shower spa would be like the bad fairy at the christening.

I muster a bright tone. 'That sounds like a lovely idea. If you email me the dates . . .' I gesture to the whiteboard. 'The logistics are unbelievable.'

She nods with energy, because it's the most straightforward thing either of us have said since she stepped into the kitchen.

'You always loved a spa day,' she says conspiratorially. 'There was a period, way back when, when you were the total mani-pedi queen.' She says it as if that version of me might be standing, available and patient, in the wings. A woman who shopped each April for a new bikini for the summer, and who had her legs waxed and her eyebrows shaped and tinted every month. A new pair of sunglasses annually, kept and labelled in their cases, her own vintage collection. Twenty-two years of curating her sunshine face.

Teddy appears again. He's trailing a walk-along duck behind the Wizzybug. He's still wearing the hat.

'Are you marshalling your fleet?'

He doesn't understand what Sophie means. She speaks to him in the over-precise way people do when they don't have children, as if enunciation is the key to comprehension. He laughs and blows right by us. Isaac at that age would have paused and looked at her carefully, as if by staring long enough at her the words might have rearranged themselves into a shape that made sense.

'And it's quite the fleet,' I say, so that her words are not totally ignored. 'At the last count he had forty-seven different professionals listed in his file. I could manage a small company now, no problem.'

'Maybe you will,' Sophie says brightly, and then, in case that implied what I'm doing now is an unfortunate interlude, she adds, 'And I guess it means you're never lonely. Now I know why you don't have time to reply to my texts.'

Our smiles are both a little forced. She stands up from the table. 'I'm going to have to make a move. Please try and make the spa day.' She leans in to kiss me lightly on the cheek.

As she walks down the path, I resist the temptation to draw all the bolts on the door. If I had a drawbridge I'd pull it right up. I press my palm to the flat smoothness of the wood and take a deep breath. How many minutes before my ears should start burning? I move to the sink and watch as she drives away; she is quickly on her phone. She might, of course, just be phoning the office and confirming what time she will be back. Or instead a call to Maggie, or Jess. *Oh my goodness, I've just seen Anna, you have to pinch yourself that it's her.*

Teddy is suddenly behind me, the wooden tag-along duck in his lap.

'Quack, quack,' he says, and makes the beak peck lightly at my hand.

Isaac

Mrs Jackson likes PE. *Think some, jump some* was her classroom slogan one week. She wrote it in huge letters on the whiteboard. I'm thinking about this as I pull on my trainers for the afternoon's sports lesson. She's taking advantage of what she says is the sun peeking through the bluster, and so we're having it a little early.

The class timetable is written on the wall and it should be Topic now, but she doesn't always stick to the plan. She says it's a lesson in life that things can be unpredictable, and that 'you never know what's coming right atcha'. When I shared this with Mummy, she said it's not up to Mrs Jackson to demonstrate this, and that she might want to concentrate instead on teaching the classroom assistants to say *you were*, not *you was*. Most of what Mummy says about Mrs Jackson isn't actually for saying to her. Anyway, I like it that Mrs Jackson has looked out of the window and brought the PE class forward, even though the person who is supposed to take it can't come because his car battery has failed, so it's Mrs Jackson who is zipping up her fleece and tucking the rugby ball under her arm. She looks as if she thinks it might escape at any minute, and she holds it how Auntie Jenny carries a chicken before clipping its wings.

'Isaac, are you planning on joining the line any time soon?'

At the recreation ground, she's still got the ball, but now just in her fingertips, like it's a bomb that might go off. Then she has what isn't one of her best ideas.

'Some of you are a lot better than others at this. I'm going to put red bibs on the fastest and strongest, and that means you have to hop when you're holding the ball. It's as close as I can get to all things being equal.'

I think she might be missing the point of sport altogether, or that if she applied the same rule to handwriting, some of the class would have to do their work wearing a blindfold. And if sports lessons start being about making all things equal, I don't know how that will work with Teddy. I can't see a teaching assistant trying to run up and down the pitch pushing the wheelchair while all the sporty boys hop alongside. She'll probably have to make Teddy a linesman instead, and put an extra-warm coat on him and give him a bright flag and a whistle to try and console him. Also, she'll have to stop writing *Think some, jump some* on the assembly whiteboard too. She probably hasn't thought of that yet.

When I get home, Mummy has just put Teddy upstairs for a lie-down because she says he's had 'half the life prodded out of him'. She's making supper, and she's put some biscuits out on the side because there was no time to go to Pret before the car park ticket ran out.

'Can I take two upstairs?'

Teddy's lying on his bed, very still, but turns his face straight away to me. His eyes are quick – nobody makes a big deal out of that, but they are – and he points floppily to the flecks of mud on my cheek, and to two of my knuckles, which are skinned from where I went down hard. Staying upright on one leg isn't the easiest when somebody tackles you.

'Good spot. That's what happens when you get tackled while hopping on one leg. Down in one. Like a tree coming down. Timber!'

Teddy frowns. 'Hopping?'

Someone else might think he's said *shopping*, or perhaps *slopping*, but I don't.

'A rubbish idea of Mrs J's to try and make the score even. She's very keen on that. You'll see.'

I'm beginning to think that he might not ever get to see, but I'm glad I said it anyway. For Teddy, perhaps just the thought of playing school rugby is enough to be going on with.

'Tell me about the game – did you score?'

To tell the truth, I exaggerate a little bit. I throw in a couple of spectacular tries that are practically true. For just a minute, it's like having Teddy running alongside me, like brothers who play rugby and football and cricket in the garden all summer long. *All things being equal*, which I could tell Mrs Jackson isn't actually what happens in sport or real life.

When I've finished describing the game, Teddy starts to try and push himself up with his arms.

'Do you think I could hop, if I tried? It might be a secret skill.'

I'm guessing the answer will be no, what with walking not really working out, and Teddy's sitting balance often being quite tippy.

I shrug, which seems like the best answer. 'You could always give it a go.'

'What, now? Right now?' Teddy gives me his best smile.

'I thought you'd had half the life prodded out of you?'

'Maybe hopping will put it back in.'

I go to the top of the stairs and listen. Mummy is clattering pans and doesn't sound like she will be coming up the stairs for what she calls 'a quick check'. I take the pillows from both of our beds, and the cushions from the bedroom couch, and lay them out in a little corridor. I help Teddy up and out, and stand behind him, holding him under his armpits. The occupational therapist wouldn't be a fan of this. Teddy is giggling, and then laughing fit to bust, although he hardly manages to even twitch one leg before we tumble sideways. He doesn't look as if not hopping will be a lifelong disappointment.

'Hopping's overrated,' I say, propping him up onto the pillows. I hold out my scuffed fist. 'See, I have the scars to prove it.'

Anna

As I see Tom walking up the path to the front door, there is a tightening in my chest – a muscle I can't name but can locate between my shoulder blades that pulls up short – and a small pausing of my breath in the lowest lobe of my lung. It's not anxiety, or excitement, or anticipation; instead a small visceral recognition that he is back, that he has returned. Am I surprised that he comes home at all? In his position – immured in the working world – would I not?

Tonight he is carrying not just his briefcase but his overnight bag. His right hand is bunched around the handles of both, and his left holds the collars of his coat together. The pavement is glittering with the promise of frost. The street lights carry a small haze around them, as if wrapped up for the chill that will come with nightfall proper. He stamps a little as he puts his key in the lock, and looks down at his feet. He is a stickler for clean shoes. Each night he polishes all our shoes, laying them out in a neat semicircle at his feet. Teddy's soft, limp, slightly twisted feet are contained in boots that would pass muster on a parade ground. Sometimes I place one of them on the flat of my palm and turn my wrist through an arc so that it rotates like something in a smart shop window. I've never told Tom that I love the way he fastidiously polishes our shoes. Perhaps I should; perhaps I should put my arms around him and tell him that it moves me – that's how best I can describe it – to watch him sit and carefully brush a buttery blob of polish into the leather of our sons' shoes.

A small shaft of tenderness. Why should that seem so difficult?

He looks tired. I can see that from where I stand by the sink, a tea towel in my hand, the television on behind me and the boys watching it quietly. He's looking older. Wearier. I have not expected to notice him ageing; I have anticipated that it will only work in reverse; that when looking back at photographs, I will think how impossibly young he seems, his smile broad, his eyes trusting, his expression sunny with possibility. I do not expect, on a Wednesday night as he comes home, to see something of his father's face emerging, smudgily, from around his jawline.

'Hallo hallo hallo,' he says, the words rising into the hallway as he puts down his bags. Is there one greeting for each for us? The boys do not rush to him. If Isaac did, it would underline that Teddy cannot, so by unspoken mutual consent they turn around from the banquette in the kitchen where they are sitting, and they wave; Teddy's hand scrunched up, his fingers cramped, so that it looks as if he is wearing a mitten, or has a small kitten paw. Isaac bobs from left to right behind him like a needle on a dial.

Tom kisses me. His cheek is cold. His fingertips touch my jaw, briefly, softly, and he turns my face towards him to coax my lips momentarily to his own. As if I need encouragement, which it seems I do. He smells of otherness: of soap wrapped in waxed paper in a Swiss hotel room; of the lemon flannel given to him on the plane; of the stale air of the train home; and faintly, so faintly, of snow, of a clear, bright sprinkling of coldness. I see him standing on the pavement in Geneva, and now, as if drawn by a thread, tugged back to the three of us, to the kitchen, to this.

'How was your day?' he asks, and I nod, murmur 'Fine,' my tone light, non-committal, and turn back to the hob to stir the bolognese, while the day – my day – sits heavy in my chest like a stubborn polished stone that I cannot bring myself to dislodge by telling him the details.

I could, of course. This is what I could say: a litany, not a litany of woes exactly, but somewhere close. I could begin with how, unusually, I hurt my back lifting Teddy from his mattress. A sudden, sharp seizing – the sciatic nerve? A disc? – that pulled me up short; Teddy carefully placed back on the mattress while I breathed through a pain that sparked and fizzed down my leg. Then a moment in front of the washing machine with the sheets balled up in my arms when I wanted to hurl them in the air, or set fire to them, rather than placidly place them in the drum. Then Sophie's visit; glossy, polished Sophie, and the feeling after she left that if I were to imagine myself as something, it would be a crumpled, grubby handkerchief, and I don't know where to begin with that.

Then the difficulty of finding parking at the hospital; round and round the rows of parked cars, the minutes ticking closer to Teddy's appointment, and a man in a Toyota barging into a space that was rightly mine. The doctor – the one with the mien and bearing of a haughty crow – querying if perhaps I was doing enough additional physio, his large, bony hand holding Teddy's soft, floppy thigh as if it were a small dead rabbit in his palm. His expression implied, *Is this all you have to show me?* as if both Teddy and I were falling spectacularly short. Rationally (and now I blink hard, because the parmesan is blurring as I grate it in soft sweeps), I know he does not mean to imply this. He is a good, compassionate man who has Teddy's well-being at heart and who probably feels sorry for us both; looking at us with a soft wash of pity rather than in judgement. I should not attribute to him words he has not said, and yet I never go to an appointment without feeling a veiled rebuke, light as the skin on scalded milk. If I tell this to Tom, he will say that I always infer more than is intended, and that it is counterproductive.

And I won't tell him about Isaac either (now as I fill a jug with water for the table); how he came home with his eyes smudged dark with despondency and his knuckles skinned and raw, and I could not bear to ask him why, because today, more than usual, my own heart is so heavy I cannot carry even one more of my children's sorrows. I will ask him tomorrow, over breakfast, what happened to his hand.

'So how was Geneva? Was it cold? Did your meeting go well?'

'Cold and then not. And yes, very well. The junior partner I have working with me is impressive.'

'Was the hotel good?' How bland I am.

'Nothing spectacular. A pool by the breakfast room. Neatly divides the guests into the smug and the guilt-ridden. Do you want me to warm the plates?'

'No, let's not bother.'

My mother-in-law never fails to warm plates; it's an unspoken rule. Tonight, out of the blue, I am ambushed by an unexpected, curious defiance and the wish never ever to warm them again. I flip out cold ones as if I am dealing cards, so that the smooth white faces stare up from the table like a series of moons.

Tom has moved away from me. He is crouched by the boys, his arms in a wide crescent around them. He stands up so that they are both held in his embrace. Isaac's legs are jack-knifing out from beneath his elbow, and Teddy's head is jammed up against his shoulder so that it lolls a little and one of his eyes is scrunched against the collar of his coat.

'Be careful.'

My voice is quick and thin, as though it is blown through a reed. How shrill I sound. He puts the boys down and arranges Teddy's legs on the banquette like a child might neatly place a doll, and tweaks at his trouser legs to make sure they are not awry. Teddy taps his boots against the banquette, laughing.

'Look what I have for you both,' Tom says now, reaching into his coat pocket. He takes out a tin of crayons. Is it disappointment that flashes briefly across Isaac's face? The illustration on the pack shows them to consist of a perfectly judged spectrum of colour. He will be able to draw something beautiful with them.

It is a sweet gift. Tom will have chosen it with care.

'They look lovely.' How limp my words sound. I should underline his thoughtfulness, egg on the boys to sound more enthusiastic. Isaac has ripped off the cellophane from around the tin and flipped the lid open for Teddy, who is tracing the breadth of them with the tip of his finger. 'It looks as if all the colours are fizzing from your hands.'

Teddy turns to me and smiles. 'I am a magician; I can magic all these colours from my fingers.'

'A wizard,' Isaac says. 'You are a colour wizard.'

Most of my good intentions freeze over before they have a chance to leave my lips. I see that clearly. It's the same with my mother, with whom I seem increasingly to parry, and who recently said to me, her fingertips pressed together neatly beneath her chin, 'When was it that you became so very difficult to help?'

What did she used to say when I was a child? *Just be nice. How hard can it be?*

It is hard. Especially when cascading furies block up any sweetness and goodness in your heart.

Tom

Coming up the path, the house seemed less than totally solid, as if it might somehow edge a little way beyond me, just out of my reach. I could see my family through the kitchen window – the boys watching television, Anna chopping, stirring, seasoning – and I had the strangest feeling that my coming through the front door would be a disruption, some kind of seismic shock, as if I would rupture whatever gauzy membrane has held the three of them quietly together while I have been gone. It troubled me as I glanced at the bricks, the soffit, the fascia. A house should radiate solidity, have roots, should feel like a physical memory box crammed full with family life. At the farm, it's as if the furniture has pushed tendrils beneath the quarry tiles in the kitchen and the oak boards in the snug. Each item is held not just by its gravitational weight but by additional depth and grip, with roots thick and waxy like the hyacinth bulb Anna had on the windowsill in a glass jar all of last spring. This house, our house, feels more and more as if it slip-slides on the surface, like an elusive pond skater, moving beyond me.

Increasingly, when I come home, especially when I have been away, I feel ridiculously self-conscious; as if I need to broadcast my return, like something shouted manfully through a foghorn, in order to inveigle myself back amongst them. Years ago, I learned Italian briefly: *eccomi* – here I am; is that what I should say? Not *hallo, hallo, hallo*, like a Mayday signal sent stoically and stolidly from a ship.

She was brusque tonight. Her cheek when I leaned to kiss her was given to me with just the smallest trace of reluctance; perfunctorily, swiftly, my fingertips touching her jaw for a microsecond longer than I think she would have chosen. *She flees from me that sometime did me seek.* Is that it? Maybe. Maybe that, and everything, also, clouded with the memory of Eliza in her swimsuit, the damp curl on her neck, and her face turned towards me, smiling, as I sat beside her on the plane. Perhaps that's why I feel I deserve to have my wife turn lightly from me; the sensation of the slightest of betrayals dusting my fingertips, my thumbs.

Anna stands by the stove, her front teeth working at her bottom lip, pulling it into her mouth, over and over. I would like to step over to her and touch it gently to make her stop, but she has just told me to be careful with Teddy – I am never careful enough with Teddy – and her voice, not just what she said, but the pitch of it, means that instead I put Teddy down neatly, tidily, fussing with his trousers. Always she watches me as if I am about to get something wrong. Always the smallest of pauses as if she is waiting for a hunch to be proved right.

Now, I lie in bed and listen intently in the dark. She brushes her hair, and then her teeth; taking floss from the cabinet, swooshing mouthwash into the sink, unscrewing the lid of her moisturiser, each sound part of a brisk, well-practised sequence. I know exactly how she does it; the moisturiser rubbed into her cheeks in increasing symmetrical circles, as if her face is a piece of furniture that requires waxing and polishing, or as if there is a stubborn stain that needs to be lifted. When we were first together, in the bathroom of her tiny flat in Primrose Hill, I remember being stopped in my tracks by her ability to draw a perfect smoky flick along her eyelid, her lips pursed as she did so, her hips leaning in to the mirror, her bottom tilted upwards in her lace-edged pants. This image of her is still so clear to me, it feels as if I could plunge my hands down, as if through cold, still water, and scoop her into my arms, and restore her to me as she was then. Before. Before.

Now, she sits on the edge of the bed in her pyjamas, a dollop of hand cream squirted from a height into her palm, her engagement ring removed and clinked onto the night stand, and her fingertips sweeping over and over her knuckles with a soft, rhythmic rasping, which is magnified by the silence of the room. When she lies down beside me, she shapes her bent arms like a goalpost onto the pillow behind her, her hands holding her elbows, her forearms pressed to her hairline, as if she is containing herself, fencing herself in. It would feel intrusive to reach out and hold her as she lies beside me.

'Anna?' She does not reply, and I think that maybe she is choosing to be silent rather than drifting into sleep.

Talk to me, I would like to say. At a party, years ago, by a river, her dress hitched up, her feet visible through the shimmering emerald water. She looked so luminously, beautifully open; turning to me and laughing, the reflection of the water dancing across her face.

Was it Theseus, finding his way back through the Minotaur's labyrinth, who unwound a ball of thread to keep track of the distance he covered? How much easier would it be if Anna did the same, so that I could follow her tracks, understand her twists and turns. *Fine,* she says, when I ask about her day, and I cannot believe that she doesn't have more words to say.

Later, I can tell by her breathing that she is asleep; she has turned on her right side so she is facing me. Her lips are pressed firmly together. If I touched her cheek, would her jaw feel actively clenched? I think that if I tried to kiss her, my tongue would find no way through her teeth. Her mouth is barricaded to me; this is what it seems. So instead, I reach out tentatively, gently, to take hold of her hand, and discover her fists are clenched, as if ready to deliver a glancing blow. When I hesitantly, lightly trace the outline of her body, she feels like a knot of elbows, knees and knuckles, as if she is sleeping in a neat coil of fury. She will wake in the morning like someone sprung from a trap, her tensile strength ready to ricochet her into the day.

Before. Before. When she used to sleep so deeply, so peacefully, it was as if she'd free-dived miles to an ocean floor. 'My mermaid girl,' I called her when first we were married, smoothing her hair from her forehead and kissing her soft, full-lipped mouth awake.

Isaac

Saturdays are best. No kitchen cleaning, no damp socks, no school. And today, a surprise outing. Not with Daddy, who has gone to the office even though it is the weekend, because he needs to catch up on things because he has been in Geneva.

At the breakfast table, there is only the sound of Teddy practising his speech therapy. He has to trace the letter 'S' with his finger in a shallow tray of sugar – over and over – and as he does so, Mummy is repeating the sound of it, her tongue pressed to the back of her teeth, to try and help Teddy shape his lips so it comes out in a sound she says must be *soft and sibilant*. She is repeating the words the speech therapist has used. Mummy keeps pronouncing 'sssss', and Teddy keeps on trying to say it too, and the sugar sprinkles a little over the edge of the baking tray, and Teddy's lips are all wibbly with the effort of continuing to try, and I am pressing my own lips together hard so that the correct sound will not accidentally spill out and make it look easy. The kitchen is full of our lips, and all the trying, and the sugar, which spills further, and the effort of Teddy's finger, over and over, drawing the snaky shape of the sound his mouth can't say clearly.

Suddenly Mummy stands up and pushes the sugar tray away. 'That has to be enough for today. You've tried so hard, and it's getting better, and shall we just cross speech therapist off as a possible job for you? Who wants to be a speech therapist anyway?'

She takes the tray away to the draining board, then comes

back to the table and claps her hands together. She takes Teddy's hands gently by the wrists to help him clap too, and says, 'Let's go out for the day, the three of us. Come on, let's skedaddle.'

Skedaddle. It's the right word for all the bustling, the preparing, the packing that is suddenly going on in the kitchen. And then, while Mummy is getting everything together, there are two things. First, as I cross the kitchen to get my jacket, I spot that Mummy has smoothed the surface of the sugar and written something of her own on the tray: *To hell with this.* She catches me looking and quickly steps over and swooshes the sugar down the sink. Then, when I go back to the table, Teddy is doing some occupational therapy of his own. He's licked the tip of his index finger and is pressing it onto the sugar that has spilled on the table, and then onto his tongue, the movement really quite good.

'Nice work.' I tap the side of my nose to say I won't tell, but I'm guessing Mummy won't mind, especially if she actually has written *To hell with this* in the sugar.

In the car, she won't tell us where we're going. *Surprise,* she says, and *It's a mystery tour.* On the motorway, she scoots into the fastest lane. *Zip, zip, zip;* she overtakes the other cars. I shrug my shoulders at Teddy and we laugh a little in the back.

The place we come to is called Compton Verney. It's a big old house, with grand gardens and art exhibitions inside. We don't go inside; Mummy says there is more fun to be had outside, especially on a day when she says the sun is having a last fandango before the clocks change. She wheels Teddy's chair to an ice house that is from the Victorian times. We peer down over the edge and can feel the air cooler on our faces. We stand in front of a sculpture called *The Burghers of Calais,* and Mummy explains that a burgher is just a salesman, or merchant. Not like hamburgers, Teddy says, and he finds this really funny. Mummy says we're probably not allowed to touch, but we do – just quickly, my hand pulled up into the sleeve of my jumper straight afterwards. The one I touch has long, knotty fingers, and the hem of his coat feels as if it is weighted with ball bearings.

'And what would you like to do now?' Mummy asks. Teddy points to a tree, and we wheel him beneath it, and he says to me, his fingers meshing into a web, 'A nest, a nest, let's make a nest for a bird.'

A bird that might live on the ground. I know this can be a true thing.

'A plover,' Mummy says. 'It could be a nest for a plover.'

I nod and begin to forage in a circle that spreads out from the base of the tree. Mummy lengthens the strap in Teddy's chair so that he will be able to lean forward but not fall onto his face. He paddles with his hands in the leaves on the ground.

I search hard. I bring large and small twigs, two feathers, one that is so long it looks like a quill pen, and a small scrap of bright blue fabric, which I hope Teddy will let peep out between the sticks. I also find a twist of shiny sweet wrapper.

'A magpie would definitely want this. Let's wrap it around the end of something.'

I find some red leaves from a tree that the sign says is called an acer, and I tell Teddy they will make the cosiest blanket for chicks.

The nest is soon the size of a dinner plate, and deeper than Teddy's boot. I stand underneath a different tree and stop for a minute and look back at where Teddy is sitting – sitting, always sitting, which sometimes I think must feel like the most frustrating thing ever – and he looks small and busy, sorting carefully through all the things I have given him, his head tipped to one side, his lap piled high. He looks like a tiny grown-up, making proper decisions; and like a picture in a book I had when I was seven, where there was a goldsmith who was actually an elf and who made very beautiful, intricate things at his workbench.

The next time I go back with some twigs, I help him to tuck them in a little better.

'It's a bit like pretending to sew, threading the sticks in and out,' I tell him. Teddy copies me, his tongue poking out of his mouth because he is trying so hard. 'That will keep the draughts out and make it super-cosy. Plover perfect.' I emphasise the Ps. Teddy always listens carefully to words, mostly because Mummy peppers everything she says to him with words that are lively. Maybe her idea is that if he is listening to bright words, there won't be a space in his thoughts to allow him to feel sad about what he cannot do. I have not asked her this, but I think it's her plan; sometimes, her face looks a little bit sad, and then she says something that sparkles. Whatever she's been thinking, it's not those words that come out of her mouth.

The nest looks solid and sturdy. The blue fabric winks out between a stick and a piece of conifer. It's easy to believe that a bird might actually choose to live there, even though it is on the ground, and winter is coming, and maybe most of the birds are already migrating to Africa. 'A robin could live in it too,' I say firmly to Teddy. My knowledge of which birds migrate is a little patchy, but robins are always shown on Christmas cards, so I'm sure they must still be around even if the plovers have gone.

All the time we are making the nest, Mummy is standing beside the lake. She looks back over her shoulder lots of times, checking that we are all right, but she is also looking at another sculpture down by the water, where the grass is too boggy for the wheel-chair. When Teddy is lining the nest with the red acer leaves, Mummy is stooped over at the water's edge and it looks as if she has dropped something, or is searching for something too. She looks like a curious bird – perhaps a flamingo – because her legs are perfectly side by side so it's like she's standing just on one leg, her hair, as it falls forward, like the loop of the bird's neck.

She comes back when we have almost finished the nest. Teddy is giving us a clap – his hands properly meeting, palm to palm. It's an actual proper clap. *Simples*, I would like to say to the occupational therapist; help him to make a bird's nest and he can clap like anyone.

Mummy is holding something in her own hands. Her palm is cupped because she is cradling it carefully, and her fingers are bluey-purple and wet because they have been in the water.

'Look what I found for you, my little nest builders.'

Her arm is outstretched, and I can see what her hands hold as she lowers them down to Teddy's level. I say nothing – *nada* – so as not to spoil the surprise, and Teddy says, 'Eggs, eggs!' his face cracking into a grin, because in Mummy's hand there are two perfectly oval pebbles speckled like a gull's eggs.

She rolls them into Teddy's palm and he uses all of his skills to place them carefully on to the acer leaves. Mummy stands back and says, 'What a beautiful, beautiful nest. What a lucky bird to live in such a fine place.'

She takes a photo on her phone and we stand and look at it a while longer as the daylight begins to fade, and when we leave, she wheels Teddy away backwards, with me also walking backwards beside her, so that we can keep looking and looking at the nest on the ground until I think I can only see the wink of blue paper, and then even that is swallowed up by the distance and duskiness, and we have to begin to imagine and think it is there rather than actually see it.

When Mummy puts Teddy to bed, later, I am in my room reading a book, and I can hear her telling him a story and it is about the nest. 'If not a bird then, if not a bird because it is flying away to Africa and following the sun, then maybe a dormouse, curled up cosy and warm, or a vole or a shrew. Maybe that. Maybe that.'

Her voice is turning all the words into a lullaby. She says things over and over, her voice soft and clear. It's hard to tell whether she is speaking or singing. It makes me feel sleepy even though it is miles until my bedtime. Teddy will love what she is saying. Mummy's words make it easy to imagine a dormouse curled up in the nest, the pebbles smooth by the curve of its spine, and the scrap of fabric and the sweet wrapper picked out by the moon.

Tom

I'm not sure whether I'm irritated with myself or with Anna. I deserve it more, for letting what was supposed to only be a couple of hours bleed into a whole day. Turns out if I'd come home I'd have been on my own anyway, Anna having whisked the boys off on a spontaneous trip out. She didn't call or text to say she was going, and when I texted her there was no answer because there's apparently no signal there. In her voice, when I got back just after they did, it felt like there was a kind of passive-aggressive pride, that I am somehow unnecessary, possibly superfluous to requirements, that she can go and have a lovely day out with our sons and does not need or require or want me to be there. *Did you miss me?* I want to say, teasingly, to Teddy, who is full of news of a nest that they have built and a sculpture he insists is called *The Hamburgers of Calais.* Anna is making a risotto while my question remains unvoiced. It is her I want to have missed me, and instead she stands with her back turned towards me, looking at a sketch Isaac has drawn of a hand while she calmly stirs in the stock. *Are you punishing me?* I would like to say.

'How was the drive?' I ask instead. 'Aren't there roadworks on that stretch of the motorway?'

She doesn't ask if I caught up on the work I went in to do. The answer would be yes; I am nothing if not conscientious. It would strike a wrong note to remind her how much my bonus hinges on this project; money has become something we talk very little about, not since she said to me sharply, 'Obviously with you working and me not, it's reverted to 1953 in this house.' I'm not sure how I'm meant to respond when she says things like that. I read somewhere that women sometimes just want to say something to give it air, like sheets pegged out on a line and pulled taut by the snap of the wind. They don't want be offered solutions, changes or options; they just want to be heard. So I listen, or at least I think I do. I worry, though; about my financial responsibility for us all, my eye always to the main chance. My father spent his working life paying attention to the actual weather – the snaggle of clouds on the horizon and the promise of rain – whereas I try to read the way a more political wind blows in the office. And now, it seems, an increasing complexity: what is not said to Anna. *Are you cross with me? Have I done something? Is there something you want to say?*

After supper, I offer to bath Teddy but she says, 'Don't worry, I've got it.' Isaac has finished his sketching and has gone upstairs with a book. If I were a man with a hobby is this where I'd revert to my shed, and whittle wood, or strip down a motorbike, or restore an antique clock? If we had a dog, would I put a torch in my pocket and stride out through the streets, instead of standing here with my hands in my pockets, wondering why I seem to have lost the ability to talk – even chat – with my wife?

When she comes back into the kitchen, her face is pale with tiredness. She goes to the fridge to take out a bottle of wine.

'Let me pour that for you. Large or small glass, modom?'

A flicker of a smile. When Isaac was first born, when she came downstairs from his last feed we'd put on some music really quietly in the kitchen, and she would joke that she was so tired she'd lost her dancing legs. She would position her feet lightly on mine, in the stance for a waltz, our hands held outstretched together, her forehead soft on my collarbone. The music would play and I would dance around the kitchen, kissing the top of her head where it lay beneath my chin, and often, her eyes so completely closed, her lashes dark on her cheeks, I wasn't sure if she was awake or asleep, and if in fact rather than dancing with her I was holding her up, the feel of her shoulder blade flat to my palm.

Remember when we used to waltz? I want to say. Instead: 'Sounds like you had a busy but successful day. Teddy is very taken with the idea that a bird might actually sleep in the nest.'

She nods, and reaches over to switch on the television. Maybe she has no words left. Maybe each one of us begins the day with a stack of words to be coined out through our waking hours, and maybe sometimes they are all spent before bedtime, leaving our mouths and tongues hollow like an empty well. She curls her legs to her right-hand side and tucks her feet in beneath her. Her arms are folded across her, the wine glass stem pinched between her finger and thumb. There is no part of her that seems phys-ically available to me. If I said as much, I'd sound like one more needy child. Instead, I go and sit on the armchair opposite. She is watching *Strictly Come Dancing*; the figures are sequinned, sparkled, with improbably tanned skin. It makes me think again of our kitchen waltzes, her hand trustingly in mine, her feet bare, her grey T-shirt damp from the feeding of Isaac. Such a thing to feel a nostalgia for; Isaac, now, tall and fine-boned, coming into the room and scooching up beside her.

Anna

A flurry of Sunday-morning telephone calls chime with Tom being out on his bike; a bright, fresh morning, the dew strung in droplets in the cobwebs on the lawn.

First it is Tabitha, Edward's wife.

'Edward's on a shooting weekend, the girls are at a sleepover and I confess I'm in my dressing gown, having just got out of the bath. Don't even tell me how productive you've been so far this morning. It's just occurred to me that it's the week after next that we're all going to the farm. Are you arriving on the Sunday or going down on Saturday night? I can't decide whether to opt for the lumpy mattresses and Edward drinking too much of William's damson gin, or doing the journey twice in a day.'

'We're going on Sunday morning. It means taking so much less stuff for Teddy. Are you bringing Christmas presents?'

'Oh Jesus, we'll have to, won't we – we won't be there again before Christmas. Roll on the Caribbean. I adore bikini shopping in November. None of our gifts are wrapped. Do you think you're allowed to take them all into Peter Jones and get them to wrap them there?'

She laughs; a deep, throaty sound that matches perfectly her boarding-school tones, her stacked jewellery, and her polished confidence. Tabitha has always walked into a room as if it's lucky to contain her, and is as frank as a freshly closed door. Once, after Isaac had made a comment: 'Is it usual for an eight-year-old to have the observational skill set of an adult psychotherapist?'

The next caller is Jenny, William's wife, asking, hesitantly, her voice barely audible, if there is anything special she can prepare; anything Teddy particularly likes to eat at the moment.

'No, no, that's kind, thank you. He'll have the same as everyone else.'

And then Tom's mum, Ruth, to discuss Christmas gifts.

'The boys here are all sorted; I'm buying them fly-fishing rods, but Isaac and Teddy, do you have any pointers?'

Any pointers that don't involve standing on a damp riverbank all afternoon, a rod and reel held dextrously between finger and thumb.

Shortly afterwards, James's wife, Stella, who has recently given birth to Mathilde, who lies fulsomely on a sheepskin rug and whacks at her play gym with her chubby pink fist. As she does so, Stella studiously avoids catching my eye and subverts her maternal pride with what looks like exquisite guilt.

'The travel cot you mentioned we could have? Would it be a total pain to dig it out and bring it to Shropshire on the twenty-third?'

Yes. Yes. Yes. Yes to all of it.

Isaac

The candle is fat, and smooth and cool in my hand. It has no smell. Mummy says it was not expensive, and that I can have it, and she has given me the potato peeler, which I am using to scrape away at the wax so that out of its blockiness is coming the figure of a man. Smooth curls of wax fall onto the table around me.

Mummy suggested some make and do; once the phone had stopped ringing, and when the vegetables were in piles in front of her ready for dealing with. She is always good at thinking of things to make and do, probably because she was a graphic designer making labels for products before she stopped work. She still has a black leather case of paints, and thick flow pens, and when she draws something, she does it in quick, fluid lines, and whatever she is drawing looks as if it is growing up and out of the page like a beanstalk. She used to try and draw me when I was small, but she says I was always too wriggly and would never sit still. Teddy lies very still, which is exactly the opposite, but she doesn't sketch him either.

Today she is not drawing anything anyway; she is peeling potatoes ready for roasting, but she has cut two potatoes in half, and on each of the flat faces she has carved out a heart. She has mixed poster paint with water and made it thick and clotty and has poured it into four saucers so that they are pooled with red, blue, yellow and green. She has ripped off a long sheet of paper from a roll and weighted it to the table using two tins of beans so that it won't curl back on itself. Teddy is sitting in his support chair, with two saucers to each side of him and the length of the paper spread out in front of him and two of the potato halves held in his hands. He raises his arms likes he's going to conduct some music, as if there is an orchestra beyond where I am sitting next to him at the table. Mummy shows him how to dip the potato halves into the paint and press them onto the paper, and he is pressing and pressing and a whole stream of gleaming hearts are dancing wetly across the page. If I was doing this, I would put them in neat lines, and either in rows of a single colour or alternated symmetrically. Teddy mixes up both the colours and the direction. The hearts are upside down and sideways, and whizz off the paper like something sparked from a Catherine wheel. 'Not on your nose,' Mummy says, laughing as he presses his red-painted thumb to the tip of it.

My candle shaping needs slower, more careful work. I want the figure of the man to stand with his legs pressed together and his arms by his sides, so that his palms are held flat to his thighs. His head is going to have to be bald, because carving hair will be too tricky and there will be a risk of shaving away half of his golf-ball-sized head with the trying. I'm going to use a small vegetable knife to trace lines on his tummy to show where the muscles are.

'I'm going to give him a six pack,' I tell Teddy, who is now sifting through the pile of shavings, and trying and failing to loop the soft, pale curls of wax around his fingers. I pick two that are as big as onion rings, and fit them neatly over his ears. 'Now you look like a pirate. Long John Silver.' Teddy stretches to try and see himself in the mirror on the wall.

Mummy isn't peeling the vegetables on the island where she usually does. She's standing at the table between us, and she says, 'Beautiful, beautiful,' at Teddy's stream of bright wet hearts. She puts a stack of wax rings around her finger too, and stretches her hand towards Teddy as if he is a king, and she gives a little curtsey and laughs when he kisses her knuckles. She says to me, 'That's such careful work. The feet will be tricky. Cut them out as a rectangular block and then pare them away.'

As the man's shape comes out of the candle, I hold him at arm's length, one eye squinting. Mummy looks up from the carrot peelings.

'He's like one of the figures on Crosby Beach.' She tells me about a sculptor who has made one hundred identical cast-iron life-size figures of himself and spread them along three kilometres of the beach, right at the shoreline, where they gaze out to sea.

I love it that she knows about this, and that she can describe them in a way that makes it feel as if the figures are lined up in a row on the kitchen table. It's like I can actually see them, and properly hear the seawater swoosh around their ankles as the tide comes in.

Anna

It's a skill, the parallel running of two trains of thought in my brain: my speech, which patters down between my children, and then my thoughts, which loop and re-loop back on themselves like an old-fashioned tape recorder with large spools of tape.

I am talking of candles, and potatoes, and iron men on beaches, and the carrots are sturdy in my hand and the peel is vivid and damp, and I can smell poster paint, and the raw-earth smell of the skinned potatoes, and the iron-blood tang of the beef, which is coming to room temperature in the roasting tin. All these things work like small hooks or burrs to anchor me in the present and yet co-exist with an ebb and flow of my thoughts; a tidal zone of my own, tugged not by the moon, but instead by my heart.

Tomorrow the dietician will come to weigh Teddy. She will nag me about feeding tubes and about my stubborn persistence in wanting to continue to give him real food until it becomes impossible. *If* it becomes impossible; I always repeat that to her.

She has a scale pan, a large one, and Teddy will lie in it like a goose trussed for Christmas, and of all the things that could be the target for my rage, it's the scale pan that gets it, because that's where it all began.

When Teddy was almost one, we were with the health visitor, the one who still yawns her way through my waking dream. Teddy is wearing the strawberry hat, but in this real version he's placed safely back on my lap, a small balloon of spit gauzy at his lip edge, and I am tugging him into his snow suit and buttoning up my coat ready to go out into a sleety rain. It's only later that I catch sight of what she's written by the date. *Floppy? Motor milestones?* It's next to the section called 'Finding out about moving', where there are sketches of babies achieving physical things: *lifts head clear of ground; rolls over; sits with support; sits alone; moves around or crawls; stands holding on; stands alone.* I shrug as I read it. *Each child develops in his or her own time*, it says on the next page. It's a plausible reason to ignore the forward-sloping looped handwriting.

A little later, when Teddy gets a stubborn cough, it is still not anxiety that blooms in my chest. 'With Isaac at school,' I say to my mother, 'Teddy is exposed to so many more bugs.' I take him to the surgery, but only after I have held him in the shower hoping the clouds of steam will help, and balanced one end of his cot on books so that he is not lying flat, and bought a humidifier, which spritzes his room with an organic decongestant. The doctor pauses on the page where the health visitor has written *Floppy.* 'His airways,' he says, with a degree of puzzlement, 'he's not clearing them effectively. I think we'd better check out that there isn't an underlying condition.' *Underlying*, before, such an innocuous word; the alternative, *lying low*, somehow carrying with it more troublesome connotations.

At the hospital clinic, the paediatrician who sits across from me is brisk and concise. 'We'll run a basic screen of his kidneys, liver and thyroid. Also some blood work to check he's not anaemic.'

He's not, and all the screenings are normal. Nor, when they do more blood tests, are his muscle enzymes raised. None of the medical team seem reassured by this; instead, a shifting of their focus, as if the answer lies elsewhere. On the next visit, the paediatrician says she'd like to involve the department geneticist. 'Just to guide us,' she says, 'in terms of what investigations might be useful.' She also wonders whether a muscle biopsy might be beneficial, and spends a fruitless fifteen minutes trying to locate

Teddy's reflexes. Her voice is opaque, and I cannot gauge her degree of concern. 'It's not unusual for reflexes to be inactive at this stage.' I report all this, conscientiously, to Tom, who at this stage is not coming with me to appointments, because we are still wrapped in complacent ignorance and cannot hear the hooves beating with what is coming towards us.

When I see the geneticist, he explains that the best place to start is understanding how Teddy's muscles are getting their energy. He says something about signalling, and I think of the train set Isaac has been given for his fifth birthday, which has a battery-operated set of traffic lights that co-ordinate when the trains can stop and go. Isaac moves the trains with total obedience. 'But what,' I ask, 'are you looking for? What are you looking to rule out?'

'Progressive conditions,' he says, and for a moment I misunderstand, and think he means something modern or contemporary rather than, as it slowly dawns on me, something that gets worse over time.

Teddy's chest infection is better anyway. While the testing continues, his chest rattles and wheezes, and he splutters into the soft muslins I hold to his mouth, and then it is quiet again, his breathing losing its soft whistle. When the antibiotics are finished, they are still puzzling about him; a doctor who watches his tongue for what seems like an age without saying why. I finally ask him. 'Fasciculation,' he says. I am no wiser.

The geneticist says, 'Don't go googling anything. Information is often inaccurate. You are better off waiting for a diagnosis.' It seems that it is no longer a question of whether something is wrong, but what it might be.

When I ask what he is trying to rule out, he says, 'SMA.' It's a crisp, go-to, ready-prepared response. The letters rise before me like three fat red balloons. I do not google them because of what he advised. It is my first and last display of passive obedience.

The following week, when Tom is finally with me, and after a preamble in which he is unable to meet our eyes, the geneticist says, 'I'm sorry; I'm so very sorry, but the test results show that Teddy has SMA Type 2.' Everyone is kind and everyone is very sorry. I could paper the walls of our house if I printed out each time someone has said sorry. My hand is patted a lot, as if I am a child who has trouble falling asleep rather than a woman who is being told I have been unwittingly complicit in sabotaging my child's life.

In the subsequent meeting with the paediatric neurologist, they call Tom Dad, and me Mum – 'Does Mum want to be present for this procedure?' – as if our individual identity has already been swallowed by what is being heaped upon us. It is all I can do to not say, *I am not your mum*, which is curmudgeonly in the face of their attempt to be inclusive. Tom is holding my hand, and wearing an expression that suggests this can still be fixed if he puts his shoulder hard enough to the wheel. The neurologist, meanwhile, draws us a diagram with his green-inked fountain pen. He explains that in order for the lower motor neurones in the spine to be healthy, there needs to be a protein called SMN. Without it, the lower motor neurones deteriorate, and then messages from the spinal cord can't get through to the muscles, so movement becomes increasingly difficult. The muscles waste due to lack of movement. He draws a squiggle of a brain, and then messages in the shape of arrows flying from it, and he makes them land in a hopeless puddle at the base of the spine. The limbs he draws are like bloated sausages without muscular definition. 'There you have it,' he says, sitting back in his chair. 'The electrical signals from the brain have no way through, and we have yet to discover a way of making synthetic SMN.'

I am given leaflets containing definitions of terms, which the consultant goes through with me, pronouncing each syllable carefully, as if saying them clearly, rather than accepting them, might be my problem: *antisense oligonucleotide*; *bilevel positive airway pressure (BPAP)*; *denervation*; *dysphagia*; *dyspnoea*; *anterior horn cell*; *hypotonia*; *gastroesophageal reflux*; *lordosis*; *kyphosis*; *intubation*; *myometry*; *myopathy*; *pectus excavatum*; *pulse oximetry*; *forced vital capacity (FVC)*; *distal*; *proximal*; *Cobb angle*; *contracture*; *continuous positive airway pressure (CPAP)*; *chest percussion*; *axon*; *atrophy*; *aspiration pneumonia*.

They are words I didn't ever imagine would be mine, and even now I would like to blow them away like dandelion clocks before they settle on my tongue.

'They'll become a kind of rosary for you,' a sharp-eyed Irish nurse says when I am rereading the leaflet while waiting for a subsequent appointment. 'That's what they'll be, and soon easy and soft in your mouth.' She smooths the corner of a bed and makes her way off down the ward.

A different geneticist has a biro with a switch at the top which allows her to alter the colour of her ink. I am distracted by wondering what happenstance causes her to flip from blue to red.

'It's brutally straightforward,' she says crisply, pushing up her sleeve and drawing a strong, straight line across the width of a blank piece of paper. She looks directly at us, as if the clue to our suspect DNA might be sketched on our retinas. 'Approximately one in every forty to sixty people unknowingly carries the faulty SMN1 gene. When two people who are carriers have a child, the chances for the pregnancy are as follows.'

She draws three offshoots down from her initial broad line. I prepare myself for an unanticipated family tree. Beneath the first offshoot she writes – her handwriting bold and confident – *Child does not have SMA and is NOT a carrier – 25%*. On the second she writes, *Child does not have SMA and IS a carrier – 50%*. The '0' of the 50 is round and puffed out as a robin's wintry breast. 'Your first child,' she says dispassionately, 'will fall into one of these two categories and should be tested when he's older.' She pauses, and then underneath the third stalk she writes, *Child has SMA – 25%.* For further clarification, she puts *ONE IN FOUR* in capital letters above it. Then her thumb flexes, ready to trigger the pen's flip switch. She draws a vivid red circle around the last thing she has written. 'And there we have it,' she says, 'or rather there we have Teddy.' She pauses for a moment whilst we look at the red circle. She clicks the pen back to blue. 'Statistically,' she says, pushing the paper towards Tom's open hand, 'you can see how terribly unlucky he's been; there was a seventy-five per cent chance – even considering his parental gene pool – that he could have come out of this unscathed.'

Afterwards we sit in the hospital café and drink coffee, and all I can focus on is the number of men I slept with before meeting Tom – was it ten? Fifteen? Which ones of those might also have had the defective gene curled up tight in the spiral of their DNA, ready to leap out and club any child we might have conceived together? Instead it was Tom who carried it undetected towards me; Tom, whom I chose because the day he walked into the meeting room I was in – which was windowless, fluorescent-strip-lit, and with a low ceiling of yellowed polystyrene tiles – it was as if what blew in around him had come fresh from the sea, with the power to make me pink-cheeked and rosy just from his proximity. And it is that I am thinking of as he tries to take hold of my hand in the café, lifting it uncertainly to his lips as if kissing it might somehow make things different. I ball up my fist so that it is as if he is holding a small pocket of potatoes, because what seems to be so particularly cruel is that that which seemed so wholesome, so gloriously, breezily fresh, is in fact the opposite: a small, mutinous gathering of darkness curled in our conjoined DNA, ready to statistically nail Teddy before he even began.

In the interim, I have amassed more details to add to the tape spool that is the sublimated soundtrack of my days. I know that there is not just SMN1, there is also SMN2, which can moderate the severity of SMA because it produces a small amount of functional SMN protein. The more SMN2 a child has, the more SMN protein can be produced. Teddy has a small amount. I think of it as a little trove of gold coins, to be spent frugally, preciously, affording him some protection.

In all the medical language I have conscientiously learned, there is one phrase that stands out. There are many technical terms to describe the scoliotic form of the spine of a child with SMA, and multiple words to describe the calibre of their muscular tone and the shortcomings of their respiratory system. And yet the phrase that is used to describe the predisposition of SMA children to lie on their backs with their legs flopped outwards – *frog-legged* – disarms me with its simplicity. It makes me think of Teddy as pulled fresh from a pond, lying exposed to the air, his heartbeat visible beneath the smooth lustre of his skin, and his small, soft, splayed feet suggestive of something that might have more traction in water. He is my beloved little froglet, whom I love more than life. When I hold him in the bath, I cradle his head so that the water laps around his ears. As he lies suspended, I like to imagine him swimming between emerald fronds of weed, with small slices of dappled sunlight lighting his zigzagged way.

I have also learned about zebrafish, which are small tropical fish used to study gene function and disease processes, and to test potential therapies. They share several genes with humans, critically the ones used to make muscles. The embryos are transparent, which allows their muscle development to be easily observed. They can be used to test drugs that may slow or prevent the progression of disease.

In a near-distant future that I cannot bring myself to fully imagine, I wonder if I will be a late-middle-aged woman who stands all day in a shopping parade, well wrapped up because it is gusty and early December. Organised Christmas shoppers will sidestep me on the kerb. In my gloved hand there will be a fund-raising tin for an obscure zebrafish research project. There will be a photograph on the side of the canister showing a shoal of fish shimmering through turquoise tropical waters. If someone elderly stops – I think they usually have more time, more patience, and are more mindful of how life can bruise and blunt – I think they might ask me kindly, curiously, why I am collecting money for zebrafish. I will try not to cry as I tell them that zebrafish may have the magical answer; that perhaps if there is money enough to study them, Teddy's limbs can grow strong.

'The red paint has run out, can you please mix some more?'

'But how . . . but how did the sculptor stick them fast in the sand?'

Isaac

When we have lunch, my wax man is propped up against the salt grinder and Teddy's sheet of hearts is Blu-Tacked onto the crockery cupboard. After we have finished eating, Daddy is reading the paper and Mummy is reading a story to Teddy, and I go to the computer to google Crosby Beach.

Each of the iron figures is just over six feet tall and weighs six hundred and fifty kilos. When the tide is at its highest, all the figures are under water for an hour. When the tide is at its mid-point, most of them can be seen. When it is low, all of them can be. The figures are naked, but the website says visitors are allowed to put clothes on them. There are photographs of people dressing them in hats and scarves and then standing next to them, grinning. There is a particular type of mollusc that has made its home on the thighs of the ones farthest out. All of them are covered in barnacles and algae, and are speckled by the seawater so that they are very mottled. *It is the intention that they will not be cleaned.*

I spend ages clicking on the different photographs of the figures, who stare and stare with their blind eyes out to sea, and what I like most is the thought that they exist in a pattern that is not to do with the hands on a clock face but instead the tide as it sucks in and out. What I can't decide is whether the fact that they are looking outwards like explorers is a hopeful thing, or if they are sad and would prefer not to see whatever is behind them.

What I also read – and I copy it down neatly in the exercise book I have on my desk – is that the artwork is wheelchair-friendly.

It can be viewed from a promenade close to the beach. The beach is accessible by steps and ramps. The promenade is flat and well surfaced.

If, on another Saturday morning after writing alphabet letters in sugar, Mummy says, *Let's skedaddle*, I'm going to ask if it can be to Crosby Beach, because it won't be a problem taking Teddy.

If the tide is at the mid-point, we will be able to put a hat on one of the men. If it's right out, we can examine their legs and see if we can spot a barnacle colony. But most of all I would like to stand there and watch the whole line of them, by themselves but together along the length of the beach. I think about them as I brush my teeth; the heads of the men freckled by the water as it swooshes and swishes around their noses and lips. If their eyes could actually see, they would see sunrise and sunset, and the long, very dark shadows of an autumn afternoon. At high tide there would only be the steel blue-grey of the water, with the grains of sand swirling in it with each tug of the tide, and their ears packed with the sweeping roar of it all. It is the oddest feeling that right this minute they are all standing on Crosby Beach, staring out to *Another Place*. I hope the sculptor did fix them cleverly in the sand, and that the tide can never snatch them away in a winter storm.

I reach out to my bedside table where my own wax figure is standing. Mummy helped me with the body, so it has neatly marked stomach muscles. The back of its head feels smooth as a new conker.

Tomorrow, after school, I am going to put it in a Pyrex bowl. If I fix it with Blu Tack perhaps it will be able to stand properly upright. Mummy will help with a plan to safely secure it. Maybe she will hold a match to the base, the flame licking against the soles of the feet, and then hot wax will drip steadily onto the glass and work like glue. Then Teddy can help pour in water to slowly cover the figure and work like the tide. It will be our very own version of *Another Place*.

Tom

Does it count as a date night? Dates presumably don't take so much persuasion. Anna doesn't want to come; she cooked roast beef for lunch, and said she'd be happy eating a cracker with some cheese. The boys have had beans on toast for supper. She mashed Teddy's with a fork, and cut the toast into tiny little postage stamps. This morning she helped them make things: a wax figure that has captivated Isaac, and a sheet of potato heart prints with Teddy. She spent ages cleaning the kitchen after lunch; carefully removing small flecks of poster paint from the grain of the table.

'Really?' she says, standing by the sink with her back to me, scrubbing vigorously at the baked-bean saucepan. 'Wouldn't you just prefer to stay in? Who goes out on a Sunday night?'

Lots of people, I want to say, but instead, 'It would just be nice to do something together before the week kicks off. It feels like we haven't really caught up since I got back from Geneva.'

She glances at me quickly over her shoulder, and perhaps there is a small, unspoken reprimand in her gaze. I'm saying we haven't spent time together, but, having worked all Saturday, I still chose to go cycling this morning. Is that what she's thinking? Perhaps I should answer as if she actually has said it out loud; to say that on my bike I feel confident, liberated, the road spread out before me, smoothed with the easy camaraderie of the other cyclists.

She wipes the draining board, and folds the J cloth over the tap, her back to me still. Teddy lies on the floor at her feet, one of his hands swiping at her ankles. She steps carefully around him, high on her toes like a ballerina. Teddy almost encircles her legs with a wild swoop of his arm as she reaches for the towel. 'Got you!' he says, as if he has caught an exotic creature.

'There's a new tapas place opened on George Street. One of the cycling guys was talking about it. We could at least text Madeleine and see if she can babysit.'

Beneath the smoothness of what I am saying, I feel a small tug of irritation that I should have to work so persistently to persuade my wife to go out for dinner with me.

Before the children were born, we went on holiday to southern Spain and stayed in a tiny house in a *pueblo blanco*. We ate lunch in a neighbouring restaurant with a small paved courtyard; Anna's face part shaded by an olive tree, a small plate of exquisite lamb chops on the table between us, a glass of sherry held to her lips, her smile broad and easy, her palm turned upwards as she spoke – 'How perfect is this?'

'Why don't you go, Mummy?' Isaac says. 'It might be nice.' He is still whittling away at the compact wax figure. He does not lift his eyes as he speaks, and his words seem somehow less weighted than my own. It has occurred to me, recently, that perhaps Isaac somehow makes Anna feel less scrutinised than I do; his words falling casually, lightly into the kitchen.

She reaches for her phone and texts Madeleine, whose immediate response is a yes. She turns to me, and nods, and I have the oddest feeling that I have just won a contest of will, conducted carefully and mutinously like a rally in a tennis game. Her out-breath, as she picks up her bag, is close to the smallest of sighs.

In the car, she is mostly silent. I am mostly aware of the volume of the indicator. Is it usually this loud? On the windscreen there is the softest mizzle of rain. When we step out onto the pavement, I lift my coat from my shoulders to create an umbrella for us both, but her step is quicker than mine, and perhaps it is deliberate, because she momentarily lifts her forehead skywards, as if she welcomes the gentle wash of the rain.

In the restaurant, we take what seems like an age to decide what to order; the waitress standing with her pen and her pad, the expression on her face suggesting that surely choosing what to eat should not be beyond us. We have, after all, made the decision to come out to a restaurant. I order chicken livers, stuffed aubergine, butter beans and some pomegranate chicken. Anna's fingertip traces along the list of tapas.

'The sea bream with salsa verde, and the fattoush, and the lamb chop.'

'Do you remember, do you remember those lamb chops, cooked in sherry, in that restaurant in Spain, the little courtyard, all the food on tiny turquoise plates?'

She pauses for a moment, her gaze fixed steadily before her, as if she is trying very hard to see down through salt water.

'No,' her eyes suddenly full on me, 'I don't remember that at all.'

The waitress asks what we would like to drink.

'Rioja?'

Anna shakes her head.

'Tap water's fine for me.'

The waitress briskly collects the menus.

The space between us feels oddly formal, as if each thing we say will be pushed across the table like a piece on a chessboard, each word carefully considered before an answer is given.

I think about reaching across and taking her hand in my own, but just as I think it, she removes it from beside her empty wine glass, and puts it square in her lap.

Anna

Madeleine can babysit. Of course she can. What else might she be doing on a Sunday night in November? And I should be grateful to her as I open the front door. She has pulled on her coat in a hurry, her scarf not properly tied at her throat, and she is carrying a rolled-up magazine that she was probably reading when the phone rang. She will pick it up again when the children are in bed.

I am lucky to have Madeleine. Her own four children are grown and long fledged. 'There's not much I don't know about babies,' she said, although that was when Isaac was small. Perhaps she wouldn't make the same claim now. Teddy adores her. She mostly lies him on the couch and pulls funny faces for him, and once she let him trace over all the wrinkles on her face with a turquoise flow pen. 'What's a bit of sick?' she said when he threw up all over her shoulder. Her hair is thinning and her bones are probably osteoporotic and she refers to the magazines she reads as books, and when she gets up from the couch she says *Oooff!* which Isaac can mimic perfectly. She went on a course to be trained how to use an EpiPen; she held the certificate out to me and said, 'I'm going to put this in the drawer next to my Cycling Proficiency.' She passed that recently too. Tom says it's her version of the University of the Third Age. I haven't the heart to tell her that anaphylaxis isn't a component of SMA. 'If there's an EpiPen to hand, I know just how to use it.'

I think I trust Madeleine to babysit because she wouldn't try and use her initiative; wouldn't try and solve something by herself, or rely on what she would call her smarts. 'Truth be told,' she once said to me, 'I don't have many of those. My biggest gift to mothering was a bosom like a shelf. I'm good at the cuddling. Can't be faulted on that.' And that's good – that's plenty – for the babysitting, but not for when Tom said maybe she could look after the children if I wanted to keep working.

While Madeleine is settling herself in (she always plumps up the cushions on the couch, as if giving them advance warning she is about to sit down), Tom takes advantage of the time and gets his briefcase ready for work. He has three different bags. It's an ongoing decision about what he needs for the next day. He's fastidious about the packing of them: his portable charger, his notebook, a calculator he particularly likes.

My decision to stop work wasn't really a decision. It was a series of realisations, a speedy dawning; that's how I think of it.

The day of Teddy's diagnosis, I was wearing a particularly good jacket. I'd come straight from the office for the appointment, and collected him from the childminder en route, because that was when Teddy was a child who was something of a mystery, not a child with a diagnosis, which is different territory altogether.

After we left the hospital, I was standing in front of the sliding doors, waiting for Tom to bring the car around from the car park because it was raining heavily and as of a few moments ago even a raindrop now seemed a threat to our child. I was cradling him in my arms and he mouthed the lapel of the jacket, leaving a small silvery trace that I would usually have quickly wiped clean. And this time I did not, because it came to me, avalanching down through my awareness, that when I got home, I would put the jacket back into the wardrobe and maybe never wear it again, and it would gather dust on the hanger, the faded colour of the shoulders becoming at odds with the rest of it. Because, I could have said to Tom but never did, *How can Teddy continue to go to a childminder who looks after eight children, helped by sixteen-year-*

olds who have barely an NVQ between them? How can I employ a nanny who will be in her early twenties and who will want to look after a child she can take to Tumble Tots and who will be filing her nails when he chokes to death on his lunch? And how can I ever find someone who will go to all the appointments if I am at work, and listen carefully to what the doctor is saying and report back to us accurately? How will we ever find someone for four days a week who will watch and watch and watch Teddy, and make sure he feels the outworkings of all of this as lightly as possible?

It would be me. No question. I knew that as I was buckling him into his car seat outside the hospital, rolling up my career in my hand and tossing it away like a tissue. 'It's not the same,' I say to the HR woman on the phone the next day. 'It can't possibly be the same as leaving a healthy child with someone else.' Madeleine has lasted because she doesn't try to usurp me. The smallest issue and she gets Isaac to dial my number.

I don't want to go out. I am tired. I am not hungry. Sometimes it is hard to remind myself that I am also a wife. Sometimes, the slightest of suspicions, like the tip of a nettle traced across my skin, that I am angry at us – at Tom and myself – because SMA is what we made, and that at the heart of us lies something dark.

In the restaurant, behind Tom, there is a rope of small white lights switched to twinkle. I'd like to ask the waitress if we can swap tables, although then the lights would be in my peripheral vision, which would probably be more irritating. Alternatively, I could ask if they might be adjusted so they don't flicker. The waitress doesn't look as if she could be persuaded to switch them off. Besides, perhaps the other diners are enjoying them. I close my eyes briefly, and try not to focus on the imprint of the lights, which is playing along the length of my eyelid. My retina feels as if it is fizzing.

Tom is asking me a question about lamb chops, about a restaurant in Spain. There are turquoise plates in his recall. Sometimes I wonder if I have cauterised all previous memories, and whether by doing so I am avoiding looking back to a time when life felt so misleadingly uncomplicated and so entirely without scrutiny.

'No, I don't remember that at all.'

However, when I try to summon it more forcefully, there it is, intact and shimmering. The sun warm on my forearms, the tables inlaid with small ceramic tiles, *queso panela* cooked in a dusting of semolina, oregano and honey. Why is it suddenly so difficult to say to him, *Yes, I do, I do remember – and also that amazing cheese?* The memory gathers substance. There were small mirrors hanging from the branches of the olive tree. At nightfall, the light from the candles on the table was refracted across their surface, so that the olive tree seemed to carry tiny candles too. It comes back to me – as the waitress reaches to take the menus – that I quoted Virginia Woolf to him, sitting at the tiled turquoise table in Spain: '"Women have served all these centuries as looking glasses . . . reflecting the figure of man at twice its natural size."' We laughed, because it had, then, no relevance to us, and yet now perhaps it throws its own precise, small shadow across the space between us.

Was he reaching for my hand? It is freshly on my lap. I think about putting it back on the table, but leave it where it lies.

'You seem . . . fraught; more fraught,' he says, hesitantly, as the waitress appears again with food.

Fraught. The word he has chosen, presumably with care, hovers over the glossy butter beans. It is probably the right word. How easy it would be to burst into tears, to press my forehead to the table and allow myself to sob. I remind myself of the importance of keeping my composure. It would be like a crack in a dam wall; who knows where it would end? What I'm not sure of is when Tom became aligned with those to whom my guard must be kept up.

Isaac's small, carved wax figure is oddly emotionally resonant; the way he held it out to me, white and smooth, stretched out across his careful palms. I loved how he listened to me about the iron men on the beach. He was rapt, I could see, intently absorbing the detail, with his visual imagination gambolling ahead of my words. He is increasingly sensitive and thoughtful. Perhaps I should say that to Tom now; blurt out this new and surprising concern, and point out that we worry about Teddy all the time but perhaps he is unexpectedly more resilient than Isaac, whose eyes sometimes, liquid and dark, make me mindful of a caged orphan leveret Tom once told me about.

Instead, 'No,' my tone impervious and contained, 'I'm just tired. It's been a busy few days.'

The rest of the meal has a steady rhythm: the boiler needs servicing; the cherry tree outside the porch needs pruning. He reminds me about going to his mother's in a fortnight for Sunday lunch. I tell him that Tabitha, Jenny, Stella and Ruth all called earlier to discuss it. We achieve a canter of conversation; a brisk tug on the ties that bind us. The waitress comes and goes and I am relieved when it is over. The mouthful of chicken livers I have eaten sits indigestible and rich beneath my ribs.

He will want sex when we get home. As he holds the car door open for me, I can read it from his physical attentiveness. I will oblige. That is the terrible word that comes to me on the journey home. I don't know when exactly it became the right one. Perhaps I have been bought for the price of a small portion of sea bream with salsa verde. It's only one more demand in a long day of demands that need catering for; it is also a perfectly reasonable expectation. He is a considerate lover and will not only be mindful of his own pleasure. He will not comment on my increasing habit of keeping my eyes closed. I tell myself this as he turns the car into the driveway, switches off the engine, and reaches across to give me a swift kiss on the cheek.

'Aren't you glad we went out?' he says, and I leave the question hanging as I gather my things.

Anna

Paula Jonson has a sharp little face; her nose beaky, her chin coming to a consonant point. It looks as if she might have been holding a book very close to her face when someone snapped it shut and trapped her between the pages, and therein altered the shape of her bone structure. It would be an understandable temptation. Her expression also suggests she has something very sour trapped beneath her tongue; a thin crescent of lime peel perhaps, or a smooth-skinned cape gooseberry.

I shouldn't be thinking that as she takes off her coat, all of a bustle, in the hallway. She pushes up the sleeves of her jumper to just beyond her elbow, as if I am something which requires tenacity and is about to be tackled.

'How's things?' she says, her folder clasped to her chest as if to prevent me making a successful snatch for it.

Things. How are things. Things, as a term, would cover the teapot beside her on the counter, or the kettle, or the fridge magnet which is just behind her and which if I squint carefully makes her look as if she has a cauliflower ear. Teddy isn't a thing. And neither am I. I assume I am included in her broad opening gambit; there's always a box to tick on her sheet that says: *Enquire about the primary carer.*

'If by things you mean mostly Teddy, he's been very well, thank you.' I try to keep my voice smooth and even.

'Well that's good to hear.'

She plumps her folder down on the side, and starts to flip

through the pages. She licks her thumb to make this speedier, and when she puts her hand flat to the counter, it leaves a small, damp print.

My kitchen amuses her. She hasn't said as much but I know it. Not amuses her in that she feels it to be a warm, witty space – which in truth it isn't – but in a sardonic way. I can see that sometimes she is itching to pick things up; to get the measure of them a little more accurately so that she can chalk up more details about us. Bags of quinoa, cocoa nibs, dried seaweed, my Nutribullet; they are all items she thinks tell her more about me than I say.

She's unzipping her portable scales now. She looks across at Teddy, who catches my eye and twinkles, and for a moment I think he might be contemplating making a dash for it in the Wizzybug.

'I'm hoping you're going to break my scale pan today, young man. Let's be having you.' She claps her hands, as if he is a little terrier who might be summoned to jump through a paper hoop at the circus.

I start to undress him down to his pants. He folds his arms to try and prevent me taking off his vest. 'The scale pan is always like an ice cube.' It's a playful rather than an actual protest, but Paula makes a show of taking the chill off the pan with her palms.

'How's his eating been?' Her chin jabs a little towards me as she asks.

'Reasonable. Better some days than others.'

At one of our meetings, she started by asking, 'So how's it going with the poached chicken, the sweet potato wedges and the finely chopped kale?' On another occasion, when she arrived and I was grating butternut squash, she leaned against the side, folded her arms and said, 'You mothers, cooking with all the fervour of martyrs.' I didn't answer her; instead found myself distracted, wondering why Catherine was pinned to a wheel.

When she's got Teddy lying in the scale pan, she has another go at interacting with him.

'How's your chewing going, mister?'

He laughs and makes an attempt at gurning his jaw like ruminating cattle. Paula takes advantage of his concentration to take a small squeeze of his flesh, just above his elbow, between her finger and thumb. She doesn't hurt him, or pinch him; that's not what she's doing. Instead, I think it is to get some kind of measure of him; whether he feels scrawny or not. Scrawny wouldn't be her word, but it's what she is looking out for. I am reminded of the witch who put Hansel and Gretel in a cage and then tried to fatten them up. Paula looks up at me and says, 'Hmm,' because I can see from the LED display that Teddy's weight hasn't increased.

Teddy's first dietician, Eleanor, was a fan of spy novels and thrillers. We used to see her in a clinic, and she always had a book pressed down on the desk beside her. She used to read a few pages in between patients. Her vocabulary was peppered with the genre. 'It's a catch-22,' she'd say, or 'What we're really engaged in is a kind of cold war.' She was very informative; she'd pick a nutritional issue each visit and give me a potted lecture.

This is what I know. Oral feeding is a problem because children with SMA are poor at chewing, so choking or coughing can happen during or after swallowing. The bulbar muscles – which are around the mouth and the throat – can be compromised so that speaking and swallowing become difficult. Recurrent pneumonias can be a sign of aspiration, and feeding difficulties are compounded by limited mouth opening. Poor head control is also a problem, and gastroesophageal reflux. See what an attentive listener I was.

Eleanor was also big on the potential solutions: Neater Eaters; valved straws; elbow supports. She'd pass them over the desk as if handing out clever spyware to help me adroitly escape from a tight spot: 'These are some of the options further down the line.'

Paula's preference is to go straight for the big guns. She doesn't dally around, ever.

'We need to think about a strategy for weight gain. I think we need to address that more directly. Are you ready to consider tube-feeding him yet?'

She knows it's a firecracker, lobbed across the room at me. Tom doesn't see it that way; if I were to recount this conversation tonight, he'd say she's trying to be helpful, or that she's just doing her job. I have a sneaking suspicion he might think her view has some merit. Paula meanwhile is already foraging in her bag and pulling out the demo tube, repeatedly clicking the port in and out to show how easy it will be to pump food into Teddy.

I place my fingers on my temples and press very lightly, because it feels as if the skin on my forehead is crackle-glazed, and that by applying pressure I will stop it falling to the floor.

'We have talked about this before. I think I've said that I'm reluctant to switch to a G-tube and for Teddy to lose the chewing capability that he has, as well as for him to lose all pleasure in eating because he's basically being given grey sludge.'

Paula wrinkles her nose, as if offended by my description of the pouches of powder she's now also whisking out of the side pockets of the bag. She even calls it 'feed' sometimes, which makes me think of silage for cattle, or grain mix for poultry.

'You just have to get your head around the compromises, Anna. Feeding Teddy orally takes so much effort for him, it depletes his calorie intake. With the tube, he'll be fed in minutes with all the nutrition and calories he needs.'

I think she can only just restrain herself from brushing her palms together briskly and saying, *Job done*. I pause, and then parry.

'The physio is always keen to emphasise that being light helps with independent movement. If he were suddenly to put on weight, his ability to move, even to sit, might be compromised. It's of no benefit for him to be fatter if it compromises his independence.'

'Physios. They're often – how shall I put it – a little alarmist. We could address that if it happens. It wouldn't happen overnight. We'd put checks and balances in place. And I do understand this is difficult for you. Feeding is such a big part of mothering.'

It's not about me at all. I'd like to shout that at her; shout it so that it makes her actually jump, because I wonder if she has ever considered that the mothers she describes as martyrs, grating away at butternut, and puréeing vegetables, might actually prefer their child to be independently chomping their way through a rump steak while they blithely catch up on Twitter. I feel suddenly so tired, so weary of her beaky little face, and of suppressing the desire to say to her, *Why don't you get this at all?*

'He was fed with a tube when he was in hospital in the spring; just for a few days while his chest infection settled. I can see its benefits; I just don't think we need to use it on a regular basis. The time may come, but I strongly feel it's not now.' My voice is smooth and persuasive. It doesn't help to be seen to be unco-operative – that would trigger her discussing me with Julia, the social worker, and filing an incident report that says: *Address consistent resistance.*

Paula looks suddenly bored. 'Let's park it then, shall we? Let's see how he goes through the winter. Meanwhile, I'll leave you a few sachets anyway so that you can remind yourself of the nutritional content.'

She can't, however, resist a parting shot, as she pulls on her coat and forgets about her pushed-up pullover sleeves so has to tweak them back down to her wrists with her fingertips.

'Remember, Anna, it's easy to focus on feeding a five-year-old puréed celeriac and playing aeroplanes with a spoon. No one wants to cast their mind forward to a young man who still has that same dependency.'

As she drives away, I'd like to shake my fist at her disappearing car. Instead, I go back into the kitchen and hold Teddy to me, his frame light and yielding, his head snuggled into the side of my neck. I look at the packets of powder and want to hurl them after her. I placate myself by envisioning a beautifully calm laboratory where the workspace is clean, methodical, and humming with rational, informed purpose. I summon up a scientist who is, at that very moment, looking down a microscope at genetic complexities and saying to her colleagues, *Why, yes, this is the way we can make synthetic SMN.*

Teddy

Mummy's put my snow domes all in a row on the table. I try and shake them one after another so it's snowing in all of them. A whole row of snow worlds, and the one with the church steeple the last to disappear. Paula the food lady's gone. When she was weighing me, she looked at me with her head on one side like a bird deciding whether to take a peck out of a worm.

When I'm shaking the last snow dome, I hear another noise. When I turn to look, Mummy is standing by the bin and she's picked up the four packets Paula left on the side. She has the big scissors in her hand and she's cutting off the tops. She holds each one above the bin and squeezes them so that they are open their widest. She stretches up her arm and the powder falls down like gritty rain. When each packet is empty, she screws it up into a ball and tosses it into the non-recycling bin. She scores four out of four goals, but doesn't seem to notice. 'Good riddance,' she says, slapping the lid down. I think about saying *Good shot*, but I don't think she's listening.

I don't know what good riddance means, but she's certainly got rid of them. I don't think that's what Paula had in mind when she left them in a neat stack, all tidy by the kettle. I think what she's thrown away is what they give me to eat in the hospital when I'm poorly. There's a tube like a clear plastic snake which means the powder slides down into me without any chewing. Mummy doesn't like that; doesn't like even talking about it. Her voice sounded a bit cross; Paula probably didn't guess, but I did. I guessed.

Mummy's putting peas in the blender now to make pea soup for lunch. It is bright, bright green. She lets me press the button for it to start whizzing. When she's pouring it back into the pan, she says, 'After lunch, we can wrap the Christmas presents to take to the farm. It seems silly doing it in early November, but think how efficient we'll feel. Top marks for Christmas efficiency!'

She has a Sellotape bracelet, which she makes smaller to fit on my wrist. I have to lean across with the opposite hand and pull out a length of tape and pass it to her when she has the wrapping paper ready. 'And tape!' she says, laughing, and stretches out her finger to me.

It's a serious business. Other people might just wrap presents with one roll of wrapping paper and Sellotape not cut neatly. Mummy doesn't. She has several colours, which all go with each other, and tissue paper to use on the inside, the colour of which, she shows me, is a contrast to the paper. She tells me the names of the colours: electric blue, carmine pink, Caribbean lime.

Each gift has a layer of tissue, and then the wrapping paper, and then a ribbon tied in a beautiful bow. As well as the gift tag, there is a small shiny bauble in another carefully chosen colour, which can be used as a decoration afterwards and put on the tree. She has a flat box of the baubles, and each of them sits in a tiny compartment like an egg in a nest. Mummy puts her fingers on her lips while she is deciding which one to choose, and tries one or two next to the paper, like when she holds an earring next to her cheek.

She chooses a bauble she says is burnt orange, and attaches it to a present where the tissue paper and ribbon are carmine pink.

It's my job as well to pass her the gifts. There is a bowl for Granny, to go on her dressing table. It's painted in very delicate colours and it's thin, thin, thin. I pass it to her carefully using both of my hands. There's a scarf for Auntie Jenny, and a small, very soft white bunny for Stella's new baby, and for William a belt that Mummy says is like horsemen wear in Argentina. For Tabitha there are cashmere socks. I put one over my hand like a glove puppet and make it bow to Mummy.

When we have finished, the pile on the kitchen table looks like a picture from a catalogue, where everything is beautiful and there's real snow and decorations everywhere and the perfect Christmas Day. When Isaac comes home from school, I know he will do a long, slow whistle; mostly because he's just learned to do this and any excuse is a good one, and also because we have totally smashed present wrapping.

Mummy goes over to the side to put the kettle on. She's talking to me, but I think not actually talking to me. She says the words out loud, but not in a way that wants an answer.

'A nice accurate impression of our daily life,' and then 'Would you like me to read you a story?' which I do.

Outside, it is starting to rain. I feel sleepy, suddenly, listening to her voice. She has a different one for me and Isaac than for all the visitors.

Tom

A thought is not a deed. I'm clear about that.

Especially when the thought is unbidden. Especially when it sneaks up, catching me unawares. The impulse to reach out, when stepping from a lift, and take a woman by the hand. Imagining the feel of it, the unfamiliar shape of it, held in my own.

A sudden yearning, which begins in the chest and blooms on the lips.

A tug in the groin.

A consonant heat in the heart, as it stirs, listens up.

A man who is married could flirt with a stranger on a train. Or in a bar smile at someone a little too directly. Know, at a conference that lasts two days at a hotel, that if circumstances were different, there could be corridor creeping.

I am not guilty of any of that.

I look only at the crossword puzzle of the woman on the train next to me, not her breasts, not her legs.

I have never been unfaithful; never considered it, never felt tempted. Never lifted my eyes to the horizon.

And now.

Eliza.

The strongest desire to say to her, *I like you*. The plain, sustaining, disarming simplicity of that, like a slice of Madeira cake on a white plate. The ease and calm of it. The beguiling frankness of her, the timbre of her voice. Now, when everything feels blocked and stilted with Anna, and instead, with Eliza, like throwing open a window wide.

The oldest story in the book. Spouses cheat, in thought and in deed. Venial and cardinal sins.

But here's the thing. Do they do it when one of their children has a life-limiting illness? That would take some brass.

If there was a scale – let's mark it one to ten – how would that kind of cheating be scored? Just how reprehensible would it be?

Maximum. Maximum score. No question.

If I look back to when the geneticist told us about Teddy and drew the line that showed how Anna and I collectively shafted him, here's the thing he didn't say. *Not only will this bend Teddy's life out of shape, but it will give you a marriage less ordinary. Just think about that.*

I am a man sitting on a train going home to his family from work.

I am a man who looked at the mouth of a woman across a desk and thought, fleetingly, how very much I would like to kiss her. Who noticed, as she reached out for her iPad, the oyster silk of her blouse, lustrous against the pale softness of her skin on the inside of her wrist. The delicate tracery of her veins.

A thought is not a deed.

I can still look my wife in the eye.

A thought is not a deed. A thought is not a deed.

See how the rhythm of the train affirms this?

And anyway, I have a marriage less ordinary. Less ordinary. Less ordinary.

Anna

Such a beautiful late-autumn morning. My running shoes call to me from the back of the shoe cupboard. I haven't run for over a year, and there is something about the light today, the cold pull of the air on the lungs, the sun still low in the sky even though it is almost eleven, and the feeling that I might run to the horizon and press my palms flat to the red of it. I stand outside the front door for a moment, my fingers curled in my palms, and imagine my steady, repetitive footfall and the losing of myself in my breath as I reach the path by the river.

Technically I could call Madeleine. She is probably returning from the shops, or perhaps from seeing a friend for coffee. She might come and mind Teddy, who is playing on the carpet with his Lego fort, and scooching across the floor like a velvety caterpillar. And yet.

The last time I ran, I hurled my trainers to the back of the cupboard, my chest heaving with hawking great sobs, my face drenched with tears. It was the rhythm of my pace that triggered it; the soles of my trainers pounding on the pavement, and the word *atrophy*, *atrophy* suddenly over and over like an ear worm that would not stop.

And then the realisation that the word pulled apart can spell *a trophy*. A trophy: something sought, proudly carried, bravely won, which isn't SMA at all. And then that notion releasing another torrent of words, like a scatter of birds wheeling up into the sky at the crack of a gunshot. *Atrophy in the trunk muscles can lead to skeletal deformities. Atrophy in the breathing muscles can lead to potentially fatal respiratory problems. Atrophy in the swallowing muscles can lead to difficulties in eating and drinking.*

I tried to swat the words away from me, and then, as they swarmed and buzzed in my head, crouched down on the pavement and made myself as small as I could, my elbows wrapped around my head, my eyes scrunched closed. An old man, walking by, said mildly, 'Anything I can do, m'dear?'

I feigned a twisted ankle, and moved to sit on the kerb, my palms pressed to my feet. That's why I came home and threw my running shoes to the back of the cupboard. I do not want to be a woman who sobs wildly on a pavement, whom an old man steps delicately around, his walking stick making gentle taps on the paving stones, his feet placed carefully to avoid his shoes being contaminated by grief.

Instead I am a woman who demonstrates resourcefulness, and who will use this time, now (coming inside and firmly closing the door), to prepare for today's appointment with the orthopaedic consultant. The purpose of the meeting will be to check for any further contracture of Teddy's muscles, and also the curve of his spine. The orthotist will be there too, and possibly the link worker, and there will likely be a discussion about a new spinal brace or a Lycra suit, or perhaps a sleep system that will allow him to be more comfortable lying down.

Always I push. Now, all thought of running is abandoned and instead I sit down and prepare to google spinal braces to see if there is a new one, one that could be more comfortable, more effective; somehow more fit for purpose. At the last appointment, I told the orthotist about an SMA project in America that has designed the first child-size exoskeleton. 'Look,' I said, taking the print-off out of my bag and smoothing out the pages, 'it has support rods that are adjusted to fit around the child's legs and torso, and a series of motors that mimic human muscles and give the necessary strength to stand up and walk.' The orthotist smiled kindly. I knew, before she said it – in a calm voice that seemed designed to placate an overexcited child – that it was a prototype, that it was a long way from being available, and that anyway such things are very rarely actually useful for children because of their speed of growth.

None of them, anyway, claim, so far, to give a child suffering from SMA the necessary strength to walk. That brutal fact always undoes me: Teddy's slim, soft, hypotonic legs, which splay wide on the changing mat and make me long for a magic spell to jolt them awake. A spangle of stardust seems as likely as a cure.

My internet search today does not discover a spinal brace any different from the one Teddy has already. The orthopaedic team will still count on me, however, to brandish something that I've printed off, or bring up something alternative or new, because that's what I usually do, like a woman engaged on an impossible, relentless quest, besieged by reality and yet sallying forth, polished cutlass in hand. The consultant never says, *Do you have questions?* Instead, *What would you like to ask about today?* always making the assumption that I have come armed to the teeth.

There's a website giving details about global clinical trials that is saved to my favourites and which I used to check nightly in case of a breakthrough. There's LM1070, which progressed to Clinical Phase II before being halted because of collateral kidney damage; RG7800 which is a compound that may be able to increase the amount of full-length SMN protein made from the SMN2 gene. There is the Avexis viral gene therapy trial; and Nusinersen, which has reached Stage II. I can also rattle off multiple different research projects. Can SMN be packaged into a virus and delivered to motor neurons? (Yes, but the mice die soon after.) Can a model of SMA be used in worms to rapidly screen large numbers of drugs for SMA? (Ongoing.) Can tetra-cycline-based compounds increase SMN levels? (Possibly; in development.) There's also a study at a European university which is using cats. As I drive past the animal rights protest that gathers outside the science labs in Oxford, I am shocked to find that I am a woman who wants to roll down the window and shout: *I don't care about the cats; test the cats, do what you like to the cats, if it helps my child to walk.*

I don't check the websites nightly any more. I can't decide whether it's a haemorrhaging of hope, the learning of patience, or, mostly, exhaustion.

Sometimes, when I take Teddy out of the bath, I roll him over to dry his back and kiss the base of his spine softly. That's where what needs to be happening isn't. I rest my fingertips gently there, and envision his motor neurons. I see them as tiny pinpoints of light, like messages from a star, firing down the spinal cord, travelling from the upper motor neurons to the lower, and to where they should project out to his skeletal muscles and thereby control his movement. The anterior horn is the front part of the spinal cord, where the lower motor neurons are located, and where the long, slender projections called axons migrate out in bundles of nerves. I picture it as a smooth, curved piece of bone, like the antler of a deer. I trace an imaginary web of lines radiating out down his legs, and wish I could magnetically draw the axons down along with me, obedient as a swoosh of compliant iron filings.

My phone pings from beside my laptop. It's a text from Sophie, confirming the date of the trip to Cowley Manor. *PLEASE COME!* she writes in capital letters.

I hold the phone in my hand for a moment and look out of the window, focusing on a spindleberry bush that is visible at the perimeter of the garden. I text my reply.

I'm sorry, that date really doesn't work for me but I hope you all have a great time.

I add an emoji of a downturned mouth to emphasise my regret, and then one of a woman dancing in a flamboyant dress to evoke what fun they will have. I press send, turn the phone face down and wait to see if Sophie responds. She does not, and I get up from my desk like someone who now feels the coast to be clear.

I go to the cupboard and take out Teddy's harness. I will scoop him up from the rug now that he is tiring of playing with Lego, and put on some music and encourage him to bob about in it for a little while. Assisted standing is good; it helps breathing, blood circulation, bladder, bowels, bones and joints.

I would give anything – anything – not to know this.

Tom

The train carriage feels warmer and a little brighter than usual. I'm resisting the urge to smile at my fellow commuters, or to start chatting to the man sitting next to me, which would obviously be unexpected and almost certainly unwelcome. Do I reek of alcohol? My face is probably skewed in a shiny half-smile.

Before I left the office to go to the cocktail bar, George looked up from where he sits at the desk next to mine. Beyond us, Eliza was putting on her coat.

'Well done on winning the Geneva project. You'll be quids in.' He lowers his voice conspiratorially. 'You've also lucked out with your junior colleague. She's very easy on the eye; it's quite the chat at the water cooler. You're the dream team. I don't know why I keep being allocated earnest, tall young men.'

As Eliza walked towards us, I wanted to shield her from the implied loucheness of his comment. I was also mindful that his eye, in reality, was no different from mine.

In the bar, Charlie, the CEO, ordered the drinks. 'This project win – it's quite a coup – and will reflect really well on your bonuses. It looks like a project that's going to generate very good margins.'

He went to take a call on his mobile, and Eliza, beaming, gave me a high five.

'Oh my God, it's like getting the perfect school report. I'm spending my extra money already!' The waiter arrived with her gin and ginger lime fizz, and she clapped her hands with anticipatory pleasure.

I could have left after one drink and caught my regular train home, but I stayed for three more, guilt peppering my fingertips as I handed the menu back to the waiter.

Afterwards, I walked back through Mayfair, the Christmas lights strung across the streets in the shape of gigantic feathers, and felt part of the upbeat buzz of it all; part of a parallel universe where I could make a young woman laugh, her face tilted beautifully towards me.

On the train, I refocus and hug the thought of my increased bonus to myself. It reinforces that I am a good breadwinner, a good provider, a good husband and father. I seek solace in this thought, guilt still inking my bloodstream.

When we were first married and had no surplus cash, we used to play a game called 'I would buy', when we imagined we had pots of money and speculated what we would spend it on. If we were to play it again now, it occurs to me that I'm not sure what Anna would choose, and the fact that I don't know bothers me. Years ago, I'd have nailed it: vibrant watercolours in neat little tubs, an expensive paintbrush, Wolford tights, hand-milled lavender soap. It occurs to me that Anna might not know what I'd like either.

I won't tilt my good mood by thinking of it as a reflection of the state of our marriage. It was only a game, and it's not the goodness of our marriage I want to focus on anyway – it's the goodness of my news. It feels physically bright and golden inside of me, although I am mindful that might just be the vodka martinis.

I am always grateful, always particularly appreciative, to be the bearer of good news because I am acutely conscious of how it feels to be the bearer of bad. Anna didn't want to tell anyone about Teddy until all the tests were completed, and then insisted that we go alone to each of our parents to explain. She didn't want Teddy to be in plain sight while we shared the diagnosis.

'That's all they'll see,' she protested, 'SMA written all over him instead of just him any more, and I will feel like throwing myself in front of him like a human shield.'

It occurs to me now, as the train pulls away from High Wycombe and the carriage thins out, that maybe that's what she's been doing ever since. It would not feel appropriate, ever, to tell her that this is what I think.

I close my eyes, and lean my head against the damp, cool smoothness of the train window, aware of my feeling of brightness dimming to be replaced by a slight burning in my gut, which is possibly the vodka on an empty stomach. The memory of the journey I made to my parents is always mentally to hand, like something I might select crisply from a rail in a wardrobe. It begins with me driving away from the house, Anna standing at the window with Teddy in her arms. Isaac is not beside her. She is waving a rattle, which Teddy does not reach to try to take; instead, his arms dangle softly at his sides. The rattle is trimmed with small silver bells, and as I reverse out of the driveway, the sunlight catches them and they flash at me like dazzling semaphore.

When I arrived at my parents', my father was out in the yard. It was a crisp morning in March, the sky blown clean of clouds, the wind whipping in from the east, his hair blown askew. He was carefully pouring seeds into the birdfeeder, and held out his speckled palm to me.

'Niger seed, goldfinches' favourite. Watch them come. A charm if it's a few of them; a charm of goldfinches.'

In the kitchen, my mother was at the stove making fishcakes, pressing potato and cod into smooth round patties. She looked surprised to see me. 'Daughters,' she always says, 'I gather they keep you posted, regularly pick up the phone, whereas sons just wander in unannounced, hands in their pockets, a bit sheepish.'

I sat down at the table, and she made tea. She has the same

cream enamel teapot she has had since I was a child. I stared at the chipped spout and avoided meeting her eye.

'How are Anna and the boys?' she asked, smoothing her hands on her apron, and then, at the window, while I floundered for a reply, calling 'Stephen! Stephen!' to summon my father to lunch. He came through the scullery door, brushing his hands against the bald thighs of his corduroys and taking off his shoes with care, even though they were not his farming boots and not encrusted in mud.

'It's about Teddy,' I replied; 'why I'm here is because of Teddy,' because a preamble suddenly seemed pointless and there was no point stalling, and because it seemed blindingly obvious, in an instant, how my parents would assimilate the news. My father's breeding notebooks were the key; years of matching ewes to tups and of noting which lambs were born hardy, which sickly ('Shan't be putting those two together again,' his head to one side, appraising). Anna and I would be understood as a very poor match, and Teddy as a sickly mite who would fail to thrive. My father's hands, when he examined lambs, were confident and sure; feeling joints, ribs, hooves; checking the evenness of teeth. I was suddenly glad Anna and Teddy were not there; Anna's intuition likely correct. Perhaps it would have been even worse than this; my father, unable to resist, palpating Teddy's spine and abdomen. Prising open his mouth to assess his tiny neat molars.

'What about Teddy?' my mother said, closing the lid of the Aga and pulling up a chair to sit down next to me. She warmed sickly newborn lambs in the simmering oven after protracted, wintry births; my father joking that if they didn't thrive, she could quickly skin them and put them in the top oven to roast. The image of Teddy laid out like a little spatchcocked chicken refused to spill from my brain.

'What about Teddy?' my mother said again. His name in her mouth still sounded a little uncomfortable. 'Calling him what?'

she'd asked when I'd phoned from the hospital after he was born. 'Theodore – Teddy for short.' Isaac was a departure enough. I could hear her trying to get her head around it, she being a woman who gave her sons English, plain, yeoman names. And perhaps after this news she would pause in her knitting and lift her eyes to the hills, and wonder whether somehow Anna and I hadn't jinxed Teddy; that if we'd given him a name from the family tree, smooth and polished and familiar as a freshly podded conker, he too would have been a boy who climbed trees, rode ponies and played cricket, instead of one who lacked the vital, secret ingredient to make movement possible.

'It's called spinal muscular atrophy,' I told them. My father reached for a pen to neatly write it all down. I told them about SMN1, about carriers, and percentages. My father nodded his head when I said one in four. He wore his stockman's expression; calibrating when a line was a dud.

'Poor little chap,' my mother said, biting her lip. 'Poor little chap.'

'It could be worse,' I replied stoically, although I thought, *Not by much*. 'He could have Type 1, which would mean we would probably have lost him already. He has Type 2 – how severely we don't yet know. It can be life-shortening but is mostly about very reduced mobility.'

'So, handicapped,' my father said mildly, the word belonging to a plethora of casual vocabulary that was acceptable in his time: *simple, retarded, spastic, mongol*. I told him there were different words now. In the following months, I would hone his vocabulary.

My mother stood up and went back to the Aga.

'And they're sure, the doctors? They are absolutely positively sure?'

It struck me it was the first time that anyone had asked this; that neither Anna nor I had questioned the diagnosis. My mother is a hopeful person; she is hopeful and kind. She has also birthed four sons who ran full tilt from toddlerhood. I nodded.

'Yes, it's a very clear, very solid diagnosis.'

She looked beyond me into the pasture.

'I did wonder, last time you were here; Teddy on his tummy, not really pushing up on his arms. Something, something about that . . .'

Her eyes were averted, like a guilty child's. I followed her glance and saw a goldfinch alighting on the feeder, pecking at the niger seeds. My father watched too, his huge hands passive in his lap.

Before I left, my mother insisted I ate some fishcakes. She produced an enormous bottle of tomato ketchup, which felt like a relic from when I was a child. 'William's boys,' she explained, a little self-consciously. She bit at her lip and looked away. It felt like an apology, as if she was suddenly remorseful for evoking the image of my three healthy nephews, up from Dairy Cottage for their supper and eating merrily around this table, snatching the ketchup, laughing and ribbing each other as her own sons had done. I looked hard at the ketchup bottle and found myself wanting to cry. I had not cried yet because I had not quite believed it to be true, standing over Teddy's cot in the blue dark as he slept and unable to imagine his muscles stymied in his limbs. But there, in my mother's kitchen, I was overwhelmed by the desire to weep, because somehow in telling my parents I had made it all real and true, and I was swept up by a wave of nostalgia for my childhood, and for a time when I believed my parents' capable hands could make anything right.

My mother passed me the fishcakes and I began to eat, finding it hard to swallow because of the unexpected emotion in my throat. She stepped to stand beside me, one hand on her apron and the other lightly touching my shoulder. 'Poor little lamb,' she said, and it was not clear exactly to whom she referred, as the words seemed to gently encompass both me – once her boy child – and Teddy too. My father nodded, wordless, because he had always preferred the doing of something to the speaking of it, and I had a sudden memory of watching him splint the leg of a lamb broken during a difficult, bloody birth, his hands swift and sure, the lamb meek and crumpled in the straw.

'Poor little lamb,' my mother said again, as if to herself this time, and I realised that this was how they would best understand Teddy, and that their work-worn farm hands would handle him as if this was what he were.

When next we saw them as a family, it was only lightly alluded to; a frayed Moses basket on a stand brought down from the old nursery and placed by the table. 'In case he's happier lying down,' my mother said, nodding towards it. Turns out that's mostly the form; people preferring to say nothing in order to avoid saying the wrong thing. Only Tabitha, the ice cubes chinking in her gin and tonic, staring fixedly at Teddy when he was a year old, giggling in his car seat, and blowing gauzy spit bubbles at her. It was just after the London Olympics. 'Any chance of a Paralympic gold for you, do you think? Shouldn't your parents be choosing a sport and being terribly pushy about it? You'd certainly get a gold for saliva.'

The announcer is calling the train's imminent arrival at my station, despite High Wycombe seeming moments ago. I open my eyes and give myself a little shake. I will not be diverted by what I have just been thinking about. I will take Anna in my arms by the fireplace in my home, which is where I belong and which is a universe away from a bar in Mayfair, and I will say to her, *How about a revitalised game of 'I would buy', with a newly inflated budget?* I will light a fire when the boys are in bed, and we can lie in front of it, our feet bare and our toes pinked from the heat, and think about spending an amount of money that years ago we would have considered inconceivable.

Anna

I can't believe it, now, squeezing toothpaste onto my brush. Tom is still downstairs, switching off the lights and bolting the door and pulling the fireguard across the hearth. My answer – the actual, truthful, unfettered first thing that came to my lips, like water fresh sprung from an underground stream – was 'A specially adapted disability desk.' He came through the door brimming with descriptions of Mayfair for the boys, and told me about winning the new Geneva business, and that they'd tripled his bonus. He scooped me up so that my feet left the floor and said, 'Merry, Merry Christmas,' even though it's only the third week of November. And then later, when we were watching the news, he nudged me, saying, 'Remember when we used to play "I would buy"? How about a revitalised round of that?'

He's laughing as he says it, his legs stretched long on to the footstool, his shoulders nestled into the back of the couch. He looks like a man who is happy; that's what absorbed me first, as if the ability to be simply happy is something he hasn't lost, and is there, shining, when the occasion demands. I don't answer him promptly because I'm thinking about when I last felt properly happy, and it feels like a tune I've forgotten. I would like to ask him how he has retained it; instead, I switch my mind to the game we haven't played in years, surprised to remember that we ever did.

How childish it seems. Were we overly materialistic? I'd like to reassure myself not. Most of the things we wanted were so very small (with one exception, after we'd been drinking tequila, and I wished for a diamond as big as a pigeon's egg).

The reason I said the desk was because the special needs co-ordinator from the primary school came this afternoon, along with the teacher. Perhaps they thought there was safety in numbers. As the SENCO undid the toggles on her duffle coat, I guessed she would similarly divest herself of more excuses for the six-month delay in Teddy starting school. Her opening gambit was a rehash of that: how it was mostly due to a delay in the installation of the ramps that will help him get in and out of the building; 'shallow-gradient ramps', she kept saying, as if this accounted for why the local education authority have so far failed to find a company to install them.

She also brought with her a hand-signed letter from the chair of governors, explaining that his research into the provision in special schools has revealed that at least twenty-five per cent of the gross internal floor area must be for circulation, and that he wanted to aim to achieve that in some of the communal spaces in school. The upshot is – and here the SENCO averted her gaze and hunted for the tissue that was tucked up her sleeve – they will require some further time to think and to plan, and so in the meantime will continue to send the supply teacher to Teddy three mornings a week to ensure that he keeps up with the learning objectives of the reception class.

'But every cloud has a silver lining,' she said conspiratorially. 'Look what I've discovered.'

She passed me a leaflet detailing a desk that moves in all manner of ways, allowing even the attachment of a hoist.

'Because there's also some concern as to whether any new wheelchair you get, now that Teddy's growing out of the Wizzy-bug, will have sufficient manoeuvrable space around a standard desk.' She beamed at me. 'So perhaps we should have a shot at getting one of these. A little collective lobbying might help.'

So far that hasn't been the case. I refrained from saying that if it was anything like the ramps, Teddy would be fifteen before he could join the reception class. Sarcasm isn't useful. I know this to my cost. It doesn't oil the wheels of anything except other people's dislike.

I have begun to wonder whether the SENCO, the headmistress, the chair of governors and the teacher all actually think that Teddy would have a finer time of it if he went to a special school instead of trying to be treated like any other child. I wish they'd just say so, rather than all this sidestepping and delaying and exaggerated regard for supposed best practice. I am nurturing particular fury for the parent who heads up the PTA, and who pointed out to me that the entire budget allocation for teaching support would be spent on Teddy's personal assistant until the funding came through retrospectively from the county council. 'We'll need to have a few bake sales,' she said faux-brightly, and I felt such sudden violence towards her that I walked away without answering.

That's why the desk was so top of mind. That's why, when my generous-hearted, open-natured, increasingly successful and perplexingly happy husband moved from the couch to the rug by the fireside and beckoned for me to join him, cosying me with his arm to encourage me to put my head on his shoulder, that what came out of my mouth was a disability desk; the deluxe model with the option of adding a hoist, hoists also being top of mind. And those words hadn't even landed in the room – Tom's response a slightly bemused, disappointed silence – before I mentally reverted to the second leaflet the SENCO gave me; this time, to her credit, a little more warily, as if unsure of the response she might get. Perhaps I was generating an audible tick like a bomb.

The second leaflet invited me to a parenting class for children with physical disabilities, in which parents and stakeholders are given tips on how to build on parenting skills and on how to look after their own emotional needs in order to parent more effectively (parents of non-disabled children presumably requiring no such advice). And it was the intention of that leaflet that ambushed me as I sat beside Tom, my knees held tented by my arms, resisting his invitation to lie alongside him.

I detest the word *stakeholder* – I'm still dwelling on that as I brush my teeth. Rather than describing someone who is emotionally involved, I see it more literally as someone actually holding a stake, wooden and smooth, and sharpened to a point at one end. A stake that might quite reasonably – or unreasonably – be rammed at a leaflet-giver who, even if unintentionally, is suggesting that the recipient should up their parenting.

I stand part-dressed in front of the mirror, stare hard at my reflection and wonder when I stopped being a person who might have spontaneously said, *a cashmere roll-neck sweater* or *a pair of patent-leather clumpy ankle boots* or *a Sonos sound system*, and instead became someone whose second thought was about the satisfaction to be gained by driving a sharp wooden stake through a SENCO's slightly quivering lip.

Tom comes into the bathroom. He still has that jaunty air, as if there is something newly oxygenated within him that is adding buoyancy.

'I'm sorry. Can we rewind on that?'

He looks surprised. 'On what?'

'On the game; the game that was always a bit ridiculous but which had a certain charm. I know you were being kind; I just . . .' My voice trails away. I am suddenly so bone-achingly tired and actually don't want to repeat it at all, but I feel I have to because I have been so joyless, so curmudgeonly, in the face of my husband's achievement, in the face of the evident happiness with which he walked in through the door. I won't be able to sleep with that image of myself. There must be, surely, something I can think of coveting.

Tom wraps his arms around me and kisses my mouth. I can smell the alcohol still on his breath. How polarising it feels, that while I was chopping food finely and spooning it into Teddy, and then wiping the surfaces and loading the dishwasher, he was sitting in an expensive bar toasting his success with his colleagues, colleagues who are presumably not wearing a raggedy old sweater that bears the traces of Teddy's pea soup lunch.

He holds me close. 'Of course we can rewind, if that's what you actually want, or we can talk about bespoke disability desks and buying one for the school, if that's what you'd prefer, if you think it would help with Teddy's start date.'

His tone is indulgent, as if I am a greedy child with a Christmas wish list.

I close my eyes, and feel that I could fall asleep where I stand.

Teddy

When Mummy feeds me my porridge, she blows on each spoonful to make extra sure it doesn't burn my lips. When she blows, it makes me wrinkle my nose, and we are laughing about that when the phone rings.

'Oh, I see, yes. No, definitely. If you think you have a cold coming, it's always better not to risk it.'

My teacher nearly has a cold and so she won't be coming today. Mummy goes across to the whiteboard and rubs off her name. Next to *Who's Coming?* she writes in big letters, *NO ONE* (she says it out loud) and puts a big smiley face by it.

'So, we could be very obedient and just do the sums sheet that Mrs P would have done with you today, and also think about words that begin with the sound "B", or we could skip it and go and visit Granma and Granpa. Hands up if you vote for going out.'

I stick both of my hands up. I love going to see Mummy's parents. She's laughing. 'We're free as birds as long as we talk about sums and B words on the way there.'

She phones Granma, with the phone tucked under her chin so that she can finish up with the porridge. Granma's voice says, 'That would be lovely, darling; what an unexpected surprise,' and she tells her to drive carefully, which is what she always says, and Mummy's already putting the phone down when Granma says it.

She's *quick, quick* packing all our things; for me an extra warm coat, and a scarf and hat. She tries the hat on me for size, 'Just in case your head has grown while I wasn't looking.' It can pull right down over my chin, so I don't think it has. We play peek-aboo with the brim right down to my nose, and then Mummy says, 'Let's get our skates on or we'll waste the morning.'

So far today we have been free as birds and now we are skaters.

Granma and Granpa's house is big and old, and made mostly of flint stones. The driveway is curved, so when you come round the corner it is standing there like a complete surprise. That's what Isaac says. He says the house looks like it should say *Boo!*

Granma and Granpa are mostly always in the kitchen. Granpa likes doing the Sudoku, and he pretends he can't do it, and sucks on his pen and waits for us to give him the answer. Then he goes on to the crossword and we fill it up with words that we just like the sound of; one day we made it fit with the names of all kinds of sweets. Granma bakes biscuits and brings in armfuls of flowers she has cut from the garden, and she plays bridge on a Wednesday, which means counting the numbers on the cards. All these things I have told Mrs P – on a day when she didn't have a cold – when we were doing a piece of thinking about my family.

When Mummy is helping me, Granma stands right next to her and says, 'Can I help you with that?' or 'Let me do that for you' or 'Surely that's something I can do?' Mummy makes her elbows stick out a bit like a flapping chicken to make a bigger space around us and says, 'It's okay, I've got it' or 'I'm on it' or 'It'll be quicker me doing it.' A little while ago, Granma said, 'You make me feel useless' and put her hands together for a bit as if she might be getting ready to say her prayers. Now she doesn't ask at all and she mainly just does the other things (not the bridge when we are there) and talks about what is happening in her life on Bledlow Ridge. The thing I like best when she stands next to Mummy is that she often makes a rhyme with her fingers. 'Here's a church,' she says, and then, her fingers pointing upwards, 'and here's the steeple.' She flips her palms around and waggles her fingers. 'Open it up and here's all the people.'

I can't join in with that part because my wrists can't twist like that. This is because Mummy says I am made differently. This is what she said to me when I was four-and-three-quarters, when I asked her why my legs and arms didn't work like Isaac's. She said that people are like cakes; they're made from ingredients, and my ingredients are a little bit different.

That's what I'm planning on saying when I start school, if someone asks me why I am in a wheelchair. We are all like cakes, I will say, like cakes in a bakery, and I am just an unusual sort of cake.

Now Granma is talking to Mummy about the field beyond the house. She doesn't go there because her hip is poorly and she's not fond of uneven ground. Granpa doesn't go because he just walks on the golf course. He says he likes his grass with eighteen holes in it. Granma says some badgers have dug an enormous new sett, and lots of her neighbours go and watch them when it starts to get dark. I like that thought; the air all dusky and the b-b-b-badgers starting to play.

'Mummy, can we go and look?'

'Look at what, darling?'

'The badgers in their sett.'

Granpa glances up from the paper. 'Badgers are nocturnal – they like being out and about at night. There won't be any playing happening right now.'

Granma looks out of the window. 'The frost's still on the ground, too. It would be very heavy going for the wheelchair even getting over there. There's probably not time, either, before we have lunch.'

Mummy's face has a new squiggle of skin just between her eyebrows, as if she is trying to see something far away. Or maybe she doesn't like what she is listening to. That, I think.

'There are always so many reasons not to do things. Why don't Teddy and I quickly nip out just so that he can check for himself?'

Whoopee.

She bundles me up in all my layers. When I look out of my eyes sideways, all I can see is wool. If there are any badgers out and about in the daylight, I hope they're not standing to the side of me, because I won't see a thing.

Mummy buckles me into my push wheelchair because this walk would be way too hard for the Wizzybug, and we set off down the path. The frost winks and sparkles across the paving stones and the grass is white not green.

We cross the lane and go through the gate into the field that leads down to the wood. Mummy stops by a sign that is pinned to the fence post and reads it out loud.

'"Permissive footpath closed. Please use original footpath across field."' She looks at me. 'What do we think that means?'

I shrug, but I have on so many clothes it might be an invisible one. She's worked it out for herself anyway. She's squinting across to the hedge.

'It means we can't walk round where the grass is short; we have to walk over the field where they've made those two furrows in the soil.'

'Over that mud?' I do my best pointing.

She sucks in a big breath through her teeth.

'Yes, over that mud.'

The frost hasn't set the mud like it has the grass. The mud has just a thin layer of coldness but underneath it is thick and squelchy. The front wheel of the chair goes round and round, and each time it picks up a new coat of mud. The two wheels at the back get stuck in the ruts. Mummy leans from one side to the other to make them pop free. Her breathing is louder and her hair has come loose from its plait. 'Bloody hell. Bloody mud.'

'Bloody badgers.'

She laughs. 'That's two words starting with a B sound, but you'd better not practise the first one.'

Bounce, bounce, bounce. That's a third one. I'm slipping down the seat, even though I'm strapped in. The front wheels are so muddy I can't see the treads any more. Small spatters of it fly onto my legs. I swizzle around a little bit to ask my question.

'How many more steps?'

'Soon. Soon. Just over by the gap in the hedge.'

'The gap with the gate?'

'What gate?'

'The gate in the gap in the hedge.'

'There's no gate in the hedge.'

'What's that then?'

Mummy stops and looks harder. She puts her hand up to shade her eyes because the sun is hanging in the sky right at her level. She drags the wheelchair a bit further, pushing a road through the furrows.

She stops by a fresh bare-wood gate. She prods at it with the toe of her muddy boot and reads out another sign.

'"New kissing gate donated by Woodbury Walkers' Society."'

She pushes the gate to its full width and measures the distance. 'Obviously wide enough for plenty of kissing, but not for a wheelchair to go through. Brilliant.'

B-b-b-brilliant.

She leans against the new gate. 'I could leave the chair here and try to carry you to the badgers. I'm not sure we'd make it, though; we might both end up face down in the mud.' She bites her lip, makes a noise like *urrgh*, then kicks once, twice at the kissing gate with her welly, so that the mud flies from it in a shower.

'Not a kissing gate, a kicking gate.'

Mummy starts to laugh. 'You're not wrong about that.'

She kneels down so that she is facing me and kisses me on

each cheek. Her face is warm from all the pushing and tilting she's been doing. She turns the wheelchair around and shoves it back across the field.

Back at the flint house, Granma and Granpa are waiting in the kitchen. Granma has chopped my food ready but Mummy says it's not quite small enough and that she will do it some more. She lies me on the couch and starts peeling off all my warm clothes. She says I am like a banana, which is another B sound. I will have a lot to tell Mrs P when she doesn't have a cold.

'Any badgers?' Granma asks.

'Nope, just a new gate too narrow for a wheelchair,' Mummy says.

Granpa says, 'Uh-oh,' writes something with his pen and holds up the crossword. He reads out 'BADGERS' from one row of spaces and then 'NO ENTRY' from another.

On the way home in the car, we are stuck behind a tractor being towed and there is no room to overtake. Mummy starts a story about a badgers' sett, where all the badger family play together under a big fat moon. She puts in some fox cubs too, and also a kingfisher, which is not strictly possible or accurate but it is my favourite bird.

'It's your story,' Mummy says, 'and so kingfishers can be nocturnal and keen on being by badgers' setts if that's what you want. And if there's a gate, you can imagine your way round it.'

I think that's probably better than trying to kick a way through.

Tom

Hyde Park is an unusual context for a new business pitch. The client we've come to see walks twice around the Serpentine daily because of a heart scare, so he takes two of his meetings while he's doing the five-thousand-step route. Charlie has tipped us off that he also likes to be given a fact about the Serpentine, and will jest that if his business goes under, he can then get a job as a tour guide around the lake. 'Get googling,' he said, when Eliza and I left his office after discussing the brief. 'Make sure you laugh at the tour guide joke, and continue your winning streak.'

The park is busy when we meet by the lake; language students in gaggles by the fountain and women with strollers power-walking and talking on their phones. Eliza comes towards me wearing a cherry-red coat. It brings to mind her swimming costume in Geneva, and as I walk to meet her, I banish the thought of her beneath the shower, her head tipped back, her body drenched. Today her cheeks are glowing after her walk from the tube. It's no surprise that the client prefers to turn his head towards her. As predicted, he asks her for a fact about the Serpentine.

She pauses for dramatic effect. 'The Serpentine was commissioned by Queen Caroline – don't ask me the date. It was originally fed by the River Westbourne and Tyburn Brook, and then then pumped from the Thames in the eighteenth century, and now from three boreholes in the park itself. Its primary inflow is from the upper chalk, and its primary outflow is a storm-relief sewer.' She says the last part with a small flourish. I find myself wanting to applaud.

The client nods. 'The sewer is a new detail to me. How do you know about that?'

'My father was an engineer, and he was obsessed with water in all its forms. We never passed a river or a lake or a pipe – sometimes even a manhole – without an explanation.' She is smiling at the memory.

'He sounds like an interesting man. And I've got two facts from you for the price of one, which appeals to the entrepreneur in me. I hope the project delivers a similar yield.'

Eliza performs a small mock curtsey and the man laughs. She is playing him like a fiddle.

I googled my fact last night, when Anna had gone to bed. The client turns to me, and I am ready to trot it out.

'My first degree was in English literature, which is how I know this. In December 1816, Harriet Westbrook, the pregnant wife of Percy Bysshe Shelley, drowned herself in the Serpentine, having left a suicide note for her father and sister. Shelley married Mary Wollstonecraft Godwin less than two weeks later.'

'Less than two weeks? I didn't know that either. I knew she drowned herself, but not the speed of his remarriage. That's full marks to both of you for something new and interesting. Storm sewers and suicides. I'm impressed.'

If Edward were here, and we reverted to our childhood selves, he'd be jeering and saying what a wetter I am; that Eliza has talked about boreholes and storm sewers like an engineer while I have spoken like a girl of unrequited love and suicidal sadness and dastardly behaviour. Worse, what seemed like a striking fact last night now seems to bloom terrible before me with proximity to the water. I can't stop looking at the lake, and wondering about what kind of a day it was when Harriet Westbrook hurried along here, head bowed, her hat firmly pinned in place, her palm perhaps flat to her pregnant stomach, a letter left on the walnut mantelpiece at home, all set to hurl herself into the water. I imagine the sateen of her dress billowing and ballooning, and then suddenly heavy as if her pockets were full of stones. I have a sudden image, too, of the perplexed baby in the amniotic sac, its tiny limbs floundering as it drowned twice over.

Eliza is speaking. 'As Tom will confirm, our experience in your market, and the fact that we can do some additional modelling . . .'

For a moment, I panic. I haven't been paying attention at all. She pauses, giving me time to relocate myself in the conversation. She catches my eye and swiftly changes the subject.

'I always think this is a particularly lovely vista, don't you – the view towards the fountains of the Italian gardens? The Princess Diana fountain gave my father apoplexy when it first opened. You'd think he'd designed it himself, or that he was responsible for fixing it. I think he was a whisker away from submitting modified drawings.'

She laughs. I have a feeling her father is no longer alive, and I am struck by the healthiness of the way she talks of him. My inability to speak openly of Dad seems small and closed in comparison. What is it with me this morning? A walk in the park and I am emotionally incontinent and unable to focus on the business in hand. The client chooses to stop by a monument and tell us about it. It's a memorial stone given by Norwegian sailors as gratitude for safe harbour during the Second World War. It is his particular favourite, alongside the statue of Isis, an Egyptian goddess. Eliza is listening carefully. The client looks visibly gratified, and who can blame him: a lovely young woman paying attention as if his anecdotes are entirely compelling.

At the completion of the circuit, he produces his step counter with a flourish and says, 'See, five thousand; well, five thousand

and twenty-three to be exact. I'll be in touch shortly with my answer.' He leaves us.

'Do you think we've earned ourselves a coffee before we go back to the office?' Eliza says.

'I think we have. Or at least you have. You batted a blinder.'

She sits at a table by the window and looks out at the lake. The water shines dully in the flat November light.

'What's even lamer is I could tell you some more,' she says impishly. 'I could elaborate for some time about the Long Water; about increasing the flow rate to keep the water fresh for swimmers, or taking carp and perch out so they don't stir up the sediment at the bottom and keep re-infecting the water with algae. I didn't want to confess to Charlie when he said google something that he'd actually hit upon my specialist subject. I have to say, my dad would be proud of my recall – obviously more went in than I thought. But poor Harriet Westbrook. What a terrible thing.'

'I know. I actually had no knowledge of it when I was a student, but of all the things I googled, it seemed the most plausible to offer up. And then when I did, possibly standing right next to where she jumped, it just ballooned in its terribleness and sadness. You were making a neat switch to what we could do for him, and all I could do was look at the water and imagine her dress sinking.'

There is a kind of craziness in speaking this honestly and openly. It's liberating and yet also makes me mindful of how carefully I speak to Anna; wary, increasingly, that I will say the wrong thing.

'But to offset it, and as a consolation, in this same patch of water there's the Christmas Peter Pan annual swim, and duck feeding. Tapestry and circle of life.'

'Are you always this optimistic?'

She smiles. 'It's a habit I'm trying to acquire.'

'It's a good one.'

'Evidently I'm not going to be setting about trying to acquire bad ones. Although being unremittingly positive and Pollyanna-ish could be kind of irritating, I guess.'

'Better than unremittingly callous. Imagine marrying someone else two weeks after your wife's pregnant suicide.'

'It's pretty inconceivable, but from the perspective of a single woman, I'd say that marriage brings out some exceptionally poor behaviour in some people.'

She's single. As we walk back along Park Lane, I realise I've fastened onto that. Not because it changes anything, but because it's something else to know about her, something she has said, candidly and frankly, like most of what comes out of her mouth. I am at a loss to think why there isn't a line of men around the block trying to make her fall in love with them, or at least fall into bed with them, but maybe there is.

I check myself, and cast my eyes forward, slightly scrunching them up to try to obscure her from my peripheral vision. It is seductive; this bright, fresh morning, and this bright, fresh, unburdened woman beside me who knows about water engineering in the Serpentine and who is determined to be optimistic and who is realistic in her assessment of how poorly people can behave.

Again I am struck by how much I like her. Is that a forbidden thought? I have enjoyed her company, walking five thousand and twenty-three steps around Hyde Park, and then a few more to the Serpentine café. It comes to me suddenly, and I am ambushed by my spousal disloyalty, that what I like is that she seems so free, walking beside me with her arms lightly swinging. Anna, by contrast, seems so bound, so contained, as if invisible sticky filaments have strapped her arms to her sides. I have an image of her as someone who has reverse-engineered from a winged creature to a pupa, and it is a thought that shocks me, because it is so brutally, visually clear.

Last week, after my flawed attempt to play *I would buy*, when

I held her in the bathroom dressed only in her sweater, I was mindful of the lightness and sparseness of her, the flattened scoops of her shoulder blades, and the bones of her spine, which seemed to be only just contained by her skin.

I am quiet on the rest of the way back to the office. On our return, Charlie asks us to come and debrief him. In the interim, I go to my desk to catch up on emails but don't read or send any. Instead, I swivel on my chair and think that the morning has been dominated by two terrible images: a long-dead woman in a sateen dress sinking into the Serpentine with her unborn child double-drowning inside her; and my own wife, who is very much alive, stickily strapped and bound in a way I have not until now perceived. And hovering above both images is Eliza.

I press my fingertips to my closed eyes to double the darkness, as if by doing so I will erase the memory of her lips above the coffee cup, the scarlet smudged stain of her lipstick caught on the white china of the rim.

Isaac

I am standing completely still. I've got my eyes closed, and I'm standing on only one leg, which makes balancing super-difficult. I'm actually peeking a little through my eyelashes, so my eyes are not shut completely. It's important to be honest about that, even though it is only to myself. I am liking the shape my body makes. It feels as if my body is a diagram in a maths book, and that someone with a protractor could measure the angle of my sticking-out knee perfectly. I bite a little at my bottom lip, which weirdly seems to help me plant my standing foot more firmly to the ground.

Standing completely still is a new thing. I've stopped on the way home, opposite a tree, and it's this I can see through my almost-shut eyes. If I look at the tree, I wobble less, although I'm not sure why. I imagine a fine wire drawn between the tree and myself, and also between my eyes and my leg muscles. I feel like a puppet, pulled up tall. Anybody walking past on the other side of the road would spot me and think I'm an idiot. I allow myself one quick eyes-wide-open check before I am blind again.

The leg I'm standing on is aching a bit, especially in the muscle directly above my knee. I clench my thigh more tightly. When I came home from school last night, Joanna the physio was there. She has a toothy smile so wide it looks as if it might slip off her chipmunky cheeks. She says, 'That's my boy,' whenever Teddy manages to do what she's asking and also even when he doesn't. Mummy looks across her each time she says it, as if she is thinking that Teddy is not Joanna's boy at all. Yesterday, Joanna was trying to teach Teddy – who looked up at me and crossed his eyes and stuck out his tongue when she wasn't looking – to be very still, but still in a strong not a floppy way. I have been thinking about it since.

For Teddy, it is usually movement not stillness that is the actual problem. Joanna made him hold out his arm at right angles, and clench his fist as if he was about to start playing rock, paper, scissors. The aim of it (and she also kept saying 'Come on, my lovely, show me your superman muscles') is for him to do it and be completely still. That looked like a long shot. Teddy's fingers waved about like seaweed, and the whole bundle of his hand bobbed around like a cork on water. The way Joanna puts it, it sounds like it should be easy. Now, standing on one leg, I realise it's actually quite difficult and wish that I'd given Teddy a bit more encouragement. At the time, I just crossed my eyes to match what he was doing, and added in a quick tongue twist when Joanna turned her back to dry her hands. Teddy laughed but she didn't spot what we were doing, and she said, 'That's it, full superpower concentration!' as if it was her corny words that were making him laugh.

Mummy was washing up while Joanna was there. She had a glass Pyrex bowl in her hands and she was wiping it and wiping it until I think it was bone dry. Round and round the inside of it she went with the tea towel, the cloth scrunched very tight in her fist. She had her eyes fixed on Joanna and was watching her trying to coax Teddy to hold his leg out straight. It didn't go to plan; it was flopping and bending like a piece of grass you might fold and whistle through.

'Let's see how you score today,' Joanna said to Teddy and reached for her pen, and Mummy looked at the sheet of paper as if she'd like to screw it up into a ball and throw it at somebody. Joanna most likely. At least Joanna would be the person for yesterday. I think Mummy might still be cross with her from two visits ago. I had just walked in from school, and Joanna hadn't yet started on her work with Teddy. Instead she was flipping through the folder she always brings with her, and she looked at me as I made my way to the biscuit tin and said casually to Mummy, 'Remind me, is older brother a carrier?'

I'm not sure what she meant, but I'm storing it up ready to take out sometime soon and ask Mummy about. In the meantime, I've logged the word *carrier* in my head, next to an image of an ancient Egyptian figure with a large terracotta pot balanced on his shoulders. He's standing with one knee lifted at a right angle, and his best foot forward. Mummy didn't answer the question anyway; she just turned her back and it was left hanging above the kitchen table, plain as a light bulb.

When I put my foot down on the pavement, it's a bit pins-and-needlesy from being propped against the side of my knee, so I do one exaggerated footstep, rolling my foot very slowly from my heel to my tiptoe as if I am walking in slow motion and my feet are made of plasticine. Walking is quite complicated when broken down and considered. There's a lot of work going on; so many muscles pulling and pushing to make one smooth motion.

All of my family are out and about walking today. Daddy is having a walking meeting in Hyde Park, and Mummy has phoned school to say she's going to be a little late home because she and Teddy have been for a walk at Granma and Granpa's and got stuck in the traffic coming back. That's why I went to after-school club, and why I can now stand one-legged on the pavement without being noticed and teased, because everyone else has already gone home.

Daddy most likely will have finished his walk ages ago, and Mummy and Teddy obviously have because they are stuck in the traffic. Teddy won't have done any actual walking, but I like describing him as walking, because if I say it enough times, one day he might pop right up and actually be able to do it, like a wish that comes true.

I stand again on one leg for a moment, concentrating hard and trying to grip tight and keep every muscle still. Perhaps if I manage to stand here long enough I'll work as a kind of counterbalance. I've learned this in science recently: to every action there is a natural counterbalance, and movement and stillness are a pair. So while the rest of my family have been blowing about walking, I can be like a tent peg, tethered in the ground and drawing them all right back.

That's a more useful thought than being some kind of carrier. It would clearly be totally impossible to carry them all.

Anna

'Just a catch-up meeting; just to make sure we're all on the same page.'

Julia, on the phone, always sounds blithe. Or perhaps only on cases like ours, where she's not actually having to roll up her sleeves and save a child from metaphorically burning. We probably count as social-work-lite. Having a designated social worker is non-negotiable. Julia also doubles up as our link worker, which she tells me is part of 'a joined-up approach between partner agencies'. Mostly she sits in my kitchen and tittle-tattles about other cases she's working on. 'Naming no names,' she says portentously, as if I am remotely interested.

Next to my name in her folder she's written: *Difficult*. I know this because she left it open one time when she went to the loo. There's also a little diagram that looks suspiciously like a game of hangman, and which suggests I am closer to the noose with each interaction.

She told me once – casually biting on a green apple and nudging her glasses up the bridge of her nose – that for middle-class, educated, affluent parents, having a disabled child is more of a shocker, 'because the shit's always supposed to happen elsewhere'. It's why she always starts by telling her clients that disorders don't discriminate by class, and that having a disabled child is the ultimate leveller. 'Your life's been thunderbolted,' she said sanctimoniously, patting my arm.

I don't know if I was supposed to be grateful for this insight.

The word 'thunderbolted' has stubbornly stayed with me, though, along with the image of my previous life in charred, smoking ruins.

Today's meeting – the catch-up one – is ostensibly a review of where we are. I bridle at the implied notion that we are in this together. What it mostly seems to involve on Julia's part is ticking boxes on a sheet in her folder.

'Tom not here?' she begins brightly, having assumed her place at the table.

Tom is never here for these meetings. We both know that, but she says it anyway, using his name in a way that is overfamiliar. Sometime she says, 'And what does hubby think?'

Today it's Isaac she has in her sights.

'Is there anything we need to record about Isaac? It's a while since we've talked about him. Do you have any concerns for his well-being, for his place in the family? I think I mentioned that sometimes it's easy to feel progressively overlooked. I'm mindful of how much time and energy you've had to spend on Teddy's application.'

'Isaac's fine, thank you.'

'Is he doing well at school? No friendship issues, no behavioural issues, no problems with his school work?' The tone of her voice is insistent.

'Yes, no, no, and no.'

She looks at me as if my words are peas spat out at her from a shooter. I couldn't be more succinct if I tried. Beyond us, Teddy is dozing on the couch, having had a disturbed night. The questions about Isaac snag on my skin like burrs. Yes, I repeat to myself, Isaac is absolutely fine. I can't bear to think of the alternative.

After arriving home from my parents', I went out onto the pavement to watch for him coming down the road. As I craned my neck to spot him, I realised he wasn't walking at all, but instead standing still, opposite the hornbeam tree, balanced carefully on one leg. He paused there for what seemed like an age, and then continued on his way home. When he appeared in the kitchen, I found I couldn't ask him about it; couldn't ask him what he was thinking when he stopped and stood on one leg as he made his way home from school.

Julia is evidently repeating a question. Is it the second or third time of asking?

'I'm sorry, what was that?' I gesture to Teddy. 'Sorry. We had a bad night last night. Both of us could do with catching up on some sleep.'

'I was just asking how Teddy has been doing; whether his health has been generally good. I know Paula's been to see you, and also that the physio's a little concerned with his progress. Didn't the SENCO come last week? Did she share the information about the parenting courses?'

I am struck, not for the first time, by how much communication goes on behind my back.

On Fridays, before Teddy was diagnosed, I used to take the boys to a singing group. At the end of it, the adults held out a circle of parachute silk, and the older children would run merrily beneath it. I think of the support agency workers as holding out a similar circle of cloth, which at any moment they might secretly and mutually signal to drop, and I will be suffocated, breathless, beneath the weight of their decisions.

When Julia stands up to leave, I hold the front door wide open, as if it will facilitate the speed of her departure. The wind whips into the hallway.

She is wrapping her scarf round and round her neck as she steps out. 'Thank you; nice to see you, good to catch up.'

All the words are lies. As I close the door, I think of the odd diagram next to my name in the folder. What I would have really liked to do is to tell her to go hang.

Tom

'What are you doing this weekend?' Eliza asks as we make our way up to the twenty-sixth floor in the lift.

'We're going down to Shropshire, to my parents' . . . my mother's – well, my younger brother William's farm now. Every ten weeks or so we all pitch up. It's a bit like harvest time; all being safely gathered in.'

At my desk, I reflect on what I have said; *pitching up*, a phrase that carries with it a sense of no-nonsense presentation, implying a ball bowled cleanly to a chosen spot. And yet it's not that at all. For several years now, when we go to the farm – and even more so when my father was alive – it feels as if my brothers and I are carrying our lives in our hands, held out like an offering, like one of Teddy's snow domes. *Look, this is my life, see what I have made of it*, as though my parents can reach out and take it, examine it at leisure, and then discuss it to see if we have turned out as they thought.

How competitive we were: who could run fastest, climb highest, score the most goals, the most runs, grow the tallest sunflowers. On torrentially wet days in the barn, begging Dad to play 'Who's behind you, Mr Wolf?' during his lunchtime, each of us buzzing with the will to reach him first. On Sunday nights, a general knowledge quiz; the *Encyclopedia Britannica* held open on his lap. As adults, a change in content but perhaps the same desire: Edward's rapid promotion and wealth; James's ownership of the moral high ground with his work with disaffected learners; William taking the mantle of seven generations and learning the land. And then, after Teddy's diagnosis, a subtle change in timbre, as if Anna and I exist somehow beyond the confines of that energy, as if we are ring-fenced instead by a small, unspoken beat of sorrow.

Is it wrong to admit that I always imagined I would have a house spilling equally with children; that my arms would be full of a tumble of limbs; and that even if the context for our family life was not explicitly rural, it would be filled with the same energetic will? And then, when we knew about Teddy, Anna stood before me in the kitchen one day and said, out of the blue, 'There can't be any more children, you understand that, don't you? Not when, between us, we are capable of this.' And when I asked her if she had enquired about the possibility of antenatal screening, her eyes filling with tears, saying, 'But for what? So that if the foetus has SMA, we would choose to abort? Don't you see what that implies about the validity of Teddy's life?'

I wonder sometimes if she has ever forgiven for me that comment, when her interpretation was not, absolutely not, my intention. Instead, the option of knowledge, as a forewarning, being preferable to the ambush that we jointly suffered. An insensitivity on my part, I acknowledge, to assume she might have the energy to mother another disabled child. An optimism, also, unshared by Anna, that the genetic axe might not fall again, as proved by Isaac. Shortly afterwards, she told me she was having her fallopian tubes tied, and I drove her to the hospital on a rainy day in March, and felt as if I was delivering my hope of a large family to be cauterised by the gynaecologist's hands.

William's boys play as we did, in a rolling maul. A tumble of bone, sinew, muscle and skin. In contrast, my mother patting the seat next to her and saying to Isaac when he was smaller, 'Why not come and sit beside me and help me with this jigsaw?' as if perhaps he might not quite keep up, or was made somehow of softer, more breakable stuff. Isaac's words, his watchfulness, marching to a different beat.

And yet our adulthood – my brothers' and mine – is composed of fragile stuff. When we sit around the dining table, our childhood selves are apparent, as if our adult skin rapidly becomes translucent. And so this weekend, again, we will gather, still bruised by the loss of my father, still in thrall to my mother's quiet dignity, and I will drive up to the house, and park my car by the dairy, and step out into the yard in which every stone in the walls is familiar to me. I will go into the house, my life held out like a snow dome, with Anna beside me, increasingly taut. Sometimes, hesitantly, the wish to take her in my arms, and to say, *Even if this is not what you thought it would be, would you wish it any different?* The anxiety, unbidden, that her answer might be yes.

Eliza is suddenly in front of my desk, holding out a printed version of the document we will be presenting shortly. She hands it to me. 'That's a wistful expression. I can't believe that what's on your mind is how best to recommend implementing a systems, apps and products programme.'

I look down briefly at my keyboard, my disquietude supplanted by the reprehensible pleasure that my face is becoming known.

Isaac

I'm just sitting on the couch watching the weather forecast and minding my own business when it comes to me. The kite. My kite. It's a brilliant idea. The weather forecaster said it will be windy at the weekend. I can say to Daddy before we leave for the farm, *Oh, wait, can we take my kite?* as if the thought has just popped into my head. Then, when Tobes and Oli and Felix are full of ideas about what we can play at – all of which will involve running or climbing or tugging or wading or digging or scrambling or pushing or reaching or rolling – I can say, *Hey! I've got my kite in the boot of the car – why don't we take it to the top field and see how high it flies?*

You only need one person to hold a kite. One set of hands. Everybody else is watching and whooping and telling you what to do, and shouting with their voices all snatched away by the wind. It's easy to join in with the yelling. Teddy will be no different.

When I play with my cousins, I mostly feel I am walking along a line painted white on the ground, trying to balance between having the best fun and making sure that Teddy is not left out of the game. Mummy often stands outside in the yard by the dairy and calls, *Be careful*, or *Don't do anything dangerous*, as we run off somewhere. My cousins laugh and say their bones are made of rubber and that if they fall over they will bounce right back up. They don't hold their bodies carefully – that's what is different. They hold them like there's no chance they won't do exactly what they want. In our house that seems a kind of luck: that when you want your legs to jump, they do just that.

When I'm sitting next to Mummy on the couch, sometimes she kisses the top of my arm or squidges the muscle in my thigh and says, *You're precious!* and I don't think she means just me but my actual muscles and bones too, because the fact that they work properly is very precious to her. That's why when we're at the farm, she stands by the dairy and shouts *Be careful*, or *Don't do anything dangerous*, because she doesn't think Teddy and I are made of rubber, and she doesn't count on either of us bouncing right back up.

Anna

It's a cold and raw late November morning when we set off for Shropshire. It feels as if I am packing the car for a polar expedition, rather than for Sunday lunch. Isaac is standing in the porch, fishing his wellies out from the boot box. I hunt for his scarf, his beanie and his gloves even though I know his cousins will be running around dressed only in T-shirts. I swear they are frost-proof, and that their blood circulates at a higher temperature, so that they scoot around, cheeks rosy, when Isaac's hands are blue. He looks so delicate in contrast. I am wary of not making him look like an overly wrapped-up mummy's boy, and yet he is often so frozen, so stiff-fingered, that when Toby tosses him a ball to catch, he drops it. I am beginning to think that motherhood consists of an astute knack of anticipating small humiliations and then trying to avert them. I stuff Isaac's gloves into my handbag and will produce them like a magician when he is blowing his breath into his cold, cupped palms.

Usually when the cousins run off in a gaggle together, Tom and his brothers reminisce about their childhood, clapping each other on the back and laughing heartily. 'Remember when we . . .' they say, and 'I swear we actually had hypothermia camping at that time of year. Who was it fell in the river trying to retrieve a spent firework?'

Sometimes I can't bear to listen; there is something so masculine, so latently good-humoured in their interaction. Beneath their laughter lie striations of muscles, of capability, of confidence. I fast-forward to an adult Isaac carefully and anxiously crouched beside Teddy's wheelchair, and worry that the *remember whens* that they might summon up will be things that were slight to begin with, and by then will no longer be possible.

Teddy is already buckled into his car seat. I've given him a Rubik's Cube to twist, and told him not to worry about making the colours match but rather to make any old pattern. From where I'm standing in the driveway, I can see his tongue poking out in concentration, and his whole hand clumped around the cube with the effort of trying to twist it. The memory comes to me of drawing circle upon circle across a blank sheet of paper with a repeatedly sharpened pencil and a pair of compasses, altering the radii until the page was covered in overlapping discs. And Spirogyro? Was that it? Twizzling carefully at the controls while a geometric pattern spread across the screen. Teddy will never be able to do either of these. Every day I have so many dawnings of what Teddy will not do, and gather them to myself as small losses as they fall around us both.

The Christmas presents are bagged up and in the boot. Tom has carried them out saying *Ho! Ho! Ho!* to Teddy, who watches him bring each load. The boxes of waders for Toby, Felix and Oliver fill the boot to the brim. They will go with the fly-fishing rods Ruth has bought for them. I am suddenly choked, imagining the three of them standing in the river, their feet planted securely, their fingers nimbly casting and winding in their line.

'Clever boy – look how many colours you've changed!' I stash a bag of extra clothes in the footwell in front of Teddy.

'Can I bring my kite? Look how windy it is.' It is Isaac who is asking, and who is tilting his head to the left to try and make his hair blow convincingly across his face. 'It will be super-blowy on the farm, won't it, Daddy?'

'It'll be whipping across the fields if it's like this here. You can bring it if you like. I'll have to repack the boot and you might have to have a box of waders beneath your feet to make room.'

'I don't mind. We can play with the kite in the top field. See, Teddy, the kite. How high do you think we will make it go?'

My gratitude for his thoughtfulness means I have to turn my head and focus on the street beyond our driveway, the cluster of a neighbour's bins, so that the ordinariness of what I see can give me a foothold into composure. I find myself on the brink of tears already, and that is before we are sitting around Ruth's vast dining table, with Teddy swaddled in extra napkins like a static little emperor.

As the houses yield to open countryside, I press my forehead against the car window. I close my eyes against the bruised-knuckle colour of the sky and everything blooms sulphurous. Tom reaches across and touches my leg.

'You're very quiet, what's up?'

His tone is kind, genuine. Behind us, Teddy is dozing and Isaac is playing a game on the iPad. Radio 4 is on softly, with the mid-morning news telling of global things darker than I feel capable of taking on board. The journalist talks of a Syrian woman cradling her two small dead sons in a barrel-bombed street in Aleppo. My blessings should be so very easy to count.

I keep my gaze fixed towards the windscreen. 'Just taking a moment. You know how hectic it always is at the farm.'

Hectic is a disingenuous word. It's hectic at one level: the hubbub of multiple voices, of boots on the flagstones; the stacks of paperwork from Defra, from feed companies, from producers of antidotes for fluke or tapeworm. It couldn't be more different from my mother's precise, tidy house, which has somehow always made me feel wanting, as if she cannot wait for us to leave so that order can be restored. The farm kitchen doesn't make me feel that. There is likely to be a syringe for injecting the turkeys next to the kettle, or a pile of sheep fleeces in the hallway ready to take to a dealer, and mud, always mud, and shoes strewn in front of the Aga. And yet it mostly makes me want to weep, with its feeling of being chock-a-block with the business of living, with life unfettered, whereas my own kitchen feels like a holding pattern, or a small state of contained siege. And then there's my nephews, who are, quite simply so healthy – so rudely, rosily, fulsomely healthy – that Isaac looks hesitant and delicate-boned beside them, and Teddy (and I flinch from the image that comes to mind) like tripe poured into his car seat: pale, soft and sinewless. It's not that Ruth and Jenny aren't kind. Jenny in particular always stands beyond me, cautiously, as if I am encircled by a grass-pocked fairy ring that must not be encroached upon.

Tabitha is different. She looks at me with eyes that are merciless and see every stain on me, of this I am sure. At least she doesn't pity me – there's a bracingness in that – mostly I think because she lacks the empathy to feel very much for anyone at all, except for her daughters, who are beautiful like she is, and for whom life will always overcompensate because of it. James's wife Stella is increasingly mortified each time I meet her, as Mathilde nails all the milestones expected in a child's first year. She is also wary of me, I think, as if I carry with me a taint of something mildewed. I am a mother for whom things did not work out as hoped – I think that's how she'd put it – and am to be stepped round a little cautiously, as if somehow I might contaminate her textbook experience. When I look at Mathilde, it crushes my heart; both in that I was so blind to Teddy's physical condition in the first year of his life, and that all that sunny possibility was so extinguished for him.

So that, yes, all that, tumbling around in my head, and I would like to say to Tom, *No, not quiet at all, just not saying any of it.*

I blink hard to force back a tear. He is watching me in his peripheral vision. Why should all this, today, crowd my mind and make me feel tearful? Nothing has changed, nothing is new; going to the farm is what it is. Stephen, sometime before he died, showed Teddy and me the little three-legged pup he had reared. 'Spirit's the thing, that's what counts,' he said, the puppy held carefully to his chest, which was the only time he'd even indirectly addressed Teddy's condition with me. But spirit isn't the only thing; I would like to have said that to my father-in-law. There's other people's embarrassment, other people's awkwardness and uncertainty; other people's advice and bossiness, good intentions, interference. That can smother the spirit. I could have told Stephen that, but I didn't. The three-legged pup is now grown and mostly looks resigned and a little bit wary. It can't properly keep up. I'm glad he didn't see that.

A housing estate is being built close to us. It has absorbed a field that previously contained sows and piglets. I used to take the boys to look at them on the way home from running errands. The pigs are long gone, and so now I take Teddy to watch the earth movers, the bulldozers, the diggers with their enormous wide-scooped mouths. He loves them. He sits on my lap with his hands on the car steering wheel and pretends he's driving one too, and I feed him halved chocolate buttons, carefully, one at a time.

Sometimes I wish I had one of the huge yellow diggers, with a broad maw capable of scooping up what every medic, care worker, health visitor, educationalist and relative thinks about my mothering of Teddy. I'd drive it away and empty it all into a vast sinkhole, and never have any of it bother me ever again.

Tom

There has been plenty of rain. From this turning in the road I can see the outer margins of the farm, and that there is still green in the hedgerow even though it is so late in the year. Anna seems not only to not want to talk, but to not even want to look at me. Her face is turned from me, so it is the angle of her neck that I see in my peripheral vision. How odd would it be to simply say, *Talk to me, please talk to me*. What do I expect her to say to me anyway? I tell myself this, my fingers drumming on the steering wheel. How, anyway, could she make me feel better about the fact that I woke abruptly from a dream this morning where I was kissing Eliza, and such was the force of it that I turned my back to Anna in bed because I could not have looked at her with my blood still brimming with the sensation? All morning I have tried to banish the memory of Eliza's full mouth on my own; carrying the presents to the car and rubbing my lips on the shoulder of my jacket as if by so doing I will wipe the memory away. It was only a dream, although I'm not sure why that fact doesn't seem to be exonerating me.

The silence between us is pained. There must be something conversational and low-key I can say; surely there is something at home that needs discussing or fixing? And yet I do not want to be a man who talks to his wife on a car journey about the possibility of achieving a saving in annual costs by changing utilities supplier.

The ditch next to the road is brimful with water. The ground will be wet underfoot if we walk to the top field. A soft grey mizzle of rain starts and I flip on the windscreen wipers. The raindrops smear across the glass. When Isaac was small, we went to Cape Town and then drove up the coast, beyond Hermanus, to Saint Sebastian. We turned off the main road and drove for an hour along a gravelled track that was so dry, the car spewed a sweeping cloud of red dust behind it. Each car that overtook us left us momentarily blind in a swirl of scorched mist. We bounced along with Isaac asleep in his car seat, the air vents closed because the dust permeated tenaciously through them, and Anna beside me in a white cotton dress and plimsolls, her feet pressed up against the dashboard, a bottle of water in her hands, laughing, and noticing, and pointing and chatting. It is this that comes to me now, as we pull into the farm driveway, laced with a sudden fear that Anna has been swallowed in a mist more insidious than one made of dry red dust. It is all I can do not to actually say, *Please talk to me*, because what I am suddenly afraid of – now reversing the car up against the stone wall of the dairy as the boys come tumbling out of the farmhouse to greet us – is that at this precise moment she can't bear the sight of any of us, and I don't know how to begin in untangling that.

Anna

The boys swarm around the car.

'Come! See! We've been waiting ages for you!'

There are new kittens in the barn and their plan is to coax the mother to allow them to hold one. Toby unfurls his palm to reveal a sardine, his fingers shimmering with oil.

'We'll wheel you, Teddy; Tom, please can you buckle him? How . . . do . . . you . . . fold . . . out . . . the chair?'

'Shall I come with you?' I am looking at Toby as Tom lifts Teddy into the chair.

'No, we'll be fine. Come on, Isaac, come, Teddy, smell this sardine!'

I turn to Tom. 'Shall I go with them?'

'No, they'll be fine. It's only to the barn. Let them be. We can get all the presents inside without them prodding and guessing.'

I watch them across the yard. The wheels of the chair send the stray straw scattering.

'Don't get scratched!' Tom calls, 'Never underestimate how protective mothers can be!'

I'm not sure whether that's a joke intended for them or for me. Perhaps it wasn't a joke at all. I think of a cat's soft, pink-padded paws, its claws ready to spring. That would come in useful. Both of the boys are up to date with tetanus injections; that's what I'm thinking as Jenny opens the door.

Jenny, Ruth and Stella are all gathered in the scullery, and it has the feel of bridesmaids waiting to ineffectually twitch at the hem of a gown.

Tom kisses them all. 'Hallo. Filthy morning. I knew it would be blowing a gale here.'

Out through the window I can still see the boys. They all have William's flame-red hair, and as I watch them retreat, they are a vivid blotch of colour against the dry-stone wall. François' langur baby monkeys have bright ginger coats so that their mothers can spot them quickly. I wonder if Jenny watches from the kitchen window as her sons meander home from school, and picks out their brightness as they weave along the lane.

'Shall I help you unload the car?' She is beside me.

Jenny is unfailingly kind. She is as plain as a dunnock and almost entirely without vanity, and yesterday will have butchered the meat that she will proficiently cook today for lunch, a hacksaw used competently, and afterwards the white rime of fat washed carefully from beneath her nails. When I think of her – and I do, sometimes, on drizzly mornings, when the rain at the farm will be sweeping across from the hills – my mind snags on the details of her life that I know. I am increasingly of the view that facts about daily lives are perhaps all that can be accurately known of another. William brings Jenny tea each morning at 6.30 and has done every day since she moved to the farm. In the winter, she cooks oatmeal overnight in the simmering oven of the Aga, and ladles it out in broad-brimmed bowls for her sons each morning. That's the fact I find myself snared by. Sometimes it is the smallest things that tell the truth of a life, and it is the oatmeal, carefully planned for the start of the day, that speaks most of Jenny to me.

'Yes, that would be kind, thank you. Most of it is Christmas gifts, and the travel cot for Mathilde. Which bedroom do you want us to put the presents in? Teddy and I wrapped them so carefully, but they'll probably be a bit squished. Feel free to put them at the back of the tree.'

Jenny stands beside me next to the open boot of the car, and looks over to the barn.

'I'm not sure the sardine is going to work. It's their fourth attempt. I've told them they can't use a shrimping net; they were up for giving that a try over breakfast. I don't know whether it was the babies or the mother they thought they would bag with it.'

She speaks, always, as if we are partway through a conversation. She doesn't say *How are you?* or *How have things been?* as if a direct question might fall between us and shatter on the floor. She doesn't ask for any update on Teddy; perhaps either because she is fearful that there will never be good news or because she has decided at some point that questions are intrusive, and that if I have things to tell, I will say them for myself without prompting. What inhabits the space between us is both what Jenny chooses not to ask and what I choose not to say, and thereby our conversation is reduced to pleasantries: a way of casseroling pheasant so they do not become tough; a magenta gladioli that will flower from May through to July. My mother's words hover over me as we carry the boxes from the car: 'When did you become so difficult to help?' Perhaps, also, so awkward to converse with.

Jenny gestures to the stairwell. 'Why don't you put them on top of the wardrobe of the little bedroom with the rose wallpaper? The boys never go in there.'

We stand, Tom and I, in the small box room, the walls heavy with the floral wallpaper and the bed covered in a thick eiderdown, and I pass the gifts to him as he perches on a chair, arranging them neatly in a pile on top of the wardrobe.

'So this is marriage,' he says. 'A husband and wife hiding Christmas gifts.' He laughs, but it is an uncertain sound; as if he needs to be reminded that that is in fact what we are.

On the mirrored chest of drawers beside the cupboard there is a rosary curled in a small china tray; the beads translucent like moonstones, the Christ figure smooth from thumbing. I pick it up briefly and let it slip through my fingers as Tom secures a large package on the top of the wardrobe.

'I'd forgotten Jenny was Catholic.' It seems suddenly to be an explanation of my sister-in-law's gentleness, her faith like a soft, rumpled shawl wrapped loosely around her, the Stations of the Cross present whatever the unremarkable, moderate accumulation of difficulties ascribed to a life.

'Not sure it has ever made any difference, has it? Unless she has a mountain of guilt we don't know about.'

Perhaps I make her feel guilty, each of us marrying a brother, then life dealing us such different hands; Jenny's sons so robust, so impervious to harm. And yet a new emerging lack of reverence for their mother: small verbal slights and disrespects, a tendency to mock – at her habits, at her inclination to exaggerate. Isaac seems so biddable, so compliant in comparison, and still capable of slipping his hand into mine.

'Pass me that one; it's just the right shape to wedge into this space here. If all these baubles on the tags make it to Christmas Day unbroken, it will be a miracle.'

'Teddy enjoyed matching them.' My tone is defensive and Tom is quick to detect it.

'I'm not suggesting your time was wasted; just that they're fragile.' He sounds pained, and shrugs as he extends his arms towards me to take another one. Downstairs, I hear Jenny calling to William from the scullery: 'Please can you come and sharpen the carving knife; I've put it next to the stone.' He will come, compliant.

I have years of history with Jenny; both as very young women coming into this house. Walking past the open door of a bedroom and seeing her in a broderie anglaise nightie, sitting on the stone ledge of the window frame, her arms wrapped around her knees and her feet blue with cold, evidently waiting for the soft murmur of William's and his parents' voices to finish in the bedroom beyond before venturing out. She is tactful, and I am grateful for this, and mindful also that perhaps she made a decision some time ago only to speak to me of her own life in a tone that is gently positive. Once, when I was upstairs changing Teddy, I overheard James asking her of news of her own family. She told him, succinctly, that geographical distance was becoming a problem, that her brother was no help, and that her mother's eyes had become milky like sea glass, her short-term memory haphazard and her limbs steeped with a new kind of lethargy. She would never have responded as candidly to me, although I recognise that I would not have asked.

Is it, then, an intractable problem, to talk openly with someone to whom life has dealt a difficult hand? Perhaps it feels morally unacceptable to complain about anything, or ever to admit, quietly, and with a small degree of understated rage, that ordinary and unremarkable sometimes brings frustrations of its own.

'Is that all of them?'

'Yep.'

'Wrapping them must have taken you hours. Let's go down and get a drink. William says his damson gin is ready for opening.'

I close the bedroom door carefully and pause for a moment on the landing. This home is both Jenny's and not Jenny's. It will somehow always be Ruth's, and I'm guessing it's unlikely that anyone has asked Jenny how she feels about Ruth choosing not to move to Dairy Cottage after her husband's death, as her own mother-in-law did.

In the kitchen, Tabitha is laying the table. She huffs with her breath on the old silver and rubs it with a tea towel, as if she might coax it into more of a lustre. She claims her skill comes from a childhood spent polishing horse tack.

'Absolute nightmare.' What is she talking about? 'One more basement extension and I swear I'll become a local planning officer and reject everything. Total dictatorship.'

Jenny laughs and adjusts the lid of a saucepan so that the vegetables do not boil over. Beside Tabitha's shimmering beauty, she becomes even more nondescript.

I should be kinder, warmer. Perhaps then I could speak to them with trust; progress from our words of pragmatic usefulness and become friends.

'Is there anything I can do to help? There must be something; just point me in the right direction.'

As I speak, we all turn, because there is a shout from the yard. Toby emerges from the barn, a tiny kitten in his hands held out like a trophy.

Isaac

The mother cat looks at me suspiciously. I think she thinks the sardine was a swizz. She ate it quickly and cleanly, pouncing on it where Toby laid it out by the side of the straw bale. My cousins debated for a while whether Toby should try and feed her from his hand, and then they ruled that out, saying she was fierce at the best of times and that was even before she had the kittens. She sprang forward and hissed when Oli's hand swooped in for one of the babies, and now she's bundled the others up behind her so that her body is like a muscly fence. The other kittens keep wriggling, though, despite her attempts to press them into the straw, and I can see tiny pink noses, and white paws, and the flicking tips of tails. As the cat twists and turns to try and contain them, her pink, milk-filled tummy ripples with movement. There is a small glisten of oil on her chin, and she sweeps at it with her paw, and then licks it, all the time her amber eyes not leaving me. My cousins have hold of the smallest tabby, which was the furthest from her in the straw. Felix has put it on Teddy's lap, and they've moved to where the light in the barn is better. Toby is trying to work out whether it is male or female.

I move a little closer to the mother and gently stretch out my hand. The corner of the barn she has chosen is the darkest, and quietest. In another part of it there are the cattle, which have just been brought in for the winter. I can hear them stamping and shifting in their pens. There's a loose bit of guttering on the barn roof, which is being tugged by the wind, and it taps and knocks with each gust that sweeps over the roof. There is one shaft of lemony sunlight that just about reaches the edges of the straw bale. Felix has shown me the place up in the rafters where the swallows will come back and nest in the spring. There are rolls of silage stacked up against the breeze-block wall. They contain the hay from the summer, ready to feed the cattle now they are inside. Toby plunged his hand into the centre of one that was cut open.

'Look,' he said, 'it's warm to the touch.'

'It's like a packet of summer,' Oli added.

Toby shook his head. 'No, it's just that when things rot they make heat.'

The same thing can be thought of, and understood, in different ways. I prefer the thought that it's summer in the middle of the bale.

The cat continues to watch me carefully. I move a little so that I am sitting cross-legged to the right of where she lies. I put both my hands in my lap and sit as still as I can. My cousins have now moved almost to the barn door. 'Let's show Mummy,' one of them says. I can hear Teddy laughing; they've placed the kitten inside the neck of his jumper.

'Look how snuggly it is. It tickles! It tickles! Its whiskers are under my chin.'

The mother cat softens her body a little, and licks at one of the babies, which peeps out from beneath her belly.

'I'm not going to mess with you. I won't take one of your kittens.' She turns to the sound of my voice, and looks fierce again.

When Toby comes back with the little tabby runt, the mother makes a small growly rumble at the back of her throat.

'Do you want to hold him before I put him back?'

I shake my head and stay quiet. He turns to Oli.

'Why don't you put it back, you'll be quicker than me.'

'You just don't want to get scratched, that's why you want me to do it.'

'I bet she'll be quick as lightning. We should have put gloves on.'

As if on cue, the cat edges forward, her neck stretched long.

'Whoa, she's going to pounce, you're going to get it now.'

The kitten makes a tiny mewl, and the mother is up on her feet, scattering the others behind her, so they roll onto their backs, their paws raking at the air. Toby is quick as a flash, slotting the kitten in next to her, although not before she lashes out with her right paw, her claws stiff and sharp.

'She missed you,' laughs Oli, 'although you jumped a mile.'

'She's not being mean; she's only being protective.' Toby pauses to make shushing noises at the cat. 'That's what mothers are supposed to do. Imagine what Mum would do if someone was trying to run off with us.'

Or weigh us. Or make our legs bend and straighten. Or try to put a feeding tube in, or suggest an operation that will put rods in our spine but that might not make anything better. That too.

The cat is madly licking the returned kitten as if she wants all traces of their hands gone.

'I think we should leave her alone now. I think she's had enough of us messing about with her.'

'Shall we show you something else instead?' Toby asks. 'Do you want to come and sit in the old tractor? It's all ours, now that the engine has totally conked and Dad's finished stripping it for spare parts. It's parked in the big shed, and we've got a stepladder up to the cab. Betcha we can lift Teddy up to the driving seat between us. Are you game, Teddy?'

Teddy is nodding and laughing. I should go back to the kitchen and check that that's okay.

We walk away from the cat and her kittens, and I have one last look back over my shoulder into the dimness, trying to pick her out as she settles them into the straw.

If she could talk, I think she would say she's spitting feathers.

Tom

I am home. Odd that the sensation can still catch me, like a fine net of belonging spilling over my limbs.

My father's chair is by the hearth; none of us sit in it without a self-conscious glance around the room first, as if to check we are not being considered presumptuous.

My mother is helping to serve the food. She is both changed and unchanged by my father's death; seeming sometimes to be listening to a conversation that is happening elsewhere, and yet now, at the table, helping her grandchildren with her customary capable air.

All the items on the table sit easily in her hands: the gravy jugs, ladles, spoons, serving bowls, her possessions down through the years. She has lived in this house her entire married life. I wonder if she glimpses her previous self sometimes – younger, fleet of foot – making her way between its rooms, a pail in her hand from the dairy, or one of us held in the scoop of her arm; running out into the yard with a shawl tossed around her shoulders, hearing my father returning from market. Her ghosts are everywhere here, quietly present. She should probably move into the cottage, but I assume part of her – most of her – cannot bear the thought of not living here for what remains of her life. I cannot see her reconciled to drawing the curtains in the Dairy Cottage at twilight, or walking without sorrow up the lane to the farmhouse for a meal, catching sight of the gable end between the trees, her heart attuned to every fall of seasonal light on the brickwork.

She moves over to the sink and turns on the hot tap. The steam clouds my view of her, and I wonder how many thousands of times she has stood there putting a roasting pan in to soak, first her sons scampering around her, and then her grandchildren, and now Dad gone; suddenly, astonishingly, his heart crashing to a halt. 'So this is marriage,' I said to Anna earlier. 'A husband and wife hiding Christmas gifts.' And what I see with my mother now is its aftermath, its undertow; the immense swell of it like water ploughed through by a ship. My mother is steeped in her widowhood, every knuckle of him known, and his goneness still the most striking part of her day.

What did she say to me once? That she had been glad when she had only birthed boys, and that the landscape of boyhood – sunny, uncomplicated – had been entirely preferable to her. When we brought girlfriends home – she called it 'casual beauty blowing in through the scullery door' – her response was rather as if looking at intriguing paintings in a gallery; something she might stand at a short distance from, her head inclined at an angle, while she puzzled them out. The girls started each sentence with 'Sorry . . . sorry,' as if excusing both their request and their physical presence in her kitchen. She often looks at her grand-daughters with something short of bemusement. 'Here,' she says, passing them a bracelet from her blue leather jewellery box, 'would you like to try this on?' Usually they do not. She is most herself teaching the boys to tie nautical knots, or to peel an apple so that the skin unfurls in one piece, or identifying the call of a bird in the garden, her index finger raised taut towards her ear as she listens.

I'm not sure how all that equates to Anna now. There is between them a kind of gentle stiltedness, that's how best I can think of it; Mum passing her a bowl of vegetables, and touching her arm lightly when the transaction is complete.

When Anna came to the farm, she burst in through the door

like the air after rain in the spring, wearing a bright blue jumper, her eyes alive and dancing with the light thrown from it. By the dam I joked that I could swim faster across it than she could, and she laughed and said, 'Bet you can't,' and shucked off her clothes to her underwear, and jumped in and started swimming. Dad liked her; respected the way she stood at the sheep-dip gate, helping one spring; the flock herded through a narrow channel that ended with her in oversized wellies. Mum described her as frank: 'I like her very much, she is frank and strong and determined.' Are they the words she would choose now? I no longer know. Perhaps those qualities have turned into something rather fearsome. Jenny certainly dodges and ducks around her; it is only Tabitha whose gaze is entirely dispassionate.

Tabitha sits three places down from me, her fork balanced on the side of her plate. How her beauty glows. She's a piece of work; Edward would probably countenance that. When he first met her, he told me that he'd never met anyone as carefree, and that he found it beguiling. That was the word he chose. Last Christmas I heard them arguing in the snuggery when they evidently thought everyone had gone to bed. Edward said bitterly, 'Sometimes I wonder if you actually give a fuck about anyone.' Not so much carefree then as careless, it seems. I catch Edward looking at her sometimes as if she is a puzzle he has somehow misinterpreted. Beauty, evidently, is not always compensation enough.

Edward is jesting now with Felix with his smooth, easy confidence.

'You call that a bicep?' He pokes Felix's upper arm. 'No, surely it's an acorn? A walnut? A tomato pip?' Felix is roaring with laughter. 'A pomegranate seed,' Edward adds, tickling him under the arm. Felix laughs again and lunges beyond Edward's reach.

I catch my mother's eye. In a moment she will say, *Not at the table*, and we will all obediently gather ourselves. How unchanged, really, any of us are: Edward the Bold, Tom the Compliant, James the Judicious and William the Peacemaker. There is a soft, easy familiarity about us all around the table; given a chance, we revert to our childhood seating arrangement. I find I cannot transpose Eliza here and am assuaged by that thought.

Mum goes each week to the graveyard to sit a while by Dad's headstone. She says she goes to keep him updated; she tells him about the prices the stock are fetching, the amount of rainfall, and how well seasoned the logs from the old orchard have become. She speaks of nothing that is sad; she says, 'Why would I want to trouble him with that?' She is of a generation that considers sadness to be osmotic. If it is not spoken of, not given oxygen, there is every likelihood it will channel itself away, especially when coupled with hands that are busy.

Looking at Anna now, I am not sure this is true. She carries her forehead as if it is just beginning to dawn on her that she has a headache.

Edward is trying to draw Isaac out, but he is more resistant than Felix.

'So are you a cricketer yet, Isaac? Don't go to your dad for any bowling lessons. Worst leg sider in the family. Appalling cover drive too.'

Isaac is barely listening, distracted by a conversation Anna has begun with Tabitha about disability allowances.

'Is there a winter nets club you could join? I always enjoyed that.' Edward is nothing if not persistent. Isaac glances once, twice, across at Anna, as if he is gauging her level of disquietude.

Edward would love a son; it's clear from his interaction with his nephews around the table. Not with Teddy, though; I don't think Teddy fulfils Edward's notion of a son. He certainly doesn't fulfil Tabitha's, who looks as if she is trying to resist covering her eyes as Anna begins to wipe Teddy's face with soft little dabbing motions. She is not beyond licking his cheek if the need arises,

her tongue quick and pink as a cat's. Tabitha is steeling herself
not to look away. Beyond her, my nieces sit neatly and tidily.
Clemmie is steadily, furtively, hiding her lamb under some cauliflower, and Scarlet has finished what little she is eating and is
rolling her napkin and threading it carefully through the silver
christening ring that bears her initial. The fine motor skills
required to do both give me a sudden, sharp pain like heartburn.
Isaac has put Teddy's napkin ring over the brake of his wheelchair
so that it looks like a souped-up gearstick.

Anna is still talking, her face intent with emotion, her fists
balled up on the edge of the table. She is talking about schools,
and lack of provision for children with particular needs, and the
level of unaccountability displayed by some of the staff. Her voice
rises and falls with intensity. Tabitha appears glassily bored and
seems to be resisting the temptation to plant her face flat in her
plate. She manages to look at Anna directly.

'Maybe you just need to be more assertive. When my friend
Antonia wrote to her child's prep school teacher, she began the
letter with "Last time I checked, I was paying your salary." She's
the kind of woman who says exactly what she thinks. Last week
she admitted to not having done an unselfish thing for as long
as she can remember.'

'That doesn't sound very commendable.' My mother's voice
is grave.

There is a moment of perfect silence, sharp as the ting of a
fork on crystal. Edward coughs awkwardly, and Tabitha shrugs
lightly and twists the stack of rings on her finger to align them
correctly. Anna doesn't look appalled. She has stopped attending
to Teddy, and bends her face to her plate. She is cutting her meat,
and looks as if she is concentrating very hard on doing so. She
obviously isn't; I can spot her smokescreen. Perhaps she is considering what a liberation it might be to be as direct and as selfish
as one pleases.

'After lunch is finished, please can we fly my kite? It's in the boot of our car. I've been watching the tree from this window and the branches are blowing like crazy.'

It is Isaac who has piped up; Isaac, who has said very little during the meal, and who now manages to steer the conversation away from Anna's slight hectoring, from Tabitha's response, and from my mother's reproof, and instead to chatter about which is the best field to go to, and how fast they will be able to run in their wellies.

I see Isaac glance quickly again at Anna. No one else is looking at her now; no one is waiting to see if she responds to what Tabitha has said. The spell is broken, the room has moved on, the table suddenly debris of empty plates and scrunched napkins. William is banging a saucepan lid with the back of a wooden spoon.

'Everyone has to carry at least three things to the sink before making a bolt for it.'

Isaac has achieved this. Now I watch as he carefully stacks three pudding bowls into the crook of his arm, and places three spoons onto the napkin on Teddy's lap, so that he too has fulfilled William's criteria.

Anna

Ruth is beside me, washing up. In the scullery, Tom and William are helping the boys with their boots. Clemmie and Scarlet have said they do not want to go outside, and Tabitha shrugged when Ruth noted the benefits of fresh air. The girls are sitting on the chintz-cushioned window seat in the hallway and playing with a miniature butter churn. The turning paddle makes a soft swooshing noise that fills my ears and makes me feel as if I am swimming deep underwater. Ruth scrubs at a saucepan with what seems like additional effort. Perhaps she is mirroring my own vigour; I catch myself not just drying the dish in my hand but seemingly polishing it as well. Ruth hands me the precious items straight to the tea towel so that they will not slip or be chipped on the draining board.

The boys are making their way across the yard with Tom. 'Stay with them and watch them,' I call to him from the window. He unlocks the car boot and hands the kite carefully to them. The boys line up to hold the tail out so that it won't become tangled. Isaac and Toby are holding one handle of the wheelchair each, and they thread the kite out onto Teddy's lap. Ruth follows my gaze.

'Quite the team.'

I nod, and let the silence sieve between us again. There is an almost audible beat between us; all the questions my mother-in-law might take this occasion to ask me but doesn't. *Has a decision been made about when Teddy will be allowed to start school?*

*Is it true that the nutritionist thinks he should mostly be fed by tube?
He looks a little paler than last time I saw him – has he had another
chest infection?*

There is no shortage of possibilities: they are all things she
might reasonably bring up but does not. Perhaps the fault is in
me; perhaps I radiate that such directness would not be welcome.
Ruth would no doubt ask Tom, if they were standing here and
doing the pots together. She is more at ease with the good-
humoured transparency of men, and with her grandsons, also, a
way of conversationally falling alongside. It could be reticence,
shyness – that is always a possibility. The anxiety of intrusion.
The fear that a conversation has the danger of sinking sand. I
am as much to blame. In the six months since Stephen died, I
have not asked, *Tell me, what is widowhood like? Do you miss
Stephen badly; is it hard living in the house alongside William and
Jenny?*

Instead we stand side by side and continue to wash the pots,
and the yard beyond us is now empty of the scattered boys, and
there is only the sound of the kitchen clock, the swooshing of
the butter churn, and Jenny in the scullery putting the tablecloth
and the napkins into the wash.

I spread the damp tea towels to dry on the steel plates of the
Aga, and as I do so, Ruth gestures to the pine dresser and to the
stack of her knitting.

'A pullover for Felix; it's his turn to have one. Look at this
tangle of wool. Goodness knows what happened for it to get like
this – one of the cats maybe. Actually, what am I saying; more
likely one of the boys trying to knit a row.' She takes it up in her
hands. 'I shall have to ask one of them later if they can manage
to sit still for a moment and lend me their wrists. I will thread
it around and around until it is smooth again. Given a little time
and patience, it will come right.'

'It looks like it will take an age.'

'Yes, it's always more an act of faith at the outset.'

Perhaps we are not talking about yarn at all. Perhaps what Ruth is actually telling me is that she would like to lend her own hands, trustworthy and steady, and somehow help me reconfigure myself. Is that what I need?

She puts the wool carefully down. 'Shall I make us some tea? We've got time to drink it before walking up to the field to see how they're getting on. No doubt there will be all kinds of shenanigans before the kite takes flight. Arguing over who's in charge will take a good part of the afternoon, and that's just my sons.'

She puts the kettle on, and reaches into the fridge for the milk. I take down cups from the shelf, and call through to Jenny and Tabitha to ask if they would like one too. Barely two dozen words have passed between us, but it feels as if what has tacitly been said is that Ruth is mindful, and that she wishes she could help. What I am battling with – now transferring Isaac's gloves from my handbag to my coat pocket in case he needs them – is that the right thing to do increasingly appears to be to say nothing at all. It's a curious thing, in this life that is mine, that the optimum form compassion can take seems to be benign indifference.

As I walk down the hallway, the tea tray held carefully in my hands, I am aware that Ruth, beside me, seems to have synchronised her step with mine. Perhaps it feels like the only way to express her solidarity and care.

Since when did I become such a muzzle on those around me; Ruth's step now halting in time with my own?

Isaac

The kite soars into the sky like a fierce bird, and twists and dives and stabs at the ground. Toby and Oliver are running beneath, yelling and flapping their outstretched palms over and over, as if this will make extra air currents and keep the kite up there longer. The wind blows stronger and the kite tugs and tugs, and it feels like my arms might be pulled from their sockets. I stand – my feet planted wide – and brace myself against it, and squint up at the bright sky to watch it dance above the trees. It's perfect. Totally perfect. What a brilliant plan.

Daddy has wheeled Teddy's chair to the side of the field so that he can watch. Teddy is sitting quietly, his arms all of a huddle in his lap. I thought he might be whooping too. It comes to me suddenly that perhaps this isn't as exciting for him as I thought it would be. What he can mostly see is me having the challenge of holding the kite and our cousins hurtling across the field, their legs at top speed. Maybe it isn't the best fun, stuck there with his wheels a bit submerged in the furrows of the ground. Maybe it feels his chair has grown roots, especially when compared to the loopy swoops of the kite. He looked much happier this morning, the kitten stuffed into the neck of his jumper. All the brightness I am feeling pops like a bubble, and then there is Toby beside me, out of breath from running.

'You've got her going beautifully. Hold on tight or you'll lose her. Oli's kite dive-bombed into the river and we've never got it back. Mum says when the water's lower we might but probably it'll have gone rotten. Look out! Look up, you're not watching it properly.'

The kite loops the loop, and everything looks perfect and strong again, and the words are out of my mouth before I have properly thought about them, as if the wind itself is tugging them free of my lips.

'I wish Teddy could do this. His hands can't hold on properly but he would love to do it.'

Toby looks across to where Teddy is sitting, and then at my hands.

'So why don't we tie the kite to the chair? Then it would feel like he's flying it himself. It'd be like those painters who hold the brush in their mouth or with their toes.'

Before lunch, Toby showed me a Christmas card that has been painted like this. Next time they do art at school, he's going to put the brush in his mouth, because he says who knows when such a thing might come in useful. I know this isn't the same thing at all – putting a paintbrush in your mouth is not the same as tying a kite to a wheelchair – but instead of thinking about that, I jump straight to Toby's solution. Wouldn't it be just like tying birthday balloons onto the Wizzybug? The outside chair is so heavy, so glued into the mud, and the kite would fly brightly above it, with Teddy feeling completely in charge.

We reel the kite back in and scramble across the field to Teddy, calling to the others. We wiggle the wheelchair free of the mud and push it to the small ridge where I launched the kite earlier, and we are chattering about our plan just like the starlings murmuring above the trees, and Teddy is waving his mittens and showing us just where to attach it, and it is exactly the same place as his birthday party balloons usually go.

Oli does one of Granny's knots, which is impressively strong, and Toby and Felix take the kite and run across the field with it in their hands, leaping and jumping at each gust of wind, waiting for the one that will carry it up. Oli and I join in, flapping with our arms, and then when a snatch of wind takes it, we all start cheering and I turn around to look at Teddy, and he is much further from us than it seemed when we were running.

Toby says, 'We did put the brake on, didn't we? What happens to the wheels if the wind is very strong?'

What happens to the wheels is that they start to turn, because Teddy is light and his wheelchair is also light, and suddenly we are all running towards him because the chair has started to move down the slope, and it's bouncing and bumping and Teddy's hat has fallen over his face, and Toby is shouting, 'Abort! Abort!' because it's a phrase he learned from a film about a crashing spacecraft and it seems the right thing to shout.

I know Teddy can't throw himself out, mostly because he's strapped in and he can't unbuckle himself even when the wheelchair is perfectly still, and also because to throw himself clear would need muscles that do just what Teddy asks, and his biggest problem is that he doesn't have enough of those. And then when I look across the field in the direction Teddy is heading, there is the river, which is full and fast and already holding a drowned kite, and the wheelchair would sink straight away, and I know – totally know – that I can't run any faster to catch up and grab it.

What I would like to do is drop to the ground, curl into a ball and press my face into the mud so that I can't see what happens next, because it will all be my fault because I should have known better, not my cousins', who do not live every day with Teddy and do not completely understand how his body cannot work. They think everything can be made strong just by fresh air and trying a bit harder. I want to be sick – all of my Sunday lunch – because what happens will be bad, very bad, and also if I had never made my plan and asked to bring the kite, none of it would be happening and Teddy would be safe. Mummy's face will be furious and also disappointed, which is worse than being cross, and she will not look at me properly but at the space just by my feet. This is what happened once when I put a mug of tea next to Teddy that I was supposed to be carrying to Daddy, and Teddy's arm jerked and knocked it over and his trousers were soaked with it and he had a small pink burn like a raspberry on the skin of his ankle. That's a trifle in comparison to what is happening now. Trifle is a word my cousins like to use; over lunch, comparing bruises: 'That's a trifle, see, look at mine.'

When I lift my eyes again – and only a few seconds have passed – Daddy has appeared out of nowhere and is running; Daddy, who has been walking through the copse down by the river with Uncle William, and who has looked up as they came through the treeline to see Teddy hurtling towards him, the kite like a red flare above him, and his harness hardly holding him in so that his body is bouncing as the chair is thrown about by the hummocky ground.

Daddy catches him. This is how I will always think of it, as if Teddy is a rugby ball that has been thrown wide of a scrum. Daddy and William run up the slope, each at forty-five degrees to the chair, and by chance it bounces in Daddy's direction, just as the right-hand side wheel topples all ready to spill Teddy out, and so he is half caught, half blocked by Daddy's body, which he has thrown towards the chair with his arms wide apart. When I finally get there, my lungs feeling like they are going to explode, Daddy is carefully lifting Teddy out. Teddy has mud on his cheek from where he came to rest, and a small bright splodge of blood coming from his lip at the corner of his mouth, and I can't tell whether he is laughing or screaming. His head is thrown back in Daddy's arms, and beyond him the kite has dive-bombed into a tree, and the string is pulling just a little, in soft, tuggy pulses, from where it is still tied to the chair. Toby and Oliver have caught up and have ground to a halt beside me, and by silent agreement we seem to have arranged ourselves neatly into a line as if we are in the headteacher's office and about to really catch it with the telling-off of our lives, William now standing there too, out of breath, stooped over with his hands on his great big thighs.

Teddy has stopped taking in great gulps of air and he turns to me and says:

'I was nearly flying. Completely actually nearly flying. Did you see me go? A-ma-zing.'

The scream is still going. The noise I heard – which I thought was Teddy but now seems to have mixed up with Teddy's laughter – is actually coming from Mummy. I know that now because it is still going on beyond me, like a wild, frantic animal. She is by the stile with Granny and Jenny and Tabitha, and they are walking with Bailey, Granny's old Labrador, and Stumps, the hoppy three-legged dog. She continues to scream as she runs across the field, and when she reaches us, she almost snatches Teddy from Daddy.

'How the hell did that happen? You were meant to be watching!' Her face is totally white, apart from a blue line that has traced exactly around her lips.

The line of boys who are about to have the telling-off of their lives has now expanded to include Daddy and Uncle William and Felix. Daddy wipes his face and some of the mud off his trouser leg and says, slowly and carefully, 'I think there's no harm done. Let's take him back to the house and check properly for bruises, but I think we've been very lucky and that there's no harm done.'

There *is* harm done. I can see that. Mummy has turned around with Teddy pressed close to her chest and is marching back across the field, her hair flying behind her as if she too might take off and be whipped up high across the river.

Toby is looking at Daddy with his hands behind his back, like a very precise soldier, and he says, 'I'm very sorry, Uncle Tom. That was completely my fault.'

'Mostly mine actually, Daddy,' I say. 'I started it.'

'It was my knot-tying; that makes me to blame too,' Oli says.

'I did the running. I helped the kite get in the air.' This from Felix.

'We thought it would be more fun for Teddy, rather than just watching.' Toby lifts his chin.

We are sharing the blame like a neatly cut pie.

Daddy brushes some more mud off his sleeve and his palm, and he touches each of our heads briefly, like he's a vicar in church giving us a blessing. He looks as if he is not really paying attention, as if he is hearing but not listening – that is what it seems.

'No harm done, although hopefully you'll learn – in fact we'll all learn – from it. I can guess it came from the best of intentions, from a thought that was kind about wanting Teddy to join in.'

'You're bloody monkeys,' says Uncle William. 'I don't know about joining in, you nearly gave me a heart attack. I haven't sprinted up this hill so fast since I was pretty much your age.'

He cuffs Toby playfully across one of his ears, and spits out some grass from his mouth like old whiskers. What he says makes me feel sad all over again, because maybe if you are the kind of boys my cousins are, you actually *are* just bloody monkeys rather than someone who nearly seriously injured their brother and should have known better. It probably means that these kind of boisterous near-miss scrapes happen all the time, when you make dens in trees, dive-bomb kites into rivers, and run flat out across a recently sown field. They do not happen if what you mostly play with your brother is board games and word games and the dealing of cards, and if, all the time, you are worrying whether he is happy and included and safe.

Anna

If fury were a coin, I swear to God I could take it between my teeth, cold and metallic, and snap it right in half.

We are driving home now. The road in front of us is dark and wet, and Tom is switching the headlights from full to dipped with a steady rhythm that has lulled the boys to sleep with the watching of it.

There was tea before we swiftly left, with Ruth at the helm quietly telling the boys to wash their hands and then cutting a Victoria sponge. I took Teddy upstairs and stripped off his clothing on Ruth's bed, so that he lay pale and soft on the plumped-up paisley eiderdown. Jenny hovered beyond me at the doorway, her hands fluttering as she gestured towards the bed, as if she was scared to intervene and somehow implicated because her boys were involved. 'Would you like me to bring you a blanket to cover the rest of him?' and 'Tea. Maybe some sweet tea? Perhaps that would be a good idea for both of you?'

And, even though I hadn't responded to her at all, 'Felix's friend's mum is the nurse at the surgery. Would you like me to ask her to come up?'

Teddy's eyes were twinkling. He wasn't concussed. I felt carefully along each of his limbs and the swell of his ribcage. His lip had stopped bleeding and there was a small bloom like a blackberry at the corner of his mouth.

'Any *ow*s? Did you hit your head?'

'Nope. I flew! I almost flew.' He extended the word so that his mouth was full of the swoop of it.

Tom had followed me back to the house, trying to catch up with me, limping a little, which meant I kept ahead of him. At the foot of the stairs, he put his hand on my arm and I shrugged it off.

'Anna, Anna.' His tone was imploring.

I couldn't bear to look at him and he did not follow me upstairs.

Tabitha, removing her wellingtons and stepping across to the mirror to check her hair, said drily, 'That looks like a ticket to nowhere, Tom.'

I heard him turn and go towards the kitchen.

'Flew,' Teddy said again, from where he lay on the eiderdown. He beefed the word up even more, made his mouth into a moue and moved his chin in circles to mimic something spiralling through the air.

My own mouth felt crammed full with unsayable, unshoutable hot words, which only social propriety stopped me yelling down the length of the landing; yelling past Jenny, who was still standing half in and half out of the bedroom, her hand on the doorknob. The words bounced from my soft palate to my cheeks and ricocheted onto my tongue:

You were supposed to be watching. You said you would watch him. I was walking with your mother, being kind to your mother. If you hadn't caught him if you hadn't caught him if you hadn't caught him . . .

Teddy was fine. Not just fine, perhaps even a little bit proud. This was evident when we came back downstairs and joined everyone at the table for tea. He had survived a danger. He had done something bold. He had had an adventure. His cousins watched him, sideways on, as the grown-ups fretted around him, because he had managed to survive something that could have gone badly for them all had he not.

'You were like a blummin' torpedo,' Toby said to him, under his breath. They were grateful to him, I sensed this as I sipped my cold tea, chewing at my lip so that it too felt on the brink of bleeding, but saying nothing and still not looking at Tom, not looking at him at all. Ruth placed her hand briefly on my arm as she passed and murmured something I didn't quite catch, and I let her hand rest there, patiently counting the seconds while it did so. Ruth was blameless, I knew this, but in her prolonged touch there was something of a plea not to judge Tom harshly – or William either. I counted the seconds while her hand remained on my forearm because I did not want to shrug her off, and yet at the same time I was not interested in her mitigating what her adult sons had done.

Tom turns to me as we reach the trunk road.

'So are we going to talk about this? I've already apologised. I left them with Teddy watching from the side of the field. It all looked fine. You know how it is with William – he can never talk unless he's moving – and before I knew it we were down in the trees. I didn't think; I just never imagined . . .'

His voice trails away. My own is crisp and curt. I would like to slap him rather than give him an answer. I ball my hands in my lap. If he were wearing glasses, I would like to snatch them from his face, to express my fury at what he cannot see. Instead I answer him, my nails pressed into my palms.

'No, of course you didn't, because that's usually the case when accidents happen. People are always not thinking, not anticipating, their eye is always off the ball. But you should have been watching. You *should* have been watching . . .' My tone is insistent. 'William's boys have no idea how it is for Teddy. You should know that. Why didn't you know that? Why weren't you thinking? It's so fucking simple. There *is* no margin for error.'

'I was thinking about William; about Mum still being in the house; about how much revenue the farm makes, about the difficulties he may or may not have. I wasn't thinking about Teddy; I'm sorry. I left Teddy looking happy at the side of the field, just like all the other boys. I was thinking of him as no different at that moment. When he was hurtling towards me, I thought my heart would pound right out of my chest. I've never run so fast in my life – and William neither.'

He pauses, and I think he is waiting for me to say something kind. It would be easy to do so, and to head off further conflict. But I will not. I cannot. I turn my gaze to the side of the road. Every minute of every day when I am taking care of Teddy, I am mindful, I am focused. Never once for a moment do I leave him in the bath in his support seat when my phone is ringing in the bedroom next door. Never once do I fail to cut a grape in quarters so that if he swallows weakly it will not block his windpipe. He will not be a child who chokes to death on a grape. Never once, when he slithers about on his tummy, am I not one step behind him, my arms outstretched, completely ready for him.

It's this I'm thinking of now, my palms itching with the desire to take Tom's head by the ears and shake him until he sees stars. *If I am concentrating, why aren't you? If I can be single-minded, why can't you?* These are the words that are barrelling around my mouth, and I swallow them down and spend the rest of the journey in silence.

Tom

They are all asleep.

I have carried Teddy to bed. Isaac stirred when we pulled into the driveway, and he ate some cereal and got into his pyjamas and I sat on the side of his bed for a while.

'Sorry, Daddy, I'm really, really sorry.'

'Hush, you've apologised enough. Close your eyes. Accidents happen, and we all got a fright, but Teddy's not hurt. Just no more kites tied to wheelchairs for a while.' I kiss his forehead.

'I should have known better. I don't want to shut my eyes because I'll just see the chair flying.'

I don't tell him that I think that is what I will see too when I put my head on the pillow, and perhaps several times during the night, my heart squeezing a beat as I do so.

Anna has showered and gone to bed, saying she wants to read. Her anger, which felt flint-edged during the car journey, seems to have dissipated into a muted sadness that somehow feels worse. I stood feeling hopeless in the bedroom when she came out of the bathroom, her wet hair wrapped in a towel, and she looked at me with an expression that made me feel I will never be the recipient of her good opinion again. I couldn't bear to stay in the room.

In the kitchen I pour myself a scotch and swill it around the glass. In a parallel universe, once the initial panic had passed, once we were triply sure that Teddy was physically fine, maybe there might have been a moment of almost good humour, of comic relief. *My God, I nearly died when I saw him coming down the hill.* There might have been a re-enactment of William, totally busted for breath, doubled over as the wheelchair crashed into me. There might have been – over tea – my trouser leg rolled up to reveal the not inconsiderable gash on my shin and the incipient purpling of a bruise, with me saying to Teddy, *Look, this is what I got saving you. See my badge of honour.* Maybe this, in a parallel world, but not in our actual world; not with Anna's displeasure hovering over the table like the mushroom of a nuclear cloud. In that same parallel world, bad stuff happens to other children: falling off horses with collarbones splintering; slipping near poolsides and opening chins on the edge of diving boards. Accidents happen and most times afterwards there is the sunny upland of relief; the good humour that comes from the worst not having come to pass. And it is this that dawns on me as the scotch burns its way down my gullet: that as far as Anna is concerned, the worst has already come to pass. There is nothing with regard to Teddy that will count as the sunny upland of relief.

I sit down with my iPad and consider the app for the Sunday papers. I have no appetite for world news. I look at my watch and wonder if Anna is asleep yet. I decide to stay downstairs until I am sure she is. I glance across at the sideboard, where there is a photograph of our wedding day. It would be inconceivable to the version of myself in the picture that I would choose to remain downstairs to avoid getting into bed with the woman who is held in my arms. She smiles across at me, cream rosebuds in her hair.

I have emails waiting. I click on the envelope icon. Eliza's name jumps out from the mid-list.

Hi – hope you've had a good weekend. Didn't you say you were going to see your extended family? Hope you had a great time. I braved Christmas shopping, which is not to be recommended. See attached for tomorrow afternoon's presentation – you might want to add something so I'm sending it to you now to give you plenty of time. Look forward to talking.

Eliza

Look forward to talking. Another parallel universe where restrained silence is not a feature, where chatting – what an unfettered word – increasingly seems the norm. I close my eyes, take a deep breath, and wonder what Eliza is doing. What, on a Sunday night, if she is without a partner, might a single woman of thirty-something be doing? I try not to think of her body wearing something soft, or to imagine her sitting on a couch, her knees tucked up to her chest. It is tempting to allow myself to think of scooping her up and holding her completely; to imagine how that might feel. To tell her how weary I am of feeling inadequate.

Teddy coughs, briefly. I listen carefully, my ear tilted towards the stairs. I wait to see if Anna turns on the landing light. She does not. Outside, a steady rain is slowly falling. Across the road, a neighbour's Christmas tree glitters with early lights.

In a comic book I had as a child, there was a character who could grow metal spikes out of his limbs and use them to deadly effect. As I stare at the clock hands turning, I can't help but feel that this is what is happening to Anna. In the face of Teddy's limb weakness, her own seem to be turning to steel. She is merciless. And yet. Her scream as she ran across the field. There was such pain in the sound of her; this is what strikes me now, and I wish I felt that she would like me to go upstairs and take her in my arms. To hold her and stroke her hair from her forehead and press my lips to her skin and tell her softly, repeatedly, *I am here for you, I am here for you, everything will be okay*. She couldn't have made it clearer that this isn't what she wants, and she probably thinks I'm not there for her anyway, not when I have failed so miserably and repeatedly in my responsibilities to them all. No doubt she thinks everything will not be okay, and that she cannot trust me to help her take proper care of Teddy. If I go upstairs now, she will turn her body from me, and I will have to lie awkwardly beside her, an inadequate father and husband in the space of a day.

Instead, I sit and watch as the clock hands edge round the face further. Across the road, my neighbour extinguishes his Christmas tree lights.

Anna

He does not come. I lie very still and can hear him moving downstairs. He takes a glass from the cupboard and presumably pours himself a drink. He must be tired after the drive; the darkness thick as soot and the rain hypnotic on the windscreen and the soft sweep of the wipers.

When I came from the shower into the bedroom in my towel, he was standing there – was he waiting for me? His arms were by his sides, and he had an air of uncertainty and hesitancy I see often in Isaac. In the shower I made the water so hot it was almost scalding, and it turned my skin scarlet as I tried to make the fear leach from my bones. As I dried myself, I realised there was a mantra playing in my head – *he is all right he was not hurt, he is all right he was not hurt.* When I came into the bedroom, my anger had begun to fizzle away, replaced by contrition because I know I was unreasonable to both Ruth and Jenny. I did not thank Jenny, who stayed with me in the bedroom in a gesture of solidarity, and I was not merciful to Ruth in signalling that my anger with Tom would pass. Tabitha I ignored, totally, after we came back downstairs and she said, 'Crikey, Teddy; that's enough spills for an afternoon. You're quite the thrill-seeker. Who knows where we'd be if you were running around out of that wheelchair.'

When I told Tom that I was going straight to bed to read, it was not my intention to actually do so. The novel I'm reading hasn't been opened in weeks. After the bubble of the car, I wanted to create physical space between us. But now, as I lie in bed and pull the duvet up to my chin, I am listening intently to see if I can hear him coming. I want him to get into bed beside me, to hold me without desire but with kindness and say to me, *I know you were frightened but it's all right, it's all right.* If he intuited that I was more terrified than angry, it would go some way towards making peace. I want very much to be lying on his chest, my hand pressed to my mouth, until the anguish in my heart has gone.

He does not come. And still he does not come. It would be easy to pad softly onto the landing and call him, but I will not. Teddy coughs but does not wake himself. Tom does not step to the foot of the stairs in order to hear him more clearly. On the road outside, I can hear cars swooshing through the rain. I hear a car door slam and someone in heels walk briskly along the pavement. He does not come, and I realise he will not come. He is choosing instead to sit by himself downstairs.

I turn onto my side and tuck my knees to my chest. When he does get into bed it will be my shoulder blades and my spine that will face him.

Isaac

I can't get to sleep. I was almost asleep – I heard Daddy tiptoe quietly away – and then I expected to be properly asleep, but I'm not. I'm in the wide-awake club, looking up at my bedroom ceiling, which I can't actually see but I think if I keep my eyes open they will adjust and I will see the outline of everything in my room. The landing light is still on; not turned down super-low as it is every night in case Mummy or Daddy need to get to Teddy's room quickly, but still properly on. One of them must be downstairs. It must be Daddy. Mummy went for a shower and didn't go back down. Teddy's room is quiet.

I wonder if my cousins are asleep. They all share a room. Perhaps they are awake too, talking about what happened in the field today.

Tea afterwards was awkward. Granny sent us all off to wash our hands and we stood in a row at the scullery sink, the water streaking brown from our hands, and Felix said, 'Crikey, we'd have been in trouble for months.'

'In trouble for ever,' said Toby.

'And ever. Like the Lord's Prayer,' added Oliver.

They flicked drops of water from their fingertips at each other.

They are mainly relieved. Not mainly: totally. They don't feel guilty, they feel lucky. They're not worried that they made a mistake with Teddy, they're just glad nothing bad happened. That's the difference, because it is a thing that is over for them now. They're not walking around thinking they actually do have to learn a lesson from it, or that they have to make sure nothing like it ever happens again in case it isn't okay.

Mummy's like a sentry guard. That's what I'm seeing her as now, while I'm whacking my pillow with the heel of my palm because it feels bumpy to lie on. She's watching all the time. When she was upstairs checking Teddy was okay, everyone was quiet, especially Daddy and Uncle William, who came in from the scullery freshly soaped and properly clean and sat at the table as if they were boys just like us. Then, after Granny had poured all the grandchildren milky tea in big mugs, and given us cake, it was like a belt had been loosened and everybody started talking more normally again. Clemmie and Scarlet had eyes round as marbles.

'And then what, and then what?' Clemmie asked, her cake untouched.

Auntie Jenny came downstairs and sat down next to Felix and gave him a big hug and everything carried on thawing – that was what it felt like – the room growing less and less uncertain and warmer and warmer instead. And then Mummy reappeared carrying Teddy, who was chuckling and doing his kitten paw wave. I wanted to shout out *Three cheers!* or *Hooray!* or *For he's a jolly good fellow!* which felt funny and old-fashioned but correct because I was so happy that he was all right, but Mummy's face was so stern and watchful, and the shout-out died on my lips, and everybody seemed to stiffen a bit in their chairs, sit up a little taller, eat more neatly, and it was as if Mummy coming in had made the temperature in the room drop, so that everyone felt awkward and uneasy all over again.

I looked down at my plate and prodded my finger into a smudge of strawberry jam and felt sad because I would have liked to have turned to everyone at the table and explained that Mummy is not a fierce crosspatch, and that she is not cold; that sometimes she spits feathers but mostly she helps make things out of wax and says words like skedaddle and fandango and only cleans the kitchen each school morning because she thinks it's a way of keeping everyone safe. I wanted to cry as she put Teddy carefully into his chair, and dabbed a little at his lip, and cut his slice of cake into even smaller squares, and then sat down in her own chair and started to sip at her tea. She is not what she seems, that is what I would have liked to say, as the table around me drew tight like the top of my duffel bag, and what seemed to have made the room difficult was that my Mummy was now in it.

In the car on the way home I was not actually sleeping. I let my head roll a little on my shoulder so that when Daddy glanced in the mirror it looked as if I was. Daddy said sorry to her. He said sorry a number of times. He tried to explain that he was trying to be kind to William, and I understand that if you are looking in one direction and trying to be kind, it must be hard to look in another one at the same time and to remember always to be responsible and on guard. Perhaps not for Mummy; maybe whatever she does, at the same time she is being watchful and on guard. She didn't say it was okay. She didn't say she forgave him. She didn't say *Sorry and start over* like she makes me and Teddy say if ever we quarrel, which in fact is hardly ever because it would not be fair sides. Instead, she said hardly anything at all. When I squinted out of my eyes, I could see that she had turned her face to the window beside her and she was looking out of that, even though it was completely dark and there was completely nothing to see.

The sound of the scream she made running across the field when Teddy was hurtling along won't go out of my ears. I want to roll my head from side to side to see if it will shake out like a marble onto my pillow. It was worse than the sound of a fingernail scraping on a blackboard; worse than when a dog was run over in the street and it screamed when the car hit it as all the air was punched out of its chest.

The sound came from somewhere inside Mummy that must be very sad. If I am one kind of carrier – whatever the physiotherapist meant by that – she is another. She is carrying something inside of her and when it spills out, that is the sound it makes, spreading all over the field. I would like to say that to Daddy; perhaps to make it into a sort of question. To ask him if he thinks that Mummy is sad.

I listen carefully. Daddy is still downstairs. I can't hear him moving about as if he is preparing to come up. I tiptoe quietly down the landing and peep into their room. Mummy is in bed, the light is off, and she is curled up on her side. She does not hear me and she stays completely still.

How small her body looks rolled up on her side. I have never thought before that Mummy is not actually very tall or big, or that one day soon I will probably grow past her so that she perhaps measures only up to my chest. That makes the noise she made even more remarkable; that from such a small body such a sound could come.

Tom

We're in the company gym. George has noted how I seem to have upped my lunchtime sessions; chiming as they do with Eliza taking her kit bag from under her desk. 'Healthy body, healthy mind,' he says as I get up from my desk with my stuff, 'or something like that. An obvious benefit anyway.' He chuckles and I don't meet his eye.

'You're kidding me.' Eliza is laughing, and looking down at where I am sitting in my shorts on the rowing erg, about to begin a workout. 'You got that at a family lunch! What's lunch in your household – some kind of contact sport?'

My shin has bruised lividly, and the gash down the length of the bone is putrid and angry. I have treated it with iodine spray, and it has rippled mustard yellow.

'It's a long story. Well, not that long. Do you know the story of the runaway train? Well, that, but not a train, a wheelchair with a kite tied to it, and a five-year-old still buckled in it, and a freezing swollen river just beyond him.'

How glibly it comes from my lips and how safe it seems now, with hindsight and in this bright space of the gym.

'Teddy?' Her face is momentarily serious.

'Yes, but he was right as rain, apart from a bloody lip. Quite thrilled, in fact, at approaching the speed of sound.'

She gestures to my leg. 'And how did this happen in that sequence?'

'Running to catch him, uphill, and diving to the right in a field full of semi-concealed flint to bring him to a halt. Classic rugby style.' I shrug sheepishly.

She peers closely at my leg.

'It's quite the gash you have there.'

'I know. And not best placed for being whacked by other people's briefcases on the Tube this morning.'

'Ouch.'

'Yup.'

'Was he scared?'

'Teddy?'

'Yes, when he was hurtling towards the river?'

'I don't think that occurred to him. Isaac and his cousins tied the kite to the arm of his chair. I think once he got going he was absorbed in the possibility of flight, which seems to have been an appealing prospect.' How daring it feels to suggest that it might not have been cataclysmic for him.

'Sounds pretty plucky to me. Confess, did you make more fuss about the gash on your shin than he did about the whole caboodle?' Her tone is arch and playful.

Caboodle. Anna's face, white-lipped; the snatch of Teddy from my arms.

In the shower, I let the water stream down my face. A caboodle. What a word for it, setting both Isaac and me free in an instant. It feels like I am washing away the residue of yesterday; the stiff, sticky awkwardness and the melancholy that crusted over my skin. Eliza makes me feel better. She makes me feel as if what happened wasn't the worst thing in the world, and that Teddy is in fact brave, proactive and plucky, rather than a vulnerable little figure to whom bad things happen. The minute I finish that thought I am flushed with disloyalty. Of course an outsider like Eliza might treat it more lightly; it's Anna's view that counts, Anna's degree of displeasure.

That's why I find myself, later, on the way home from work,

standing on the platform at Marylebone holding an enormous bunch of cream rosebuds. They are wrapped in a vast skirt of ivory tissue paper with a gleaming fuchsia-pink inner lining. During the journey home I begin to find them increasingly unsatisfactory. What felt like another way of saying sorry, or of implicitly promising to be more mindful, suddenly feels like a stiff, overly starched piece of frou-frou. They are scentless. The buds are clenched tight and I suddenly doubt whether they will ever in fact bloom. Perhaps it would have been better to have gone out into the garden with some scissors and my phone for a torch, and cut a small twist of elaeagnus and dahlias rather than this huge bunch of flowers that is beginning to feel like an inverted tutu in my lap.

I am mindful of all the flowers I have bought for Anna previously. A bunch of magnificent, tousled, blowsy red roses one Valentine's Day before we were engaged; three hundred paper-white narcissi when Isaac was born. An enormous bunch of cornflowers and bishop's ammi returning from work one day, because when I left in the morning I'd turned and seen her at the window and her face was so lovely to me I wanted to return to her with an armful of flowers.

In the car park at the train station there is a large refuse bin by the café. I stand by it, the rosebuds held downwards in my left hand. It would be a waste to discard them; perhaps I should gift them to someone else who has got off the train. Therein lies more awkwardness and possible misinterpretation, so I stand there, uncertain, for a little while longer.

I find that I am crying, which is unexpected and painful. I am a man at a station holding a very expensive bunch of flowers, who finds himself suddenly unable to go home and give them open-heartedly to his wife. I'm not sure how to begin to think about that, or how it relates to another woman in a gym.

Anna

He hands them to me like an awkward child who has been primed to do so, with a touch of hesitancy and formality. The flowers take up the arm's length of space between us. He steps back after he gives them to me. They are an obstacle, not a gift.

'They're beautiful,' I say, even though I hate them instantly. There is something frigid about them, and entirely without warmth. The whole way he handed them to me, and most of all that they are not the right thing, not the thing I wanted at all.

'Gosh, I don't think I have a vase big enough. Let me just try and find something.'

My words are hollow. The flowers lie on the kitchen counter, the size of a large toddler.

Last night, he came to bed after I'd fallen asleep. I was aware of him when I turned over in the night, but he seemed to be keeping as much to his side of the mattress as I was to mine. This morning, after he'd left for work and I was cleaning the kitchen, I wondered whether what I want from him is actually impossible for him to give. He's said sorry; he's apologised several times, but what I want is for it *not* to have happened, for him to wind the clock back, and he obviously can't do that. Failing that, I wish he had intuited that I wanted him to come to bed; to have guessed that what I needed most was to be held. To have understood that my anger came mostly from fear, and then for all that is jarring and jangling between us to have fallen away and for him to have made me feel safe.

He did none of that, and now there are these flowers, which are a well-intended substitute but which make the omissions more glaring, and which are rustling and bustling in their ridiculously excessive wrapping and impossible to undo because they are knotted so tightly with green florist's string. As I wedge them into a too-small vase, an unseen thorn jabs into my thumb. It feels utterly appropriate that this has happened, and that I am bloodily snagged on the flawed gift of them.

During the night, I wake thirsty and go down to the kitchen to get a glass of water from the dispenser on the fridge. In the half-light from the street outside, the roses are visible on the island. They look haughty and imperious, the white of the buds throwing a ghostly shadow. I shiver as I look at them. Irrationally, spontaneously, I want them out of the house. They carry with them an evanescence that feels somehow harmful. They are emblematic of how Tom and I seem to be floundering, and how at odds we are with ourselves. I stand by the island and reach out to touch them with my pricked thumb. The spirit in which he gave them to me – awkward, restrained – now makes me want to cry. All the flowers he has given me previously have been heartfelt affirmations of his love, and now these. I wish there was a way to accelerate them withering so that they can be gone. As I tread softly back upstairs to bed, I take pleasure in the thought of being able to upend them into the bin.

Teddy

On Sunday, Daddy goes to buy the paper, and also sweets for me and Isaac. Today he's buying the Christmas tree as well, and I am going with him, because he says I will be a champion Christmas tree chooser.

In the village shop, first, there is the choosing of the sweets. I choose for Isaac, which is simple, and then for me, which Daddy says is like a meeting of NATO. He takes out the index card Mummy has written to remind him which sweets are definitely not allowed. I try to make some of them allowed before he has got to the part where they are written. Tooty Frooties are my goal today, but no luck.

'It says here too choky. Tooty Frooties, my boy, are on the list of banned substances, just like you're an Olympic athlete.'

'Wouldn't they be good for my bulbar muscles?' Bulbar is my new word. The dentist said it this week when he was trying to help me open my mouth wider so that Mummy can clean my teeth better. 'Like a lion,' Mummy says, 'open your mouth wide and roar like a lion.'

'I think your bulbar muscles are going to get plenty of practice with . . .' Daddy stops and reads the list again, 'jelly babies, which just about make it under the wire, or some Haribo fried eggs.'

We drive to the farm shop, which is selling Christmas trees. Daddy puts me in my Wizzybug, and I can get up the ramp into the barn, where there are rows and rows of trees, some lying on their sides in piles, and some held tight in white netting. There is a long table with food for tasting: small squares of mince pies, and ham, and little slices of blue cheese.

'I'm hungry! Please can I have some of that?' I point at the meat. Daddy picks a piece up with his fingers because there are no knives and forks, and everyone is just putting it right in their mouths.

'This could be tricky,' he says, and it's true, because the pieces are much bigger than I can manage. Daddy thinks for a moment and then takes a neat bite and chews it very quickly for a couple of seconds with just his front teeth. Then he takes it out of his mouth and pops it right into mine.

'There, that's like you are a baby bird; although obviously much naughtier, and despite your best attempt, not able to fly.'

'Could we do this with Tooty Frooties as well?'

'Nice try. But even for you I'm not softening Tooty Frooties. I think the kings of England used to have people who tasted their food for them. Maybe you could have someone who just chews yours for you.'

A man comes and asks us which tree we would like.

'Sharp eyes now, Teddy,' Daddy says. 'No wonky or broken branches.'

The man shakes out some trees for us. He holds them by the very top, and when he jiggles them the branches fall open.

'Too tall,' Daddy says, then 'Too wide,' and on the sixth one I say, 'Perfect,' because it will be when all the decorations are on it.

The man takes the tree away to be wrapped in white netting and he gives Daddy a little ticket so that he can collect it from by the till. Daddy chooses a garland made of holly, which is bright with red berries; it will go on the front door and show that it is Christmas to the street. While he is doing all this, I spot a door at the back of the barn which is open, and as I wizzy towards it, I can see that there are small animals in the yard outside.

'Look!'

Baby goats. Daddy tells me they are called kids. There are about ten of them, in all sorts of colours. The mothers are there too, but they are mostly eating straw from a wide net hooked up against a post. The little ones are more interested in me and the Wizzybug. They come all around my legs. Their horns are very tiny and look like snail shells peeping through the tops of their heads, and their little hooves are so shiny it's like they've been polished with shoe cream. I move to one side, and they follow me, and then to the other and the boldest ones still do. I do a little zigzag and the kids come along with me.

Daddy is laughing. 'A new career for you, Teddy. Goatherd. Grandad Stephen would have liked that. I wonder if you're too young to get a Saturday job here?'

I'm laughing too. This morning feels like a Christmas present already: the ham, and the tree, and the goats, who are still milling and spilling around my feet.

'Please will you take a photo on your phone for Mummy and Isaac?'

Daddy leans down by the straw so that he can get all the goats in.

'Say cheese.'

'No, roast ham!'

When we are queuing to pay for the tree, I say, 'Now I know exactly what I want from you and Mummy for Christmas.'

'A slide for the garden?'

'Nope.'

'Table football?'

'No, a goat. A kid. Exactly like you could buy from here. You could ask the man when you pay for the tree. Maybe there's another kind of ticket.'

Daddy is laughing. 'How about a Lego set that makes a space station? We could build it with Isaac.'

'No, definitely a goat.'

All the way home Daddy comes up with things they might buy me, and I say, 'Nope, a goat, still a goat,' to each thing he suggests.

When we get home, I give Isaac his sweets and show him the photo.

'I am a natural born goatherd. They love me.'

Isaac gives me a fist bump. 'Respect.'

Daddy says, 'Don't tell Uncle William, or he'll be buying some for the farm.'

Mummy calls to us from the kitchen. 'Wash your hands thoroughly, Teddy. Tom, can you help him with that?'

Anna

I'm standing in front of my wardrobe mirror, and tugging at the shoulder seam of my dress. It's not new, but I've hardly worn it. It's made from black lace with a front button fastening, a knee-length scalloped hem, and panelling at the waist. It has an exposed lace collar and long sleeves. I can't decide if I look appropriately Christmassy or like an Italian widow. I put on a pair of diamanté earrings and pull them off again. At the back of my shoe rack are a pair of black high heels with a flat grosgrain bow that fastens across the ankle. Also, some delphinium-blue suede ones, which would bring a pop of colour to the dress. I've got those in my hand when Tom comes in and says immediately:

'I'd forgotten about those. They'd look great.'

I put them back on the rack and take out a square-toed pair of low courts. They are dreary, sensible shoes but far more appropriate for nudging a Wizzybug in and out of a lift. Tom will say that he will take care of that, but usually someone senior walks past and there is all the business of greeting and glad-handing and Christmas party joviality, and the lift door will open and close three times with the wheel obstructing it, and I will be trying to budge it out of the way so that other partygoers don't get irritated. The delphinium-blue heels wouldn't help with that.

If I'd had a daughter, I'd have told her that, unless stepping from a building directly into a car, it's good to have shoes capable of running a dash in case the need arises. In my youth, tucked

in my bag, always a pair of flats or runners. Perhaps it was indic-
ative of a kind of controlling; the wish never to appear vulnerable,
to be always able to escape on my own terms. The get-away girl.

The company Christmas party offers no possibility of escape
for at least three hours, not that Isaac and Teddy see it that way.
They're decked out in their Christmas jumpers and I can hear
them in Teddy's bedroom horsing around singing 'Jingle Bells'.
Isaac is reminding Teddy of all the different kinds of food there
were last year, and also the non-alcoholic cocktails, which were
coloured in layers like liquid traffic lights.

'And the games, remember all the games they make up in that
special room?'

The games indeed. Practical and social. Adult and child. It's
the contrived interplay that kills me: Tom's colleagues being overly
attentive and complimentary about Teddy lest they are perceived
to be insensitive; stepping neatly around the Wizzybug and
crouching at his level, the men twitching at the fabric of their
trousers first so that they can bend unobstructed. The women
saying, 'Oh, so this is Teddy!' in faux-bright voices, as if he is a
rascal whose adventures are water-cooler chat. All of this, coupled
with my own speedy calibration of which of the actual games he
may or may not be able to play.

When he was three, there was a mini bucking bronco in a
soft padded ring that made him weep with longing, and, only
marginally less upsetting for me, a game kindly devised by Tom's
executive assistant with Teddy in mind, but which was so dull
that none of the other children wanted to play it and Teddy was
stuck by it looking as if he was in charge of a lame stall at a
fete.

Charlie, the CEO, always seeks Teddy out and says, 'Hello,
Trouble, how are you this year? I assume up to mischief?' He
speaks very loudly as if what Teddy suffers from is deafness
rather than SMA.

And then there is the small talk with the other wives. Most of them have very successful careers in their own right, and I feel their politeness, their highly accommodating, slightly patronising tone, like a neat poke in the ribs. It makes me feel small and entirely without achievement. The wives who are full-time mothers – especially those of the directors, whose children are mostly in their teens – are glossy and immaculate. With them I feel like a dull, slightly shabby mouse; their hands, when they reach for a drink, display perfectly shaped, perfectly polished nails. I yearn for pockets into which I can stuff my hands deep.

At least it's only once a year. I am putting on blusher. Have I said that out loud?

'You look lovely.' Tom's tone is encouraging, which is a little bit unbearable too. Neither of us acknowledge that he is implicitly coaxing me to go.

In the car, he puts on Christmas carols, and Isaac and Teddy sing along. I close my eyes so that a string of traffic lights becomes a smudge of lollipop colour through my lashes, and wonder how I have become so joyless.

And then, when I am standing with a drink that is rapidly becoming warm in my hand, it is as I expected. The other women are mostly a trial, although I am fearful that this is due to a lack of grace on my part.

'How has your year been?' one asks me, with what may be genuine warmth.

'Thankfully uneventful.' Might this be one of the most negative responses possible? My words drop into the room, which is bright with expensive decorations, and the other woman looks almost puzzled, as if she is unsure how best to respond. For a moment, I don't know which I hate most, the party or myself, and I grip the handle of the Wizzybug tightly. Charlie appears in my peripheral vision, bobs down to Teddy to ask his annual question and shows no real indication that he has understood Teddy's reply. It will have been about the kite. It has become his go-to story; he's shared it with the physio, a doctor, the dietician and his teacher. He says, 'Mummy screamed!' but he laughs as he says it as if it was all high jinks. It occurs to me now, as another woman approaches to talk to me, that the relationship between perception and reality is always highly mutable. Whose account is truest?

Tom is next to me now, his palm in the scoop of my back; steering me between clusters of people, facilitating conversation. 'This is my wife, Anna . . . Have you met Anna, my wife?' Perhaps he is also making sure that I do not turn and flee, which would be my inclination if the boys weren't here. A woman I am introduced to moves her arm hastily and spills a little of her drink down the front of her beautiful aquamarine slub silk dress.

'Oh God, what a rubbish corporate wife I am. I should never be allowed out of my studio and my overalls.'

The notion of being an effective corporate wife comes to me as such an alien thought, the woman might as well be speaking in tongues. She moves away, dabbing at the smudge on the fabric with her napkin, and is supplanted by someone else, who asks me what I do, and then, when nudged by her companion to indicate Teddy just beyond me, says without missing a beat, her expression smooth as a mirror, 'Oh, sorry, I see you have a lot to keep you busy.'

I nod, and am moved on by Tom's hand, still placed in the small of my back, and it feels as if we are a small shoal of fish, purposefully swimming through the glaring brightness of the room.

He steers me towards the room that has the children's games in it, where Isaac has just taken Teddy. They are standing with a young woman whom Tom introduces as Eliza. There is a game that involves blowing ping-pong balls into a goal. There are straws with which to do it, and Isaac can easily blow the ball from one end of the little table to the other. Eliza gives Teddy a straw, but it flops ineffectually from his lips.

'Wait, hang on a sec.' She goes over to a desk and comes back with some scissors and tape. She is deft and practical, cutting a hole in one straw and feeding the other into it, and then securing the junction so that the two straws can blow as one. 'Shall I be your partner?'

Teddy grins and she says to Isaac, 'Right, game on.'

They are evenly matched. Each time Isaac comes close to getting the ping-pong ball into the goal, Eliza and Teddy manage to blow it away. When the pace picks up and leaning out and across from the Wizzybug becomes tricky, Tom lifts Teddy out and holds him like a torpedo, his chest supported by the length of his forearm. Eliza ducks and weaves around him so that she can retain purchase on her part of the straw.

'You're champion at this!' Tom makes Teddy soar around the edges of the table. Teddy offers his hand in a soft high-five to Eliza.

They're all laughing, laughing with real merriment. I watch with my arms folded across my body, my jaw tight, although I'm not sure why. They look like a happy family; like a laughing, happy family, and there is something about their grouping, about the way they stand, which is jolly and free. Eliza, now smoothing the seal of the conjoined straws to check the tape is still secure, and taking off her heels, saying to Isaac, 'Right, steel yourself, it's going to get dirty.'

When we finally leave the party, the boys bubbling with how much fun they've had, we are standing on the pavement by the car at the same time as Eliza comes out. She's wearing a very beautiful high-collared shearling coat buttoned right up to her neck. Her hair, which was pinned up neatly earlier, has tumbled around her face from the ducking and diving of the game. Her cheeks retain a rosiness from all the straw blowing.

She pauses by the car a moment as Tom puts Teddy into his car seat. She leans in to the boys. 'Bye, guys. Beware, Isaac; next year, it's a grudge match.'

She stands up from the open car door and, without seemingly intending it, is in close proximity to me. She is taller than me, although that is perhaps her shoes.

'Thank you.' My words come out a little stiffly, which was not my intention. I try again. 'I'm very grateful to you; thank you for helping the boys to have such a happy game.'

'My pleasure.' She gives me a warm, unfettered smile. 'I've been looking forward to meeting you all; I've heard a lot about you and it's lovely to put faces to names.'

Driving home, Isaac says, 'Eliza is really nice.'

'She's fun, fun, fun,' Teddy pipes in.

'Isn't she?' Tom says, after a small pause, and it tugs like a small fish hook on my skin, because I'm not sure whether it's a question to me or an affirmation of what the boys have just said. The tone of his voice makes it seem to be an answer to which he has given speedy, yet careful forethought. Either way, Eliza is undoubtedly both, and also clearly beautiful, with her merry smile and bright eyes.

Taking off my dress at home, I wonder, for the first time, about Tom being in Geneva with Eliza; of them in meetings together, having dinner, waiting in airports for planes. What do they talk of? What does Tom share? How stupid that it's the first time it has occurred to me that the junior consultant on his project might not be a spectacled young man.

I'm very grateful to you. I said that to her because it was what I felt: grateful to a young woman who with no nonsense or fuss modified a game for my boys that had them pealing with laughter. And it strikes me – now, putting my dress back into the wardrobe – that perhaps Eliza has more insight into my family than I guessed. I wonder what Tom has said to her; how much about Teddy, about us all.

He emerges from the shower, towelling himself dry.

'You haven't said much about Eliza. I imagine she'd be very

resourceful to work with, judging from her ability to modify straws.' I avoid the word *fun* and try to keep the suggestion of a joke in my voice.

'Yes, she is.' His tone is casual, disinterested, almost studiedly so. 'She's a very good team player, although I hadn't realised that extended to ping-pong blow football.'

I wipe off my make-up with a large square cotton pad. I think of Eliza, setting off down the street in her beautiful coat. Tom stopped what he was doing and watched her walk away, his hand on the open car door, his gaze steady. To whom, I wonder, might she go home?

Tom

I'm almost never home at 5 p.m. on a Tuesday afternoon, but a meeting in Milton Keynes finished early. Isaac is back from school, and sitting beyond me reading a book. I'm looking at bank statements when the doorbell rings.

I glance at the whiteboard as I move to the hallway. It tells me it's going to be Julia, the social worker. Her face isn't familiar.

'Oh, hi, Tom,' she says brightly. 'I don't usually get a chance to see you. Is Anna in?'

My immediate instinct is to say *Of course*, and I am struck for a moment by my assumption that she is always at home. Julia has stepped inside anyway, and is shrugging off her jacket.

'She's just upstairs with Teddy. Can I make you a coffee while you wait?'

I make the coffee, and also some small talk about the weather, and gather the bank statements ready to leave the kitchen. Julia is foraging in her bag.

'Oh, by the way, has Anna mentioned the fun days to you?' She hands me a leaflet swiftly. 'They're really well organised and loads of fun. We invite parents of children with life-limiting illnesses, so there's lots in common, and the kids have a great time and always make something nice.'

She glances down at the leaflet, as if she might be running short on detail. 'Yep . . . a cake or a Christmas bauble. Glitter and icing sugar; what's not to like?'

Anna has never mentioned fun days at the local children's

hospice. I don't think she's ever been there. She's hardly mentioned Julia either. When I asked once – a broad question about Social Services' role – she replied, 'I deal with forty-seven people in relation to Teddy's daily life. Would you like a synopsis on each of them and what they contribute?' I'm guessing Julia might be a particular bugbear; something about the way she rustles and bustles, and a certain pushiness about her that I imagine would chafe. She's still talking.

'This is our special Christmas fun day. No expense spared! Places fill up quite quickly. Maybe check Teddy's commitments, and if he's free, I can quickly text a confirmation of his place?'

I feel bamboozled into picking up the diary from beside the phone, and turning to the date written on the leaflet. She's watching me carefully, blowing a little on her coffee, and glancing in the direction of the stairs in the hallway from where Anna will appear.

The afternoon is free. I feel a little cornered, momentarily, but relatively confident that Teddy will enjoy making a bauble or a cake. Has Anna been to one before? I can't remember. I resolve to ask more questions; to pay more attention to the detail, to log the people she deals with more clearly.

'Yes . . . that looks like it will work. Obviously, confirm it with Anna, but maybe text a place provisionally. I'm sure Teddy will love it.'

'Love what?' Anna steps lightly but swiftly into the kitchen, and the way she says it is less like a question and more like the throwing-down of a gauntlet.

Julia beats me to it, and erases the hedged conditionality of my answer.

'Tom's just confirmed that you and Teddy can come to the fun day at the hospice.' She turns to Teddy, who is held in Anna's arms, and opens her mouth and eyes really wide. 'Lucky you!'

'But,' Anna looks directly at me. 'But—'

This time it's Teddy who interrupts.

'What do you do at a fun day?'

'HAVE A GREAT TIME.' Julia enunciates the words clearly, which I can see irritates Anna, and holds out the leaflet to him so that he can see the illustrations of a cupcake topped with a sugar-paste reindeer, and also a paper Christmas tree drenched with green glitter. 'I think you'll be choosing between making one of these and one of these.' She points to the images. 'How exciting will that be?'

I am aware of Isaac, who is suddenly beside me, and also of Anna, who has the air of someone who has been ambushed and scooped up by a very large net. Isaac is silent, but has his gaze fixed on Julia, who is now reiterating to Anna that the only reason she came was to invite Teddy to the fun day. She seems to be making a dash for the door, speedily zipping up her jacket to go back out into the cold.

Isaac is now standing very still by the table in the hallway. The angle of his elbow draws the eye to what is on it: Christmas decorations, made from salt dough and spread out along a length of greaseproof paper. There are snowflakes, and stars, and tiny leaping deer, and each one has a red gingham ribbon threaded through a hole at the top. I don't know how I could have missed them when I came through the door.

'Oh wow, look at those!' Julia says. 'Someone's been very busy.'

'We made them with Mummy after school. Teddy rolled the rolling pin all by himself and pressed the stencils down with the flat of his hand. I did the threading but he helped pull it through the other side.' Isaac's voice is quiet and neutral.

When I come back into the kitchen, the Harriet House leaflet is on the side where Julia left it. Harriet House. Considering its function, it is reputed to be a lovely, happy place. Harriet was a child whose bereft parents fund-raised to set it up. All the effort invested in choosing a name for a child; all the happy future scenarios in which parents imagine its use, and I realise all anyone should ever hope for is that it's never marshalled for a hospital ward or a hospice. It's this I'd like to share with Anna as she turns from settling Teddy by his snow domes at the table, but she's in no mood to hear it. She glances at me, stony-faced, and starts to make supper.

Isaac

I can hear them talking. Arguing might be a better word, but it's quieter and colder than that. Shouting might wake Teddy anyway, and he's taken a long time to get to sleep. Mummy checked twice to see whether I was sleeping before she went back downstairs. I pretended I was. I slowed my breathing right down and flung my bent arm over my face so that she couldn't see my eyelids fluttering a little bit.

Supper was horrible. Mummy was brisk; that's the best word for it. She served the stew on to the plates with a flick of her wrist, and she chopped Teddy's food up with a much quicker action than usually. *Chop chop chop chop*. She didn't look at Daddy, and I think maybe he still doesn't know quite how he made her cross. I could have told him; could have told him the minute Julia reached for the leaflet in her bag that it would result in some spitting of feathers.

It was only after we'd finished eating – and I had told three stories from school that weren't really funny, but the mood at the table felt like a great big sheeny bubble that needed to be popped – that Mummy gave the first sign. She was carrying the plates over to the sink and she nodded towards the diary and said, her voice with a bite in it, 'Anything else you've committed me to go to without consulting me?'

Daddy stood up with the casserole dish in his hand and looked a bit confused. 'I thought I was being helpful; it seemed like a nice thing to do, and I didn't realise you'd never been there. Is there a reason? Have I missed something?'

It looked like he'd missed everything. For a start off, that Julia is definitely not popular. Mummy scooped up Teddy ready to take him upstairs for his physio and expectorating and bath time.

'I haven't got time for this. Just like I don't really have time to go and make a glittery Christmas decoration when we've made twenty-four since after school today.'

She left the kitchen, and Daddy looked like someone who has dropped something without realising, like the little wooden horse in the story who puts all his hard-earned coins in his tummy and sets off along the road without knowing there is a hole in it and when he gets to his destination he feels very light, which is puzzling until he realises he is completely empty and that all his hard work has been wasted.

If Daddy makes mistakes, he will be the same as all the other people who Mummy doesn't like because they get it wrong. That's what it is; they get it wrong and it makes her cross. I know what her anger is like, not because she gets angry with me, that hardly ever happens, but because I've been in enough rooms – at hospital appointments, at home visits – to see it happening. Her anger is a bit like when the wind blows on the beach on a hot day, and a sweep of sand is blown at you, gritty and right in your eyes. Daddy, downstairs now, will be like in the whirl of a sandstorm.

They've closed the sitting room door and I can't make out what they are saying; just the rise and fall of their voices like waves washing up on a beach. I blow out through my mouth and it makes a soft noise – *whooooo*. It reminds me of the straw-blowing game we played at the company Christmas party. That was the opposite of angry. Who taped the straws together – Eliza? She looked at Daddy with a face that was full of laughing and fun. That's probably very different from the skin-scorch of a sandstorm.

Anna

I've come. I can't quite believe it, but more from sheer bloody-mindedness I've honoured the commitment, now parking my car outside Harriet House. Pulling out would be to acknowledge Julia's victory, so I'm making it pyrrhic by coming anyway. How bad can an afternoon be?

It's stiflingly hot in the day room. I'm flame-cheeked after only a few moments, and I can't look at any of the surfaces without thinking of bacteria multiplying in the heat. Teddy has been immediately swept along by a young play assistant and I am given the option of joining the parents' circle time.

'It's mostly a chance to share the fact that you haven't done your Christmas shopping yet, and that you've missed all the internet food delivery slots.'

'I think I'll just wait in the day room, thanks.'

'Of course. Nothing's compulsory. You don't have to participate if you don't want to. Take a little me-time.' The receptionist gestures towards the large fish tank in the corner of the room, as if there might be the possibility of snorkelling or stand-up paddle-boarding in it.

A darting question comes to me, unexpected and random, about whether Eliza, if asked the same thing, would join in. I expect she would, and the perception shimmies beneath my skin, quick and silver as a blade.

The book I have is the one from my bedside table. I can't

remember the beginning and so open it at the start to remind myself of what I have already read. I haven't even completed a page before another woman comes in. She's hot too. She's wearing a skimpy scarlet top over an emerald-green bra, and neither contains her flesh so it spills over whitely. I dip my head further to avoid eye contact, but she comes and sits beside me, chummily, pulling up her chair so that our knees are almost touching.

'You're a new face. I recognise everyone. First visit, is it?' I begin to chew at the side of my mouth. 'Don't be shy, we're all in the same boat, or at least mostly. There's not much that happens to you as a parent that someone here hasn't had happen to them too. I could tell you some tales. What's wrong with yours? Straightforward or complicated? Don't get me started on my Tara, I'll have you here all day.'

I don't doubt that she would. She reminds me of a truffle pig, sniffing out misery, hungry to suck up medical details. From the corner of my eye, her mouth is like a mollusc, latching onto my skin, keen for purchase. It's unbearable.

'My Tara's been coming for three years; respite care on a regular basis. It's a home from home, which is not the sort of thing you'd ever think you'd catch yourself saying about a place like this. I can't fault them. Every blessed member of staff. Tara loves them like they're family.'

I clear my throat. 'I'm really sorry, thanks and everything, but I'm quite keen to read my book.' I wave it a little ineffectually, trying to disguise with my thumb that I am only at the beginning. 'I've got to a really good bit.'

The woman sees straight through me and takes umbrage.

'Suit yourself. I was just trying to be friendly.' She stalks off to the coffee machine.

All the walls are painted a garish primrose yellow. I note this walking towards the toilets – because locking myself in the loo suddenly seems like the best thing to do. Someone has evidently decided that a cheery colour is compulsory in this context.

I stand in the cubicle for a few moments, my forehead pressed to the locked door. Then, stepping outside again to the basin and the mirror, I wash my hands, splash my face, and press my palms to my cheeks. I drag down my skin so that I can see the pink rim of my inner eye. How lacking in grace I am; in fact, worse, I am a snob, and as mean as a snake. There is no excuse for the fact that I wanted to shout at the well-meaning woman, *I don't want to be your friend. There are no circumstances in which we would be friends. Just because we both have poorly children does not mean we are friends.* I am dreadful.

I take a deep breath, and resist the temptation to storm into the activity room, sweep Teddy up into my arms and leave. I press my hands to the side of the basin and feel a hot sweep of fury directed at Tom, because it is his fault that I am here; his fault that Julia managed to snooker me into coming.

'What is happening to me? How did I become like this?' I say the words out loud, and they bounce off the mirror and smoothly back at me.

How lovely it would be to walk out of the cloakroom and stop in front of the first person I meet and say to them, my arms outstretched as if I am holding an enormous parcel, *Please will you help me carry this?* because suddenly every one of my limbs feel so very tired, and I am so weary of fighting and worrying and questioning and harrying and thinking and catastrophising. The woman I snubbed no doubt had insights to share, and intentions that were kind and good.

When I open the cloakroom door and step out into the corridor, the first person I meet is Julia.

'Ah, Anna, so you came, that's good.' She speaks as if I am a child who must be cajoled. Her voice is a little crowing.

I recalibrate my equilibrium and make my face as impenetrable as possible. 'Yes,' I say smoothly, 'I can't wait to see what Teddy chooses to make.'

Tom

The office cleaner is wheeling a trolley piled high with glasses, napkins and plates from a boozy festive lunch before the office closes for Christmas. George produced a bottle of vodka and some shot glasses and tutted when I declined. 'All work and no play – oh, wait . . .' He smirked and winked in Eliza's direction. I want to finish the proposal that is due early in the New Year. It will sit more easily with me over Christmas, the knowledge that it is done.

I'm distracted by the cleaner, who methodically makes his way between the desks, picking up glasses from where they are perched on printers and photocopiers and filing cabinets. He catches my eye and gives me a thumbs-up.

I return the gesture, and throw in a 'Merry Christmas' for good measure. Even if he speaks no English, this will be understandable. The man nods, but I sense that it may not be merry at all.

I refocus on my screen – three charts to go – but look up when I hear someone else come into the office. Eliza.

'Hello – I thought you'd left, and that it was only me, the cleaner, and some canapés here. I'm just about to send the project activation timeline so that they get it before the break.'

'That's efficient. And yes, everyone's disappeared so quickly. I just popped out to get a couple of things my mum needs. I'd recommend you don't hang around too long. The Christmas spirit is evaporating fast downstairs; the guy on reception is taking down the Happy Christmas banner. He says it'll be one less job to do in the new year. That's not really in the spirit of the season, is it?'

She comes behind my desk and looks at the screen. I try not to be conscious of her thigh and her hip in proximity to my shoulder. I click through the charts slowly so that she can see the document.

She appraises it carefully.

'That looks good. All set to go.' She gives a playful punch to my shoulder. 'Well done us, yay!'

How pathetic I am, that her warmth and her praise channel straight to my core. It's the oldest story in the book: when a wife can only find fault, the praise of another woman is like walking into sunshine.

I can't get anything right with Anna. That's the logjam I'm in. Last night, when I got home and she'd spent the afternoon at Harriet House, a mutinous, sulphurous glow seeped into the whole evening. 'Was it as bad as you thought it would be?'

'What do you think,' she replied, turning away.

Teddy seemed to have quite enjoyed it. He'd chosen to make the Christmas tree, and Isaac held it up to show me, dangling it from his index finger so that it twirled round and round. 'Isn't it cool?' Isaac said. 'And really good scissor work. Look how neat the branches are.' A shower of green glitter fell softly onto the island.

I don't think another apology – whatever form it takes – would make any recompense. The flowers I bought after the kite episode were in the kitchen for less than forty-eight hours. Whatever they were meant to be – peace offering, apology, fresh start – spectacularly misfired. There was no evidence of them in the bin or on the compost heap either – pathetically, I checked. Perhaps she couldn't even bear to have the remains of them anywhere near her. The fact that I guess this, and also sense that she hated them, is unsettling. How odd it is to have insight and knowledge, and yet feel so totally estranged.

Eliza has finished reading and is asking me something.

'Are you going anywhere over Christmas?'

'We're at home. Anna's parents are coming and then I'm not sure what's happening between Christmas and New Year. And you?'

'Oh, at my mother's, and then with some friends renting a house in Cornwall. Walks, log fires, jigsaw puzzles, wine; I'm sure you know the drill.'

'I think I remember it.'

I save the document, and press print. 'Well, that's me done for the year.' I push back from the desk. 'Time for that speedy exit. There's a very large turkey that needs hunter-gathering.'

'I should be getting home too. And I'm guessing if we don't leave the building soon, the Spirit of Christmas downstairs will be dusting off his banner for Easter.'

She moves across to her own desk and starts gathering her things. It is an unsettling sensation, the feeling that implicitly we are synchronising our exit; an awareness, as we pack our bags, of what the other is doing.

In the lift, we stand next to each other with our shoulders almost touching. The temptation to turn to her is overpowering. I lean down and fiddle with the catch on my briefcase, and use it as an opportunity to shift myself a little further away. The sensation, in close proximity to her, is of a magnetic field that will draw me even closer.

As we wait for the lift door to open, she turns to me and says, 'Merry Christmas, Tom,' and there is in her tone such warmth, such open directness, that when I say it back to her, the words feel of great import rather than the seasonal greeting that I will also say to the man at reception.

I pause to let her step into the first section of the revolving door. She turns and glances over her shoulder at me as she steps lightly down the street, one small quick wave, her fingers spread wide. I stand on the pavement and swallow down the words that I would like to have said to her. *I'll miss you*. Because that is what I feel, with conviction, as she disappears from view.

Anna

It's Christmas Eve, and Teddy's bedroom window is wide open.

He's in his pyjamas, with a blanket wrapped snugly around him, propped between the windowsill and my body. Isaac is next to me. My right arm is around him and his head is pressed to my shoulder. Where the boys' heads meet, there is the soft muss of their hair. They smell of shampoo, soap and toothpaste, and freshly laundered pyjamas. They are lit by a thread of perfectly clear, static white snowberry lights that are strung around Teddy's bed.

Downstairs, I can hear Tom preparing the turkey. He does this each year on his last day at work; fetching it from the local butcher's, queuing outside with everyone else who has pre-ordered, and then carrying the green-and-white box high on his shoulder as he comes up the path, as if it is something bravely won in battle rather than bought in the high street.

Ever since we have been together – and I can see fifteen turkeys lined up neatly side by side – he has prepared the Christmas turkey. If I were to go down to the kitchen now, I know what I will see: an enormous plastic-lidded container filled with water and spices, the turkey taken from the box, ready to be carefully lowered in. He will have sliced oranges, ginger, onion and parsley, spooned in maple syrup and honey, and scattered cinnamon sticks, allspice, mustard and caraway seeds and star anise. As if to confirm what I know, the fragrance of oranges and ginger drifts up the staircase.

The insight makes my heart sore. The years of familiarity, of co-existence, of knowledge; the primordial intimacy of both being woken at night by a sudden, thunderous hurl of rain. He is my husband. Beneath all the attrition of our interaction, this is what he remains. This stark simplicity hits me forcefully, our boys in my arms. How simple and how infinitely complex it is: the ongoing, emotionally labile daily transactions, the solidity of our shared history, the weft and weave of the things that bind us. How have we become so lost?

'Can you hear him?' For a moment I falter, bewildered as to why Isaac is also thinking about Tom brining the turkey downstairs, but then I realise his question is to Teddy.

They are pressed to the sill, listening for Santa's sleigh bells. They do it each Christmas Eve, before bed, the window flung wide. In other rituals, I have baked the clementine cake, arranged the porcelain crib figures at the table centre, and decorated the tree with two more new baubles marked with the boys' names and the year.

The sky is clear and sapphire black in its glittering darkness. There are fistfuls of stars, flung wide and bright. The night air is cold, and I tuck the blanket more closely around Teddy.

'Listen, listen carefully.' I feel both of their bodies strain forward.

How irresistible it is, to lean out of the window into a night that is gift-wrapped with magical stories of shepherds, and kings, and tiny babies in mangers; a night that despite my agnosticism convinces me each year of the possibility of a place of calm and newness. I find my own body tautening and leaning with theirs.

Isaac knows that Santa doesn't exist. His part in this charade is typically generous.

'Was that a sleigh bell?' He nudges Teddy's elbow. 'Listen, I think I heard something. He's on his way, I know it!'

Teddy turns his right ear to the night air, as if to hear more keenly.

'He's coming! He's coming! I can hear the reindeer as well – not just the sleigh bells but the reindeer too.'

I wrap my boys more tightly in my arms and cherish the moment: Isaac's kindness and Teddy's open-hearted belief in magic. It feels for a moment as if the world has laid down its sword; that as I stand by the window, everything I feel is for the good. I am enveloped by complete and total love for my sons, and by a momentary banishing of all the demons that harry me.

Behind me, I hear footsteps. Tom.

'A-ha, so here you all are. Is that Santa I can hear setting out? I hope those reindeer are hungry; there's a stockpile of carrots and apples by the chimney.'

He puts his arms around us. I can smell oranges and cinnamon on his skin, and his wrists on my upper arm are chilled from steeping his hands in the cold water.

'Merry Christmas.' He kisses my hair.

'Merry Christmas,' I say softly. Am I in fact saying *truce*? That's what it feels like as I lean forward, fleetingly, to kiss the soft skin on the inside of his wrist.

There are many words in a marriage that are not what they seem; many moments that appear to be one thing but are in fact something different entirely. If held up to the light, a complex series of unspoken codes.

I made a designated trip to the municipal tip to get rid of the roses. The compost heap in the garden and the recycling bin were not far enough away. I stood on tiptoe and hurled them deep into the vast skip. Then, on the evening of the hospice fun day, I punished him by resentfully sulking. I regret both things now, tucking the blanket again around Teddy. *Truce*, I feel myself saying again, as we stand together at the window.

Tom

Anna has never been a fan of New Year's Eve; she says it makes her feel melancholy. She's gone to bed, and I've got the television on quietly. On the screen, the sky behind Big Ben is dissolving with fireworks, and I am a man who is unexpectedly beginning the year sitting alone.

I had a teacher once who said that the question to ask oneself on New Year's Eve was *What could I have done differently or better?* The answer comes to me now: *Most things, actually.* It brings with it an up-swell of despondency. Perhaps hindsight is mostly a stick to beat oneself with.

It's been an odd Christmas. A small moment, at the beginning of the holiday, when it felt as if Anna had somehow yielded and softened a little; as if my shortcomings were momentarily wiped from the board. And then the steady slide back into what feels like a protracted stand-off: no, I could not take the boys sledging on the common when there was a thin skim of snow. 'It's closer to ice, which would be perilous for Teddy, and how do you think it will be if I have Isaac with a broken bone too?'

Outside in the street I can hear people laughing and shouting. Eliza comes to mind, as she has done so often during the last ten days. I imagine her in Cornwall, perhaps on the shoreline of a crowded beach, fireworks going off in a harbour, the sound of them booming across the expanse of the water.

Will she share, on the way to meetings, or in the lift up to the twenty-sixth floor, how she has spent her time? There will be glimpses of a life very unlike my own. I conjure her up sitting at a window, calmly watching the first light of morning over the water.

Upstairs, I hear Teddy coughing. I put down my glass and go to him so that Anna can sleep.

Anna

The truce didn't last long. One moment it was there, palpable, and then when Teddy started coughing the day after Boxing Day, it dissipated like water, spilling through my fingers. I stand on the landing in the half-light thrown from the moon. It is three days into the new year and he is still no better.

Teddy's coughing kills me. Actually, it's his breathing while he's asleep that mostly kills me. I pause by his bedroom door while the minutes tick by and my feet mottle blue, attuning my ear to the possibility of hypoventilation. If his breathing becomes too shallow or too slow it will lead to an increase of carbon dioxide in his body. It is always shallow in sleep because of the underdevelopment of his chest wall, but tonight it sounds worse.

I move from beside the door and go to sit beside him. I flip through my mental checklist; dyspnoea, which is difficult or laboured breathing; cyanosis, which is a bluish discoloration of the skin. I lift his hand gently into the glow of the night light and check each of his fingers, because cyanosis can be detected in the colour of the nail beds. With SMA, the inspiratory muscles are weakened, which results in a reduction in lung volume. If Teddy's breathing is compromised, he will be at risk of desaturation, because the level of oxygen in his blood will fall too low. I put my ear close to his chest so that I can listen more carefully.

The drill is wearyingly familiar. If his breathing worsens, I will contact the respiratory consultant, and Teddy will be given a polysomnograph to document the signs of hypoventilation. There will be a discussion about nocturnal non-invasive ventilation, and airway clearance, and Teddy's eyes will focus on mine as the mask is taped to him and he is connected to a small ventilator. They will check his peak flow, and use what Teddy calls the cough machine to assist him in clearing. I hate that part most, even though it is speedily productive, and I will stand by him, holding his hand and trying not to cry as his little pigeon chest bounces and jumps as he hawks mucus into his mouth.

I'd breathe for him, if I could. It's the corniest thought, but it has traction. I find myself, beside him, breathing more deeply, expanding my diaphragm to its fullest width, as if I might osmotically transfer oxygen from my body to his.

I put my face on the pillow next to his, and softly kiss his cheek. I hear Tom, from the bedroom, calling softly. 'Are you coming back to bed?'

I don't answer in case I wake Teddy. He can infer that I am not by the fact that he doesn't hear me returning.

Anyway, if Tom is awake and I get back into bed with him, he'll start asking about going out. It won't be an argument, just a persistent chewing away at discontent, like cud mouthed and re-mouthed in an effort to make it digestible. It began yesterday, when he read a review of a film he'd like to see.

'How about going out tomorrow night? We could check with Madeleine, I'm sure her family will have bailed by now.'

'No,' I heard myself saying firmly to each thing he suggested. His frustration was palpable.

'Remember, the SMA website says it's important to make time as a couple.'

I resisted replying, 'It also says it's good to have someone you can say anything to. Where would you like to start with that?'

A fresh sadness shuffles up next to me on the pillow, because I can't tell him that I increasingly feel myself to be smothered in the darkest of fogs, and that all I want to do is be next to Teddy, on guard, making sure he breathes in and out. All of my fierceness – and I know that some of the healthcare team think I am too confrontational – all of it is driven by a terror that won't go away. That one day his breathing will become so compromised that his chest will cave in, and it will be because I have not been sufficiently on guard. Or perhaps he will choke to death because I have not spotted that he needed a video-fluoroscopic swallow study. The thing that also kills me – and I see it so vividly, now, in the lucid self-awareness that comes in the middle of the night – is that not only am I half responsible for carrying the gene that gave Teddy SMA; I am wholly responsible for giving him, and making sure he gets, the best possible care.

I begin to fall patchily to sleep, kneeling beside Teddy's bed so that my head remains close to his. One of the websites I go on is called Cure SMA, and has the tagline *Make today a breakthrough*. Would that I could. If it could be effected by boiling potions in the kitchen, or foraging for bittersweet herbs, or spooning fish oil into Teddy's little bird mouth each day, I would do all those things, gladly. Another site I follow is called Fight SMA, and I'd do that too, with the relevant boxing gloves held up square to my face. I am intelligent enough to know that I don't have anything to contribute, other than painstaking mothering and a determination to hammer on until I get the best for my child. The actual battle can only be done by the scientists, with their terminology that I can absorb but that will never truly be mine.

I am thinking of their words as I drift into sleep: *mediated gene therapy, viral vectors, splicing modifiers, chemical and functional genomics*. I imagine stringing them around the bed as talismans like the Christmas snowberry lights, and hope that one day a permutation of them will allow Teddy to breathe deeply and well.

Isaac

Back to school. All the Christmas tree decorations have been taken down, and people have put their newly bare trees up against their garden fences ready to be collected by the bin men. It must be sad to be a Christmas tree; one minute all covered with baubles and lights and in the warmth of the house, and the next minute with everything stripped off and junked out in the cold. Last year, Daddy didn't put ours out in time and it wasn't taken away, so he dragged it round to the compost heap and left it to rot. In July it was still there, the branches all brown and limp, the needles in soft, dry piles alongside. A line of ants made their way steadily to and from it, and sidestepped around a red decoration Mummy had missed – a small velvet heart that was faded by the sun to a scrap of pink. I watched a bird tug a thread of it away in its beak. It was a good reminder that even lost things aren't wasted.

Mummy is waving from the kitchen window. I blow out a puff of dragon's breath to show her it is cold. Teddy is in her arms and sort of waving too. Mummy says soon he will be able to start school. Soon. Teddy is probably fed up with the promising. The whiteboard is covered with Mummy's writing; she says there's 'a whole rash' of appointments coming. I don't like those words; it makes each appointment sound like chickenpox on Teddy's body; red and itchy and oozing to the touch. This week there's one at the breathing clinic, the spinal clinic and the muscle clinic. The dietician is coming to see if Teddy ate enough over Christmas;

and also the speech therapist, so Mummy has bought an extra-large bag of sugar.

Teddy got a cough in the holidays and Mummy was by his bed all the time, and I heard Daddy ask her to come to bed, saying that she shouldn't sit there all night. I think she did it anyway, because in the morning her eyes looked as if they had been scribbled underneath with a bluey-grey crayon.

When Daddy talked to her, he said, 'Are you actually listening to me?' and she said, 'I'm tired, sorry,' and he said, 'No wonder.'

And then, when I was supposed to be asleep, the night after Teddy's cough seemed to be getting better without it turning into one of the horrible ones that mean he has to stay in hospital, Mummy and Daddy had a conversation in their bedroom and I heard every word.

'I just think it would do you good; to have a break, some relaxation. We don't have to go far. I'm not suggesting a plane ride away, just a weekend, just a weekend somewhere for the two of us. You choose. Choose anywhere. Maybe just one night away; some time for you to relax and for us to be together.'

'We're together here. What's wrong with us being together here? I'm less worried here than I'd be anywhere else. Who am I going to leave the boys with for a whole weekend, or even just overnight? Who would I trust with that? No one, that's who. I don't want to leave Teddy, with Isaac then feeling doubly responsible because he's here and I'm not.'

'But just a weekend, even a night . . .'

Daddy's voice trailed away. It sounded a little like he was pleading; as if what he wanted and why he wanted it was very important. Mummy sounded determined, as if there would be no persuading her, no changing of her mind. It's still making me uncomfortable even though it was three days ago, because I don't like them having an argument that is not shouty hot words, but instead one where they are stuck with glue to different sides of the room.

In the few days Daddy had left before going back to work, he kept suggesting things – the cinema, and going out for dinner – but Mummy said, 'No, no, Teddy isn't properly better yet. I don't want to go anywhere at all.'

After one conversation, Daddy went outside to stack the new logs into a woodpile. I knew he'd be doing them beautifully, very neatly and tidily. Grandad Stephen used to say that you can tell a lot about a man by his woodpile, so Daddy's is always very carefully made. But when I got there, my gloves pulled on to help, Daddy had finished already and was just sitting on it, and looking across the garden, which was mostly bare and empty and just clumped, frosty soil, and I didn't know what he was looking at but his face looked very sad and as if whatever he was trying to see was keeping itself just out of sight.

'Did you have a good Christmas?' Harry has swooped up next to me in the playground.

'Yes, yes, did you?' It's not a lie, because my presents were just what I hoped for, and Daddy's turkey was what everyone called 'a triumph', and we played charades and I guessed Granma's really difficult one, and so all that was happy, properly happy.

What I don't say to Harry, because I'm hoping the feeling will go like when fog lifts and everything is bright and clear beneath it, is that in the days after Christmas something different happened, what with Teddy poorly and Mummy tired and not wanting to go anywhere, and Daddy by the woodpile but so lost in his own thoughts that I had to tug on his hand to make him realise that I was there. I say none of this to Harry as I stand tidily next to him. I'm quiet, which is just how Mrs Jackson likes it, and probably the best way to start the new term without being told off before we've even gone in.

Anna

Vigilance is tricky; the balance between being observant and obsessive. The need to mindfully watch, but not to have my brain on a spooling loop, re-processing each moment in the day in case there is something I have missed.

Fasciculation is hardest; a small involuntary twitch that can occur in any muscle in the body, but in children with SMA is mostly in the shoulders or shown in a fine tremor of the hands. It can be a sign that overall muscle strength is diminishing. Sometimes, when I pass Teddy his sippy-cup, I hold it out for a moment longer than is necessary in order to see the steadiness of his outstretched hand. In the bath, I lie him across my arm and watch his shoulders for any flickers of movement. Proximal muscles are situated close to the centre of the body, in the shoulders, hips and neck, and are more affected by SMA than the distal muscles, which are in the extremities of the hands and feet. In the bath I say to him, 'Swim, swim little froglet,' and scan his body, looking for fasciculation.

Now, lying in bed, and replaying tonight's bathtime, I also listen for Tom's car. He is out with clients and will not be back until late. Then I'm listening for Teddy too; my ears straining in the darkness because it sounds as if he is stirring. I walk softly down the landing; by the glow of the night light I can see that he is still sleeping. Isaac, then? He sits up as I come in.

'Hey, honey bunny, why are you still awake?'

'I think I was asleep, but then something woke me up and now I'm not tired.'

I go over to his bed, and get in beside him. How long since I have done this? So many nights are spent beside or in Teddy's bed. He pulls playfully away from me.

'Ow, your feet are freezing.'

'I know. I haven't been in bed long and they're not warmed up. I promise to keep them on this side of the mattress so that they won't touch yours.'

'Deal. Is Daddy home?'

'He's out with clients, but he'll be home soon. Snuggle up to me – except my feet – and then you'll fall back to sleep.'

'And then afterwards what will you do?'

'I'll creep out and take my cold feet back to my own bed.'

There is a small pause.

'Mummy . . .'

'Yes.'

'You know on Saturday when Daddy's taking me to Harry's birthday party with the climbing wall?'

'Yes.'

'What will happen when Teddy's at school if he gets invited to climbing wall parties? Teddy won't ever be able to climb walls, will he?'

'I don't think so, but sometimes unexpected things happen.'

'You know when you tell Teddy that one day the doctors might be able to make him better, is that totally true, and will it be in time for him to go to climbing wall parties?'

'I hope so. Somewhere in the world where it's still daytime, there's probably a doctor or a scientist working right now who might discover something amazing to help Teddy and all the children like him.'

'That's a happy thought.'

'It's a lovely going-to-sleep thought. Now no more talking, or you'll be tired for school tomorrow. Hush now.'

He cuddles up to me. I am overwhelmed by the reminder that

he's still small too; the lightness of his frame now resting on me, his head on my shoulder and his hand holding mine. How different his breathing is from Teddy's shallow refrain.

When he has fallen asleep and I go back to my own bed, it is now with double worries: was it fasciculation at bathtime tonight, and what can I do about Isaac feeling anxious about Teddy's future? I lie wide awake in the knowledge that I can't safeguard either of them. It's a terrible thought. I lie on the mattress and feel totally at sea, bobbing and floundering in my crushing anxiety.

Tom

'How much more do you think he'll need for the first presentation?' Eliza asks.

We are sitting in the board room with Charlie, and she is flicking through the timeline document that I sent before Christmas.

'I think we should reinforce it with some more European data, at least while it's relevant.'

'Isn't the meeting on Monday?' Charlie sounds irritated.

'Yes, but we can always come in over the weekend and beef it up.' Eliza's tone is emollient. 'Would that work for you, Tom? I can be completely flexible if you have commitments.'

'Yes, I guess so. Saturday would be fine. It shouldn't take all day.'

'Great, that's a plan then. And I found out today that the new Peruvian fusion restaurant that's opened round the corner has signed up with Deliveroo. At least if we're in the office on a Saturday we can have a gourmet lunch at our desks.'

'Chalk it up to project expenses,' Charlie says, his equanimity restored.

It's only when I am back at my desk that I remember the climbing wall party I'm supposed to be taking Isaac to because Anna hates them. I can simultaneously hear Eliza on the phone talking to someone. 'Yes, I've just committed to working on Saturday, but I can get the train late afternoon and be in Sussex early evening.'

I send a quick text to Anna.

Looks like I have to work on Saturday – I'm sorry. Any chance that you can get M to look after Teddy and you take Isaac to the party?

She is quick to respond.

I can contact her and see. Wouldn't be my choice, but if you have to go in . . .

I suppress my disingenuousness.

Sorry, can't be avoided. Will make it up to Isaac. Thx.

I get back to work, a soft sifting of guilt in my chest. Reprehensibly, my overriding thought is not of Anna, single-parenting at the weekend and having to go to a party I know she doesn't want to attend, but rather of lunch with Eliza, by ourselves, in the office.

Anna

'People do this up sheer rock faces with no safety ropes, just holding on by their fingertips. Daddy showed me on YouTube, in Yosemite National Park in America.' Isaac's face is animated beside me as I park the car at the university sports centre for the climbing wall birthday party.

'Don't go getting any ideas.'

He laughs. 'That would be fun, though, wouldn't it, to just climb up using your own strength and nothing else. That would count as very brave, wouldn't it?'

It's hard not to shudder at the thought of anyone inching their way along a ledge with a cavernous, dizzying drop behind them. The bone, muscle, tissue, the thin ropes of the veins; the composite preciousness and fragility of it all.

'It would be exceptionally brave. Have you remembered Harry's present?'

'Yes, it's on the back seat. Daddy picked football goalie gloves with me. Our wrapping is a bit rubbish.'

'I'm sure it's fine. I bet Daddy's wishing he could have come here with you rather than have to go in to the office.' I'm not sure this is true, but I say it anyway. When Tom left this morning, there was a palpable spring in his step, choosing to take the car because there would hardly be any traffic, and then a snatch of music audible on the radio as he drove away, the window partly down.

At the reception desk at the climbing centre I check my phone

for any missed calls from Madeleine. I left her Play-Doh modelling with Teddy. 'None in your mouth' was the last thing I said
to him, worrying that if he swallowed it, it would plug his windpipe. I read recently of a child who choked to death on a jelly
cube, and none in the house since. Eliminating danger is a full-
time occupation. Standing watching Isaac on a climbing wall may
be a form of torture.

Harry's mum is beside me. 'Hey, Anna, it's lovely to see you.
I haven't seen you in so long. Did you have a good Christmas?
Harry says Teddy will be starting school soon. Did you not bring
him to watch? The boys are so excited. I think there's some sort
of safety briefing, but in fact it's all quite tame.' How relaxed she
is. All those femurs, collarbones, wrists and ribs queuing up for
coloured bibs.

I don't think she's expecting me to answer any of her questions.
She swooshes by me, and greets another mum. 'Oh my goodness,
do your glutes and hamstrings hurt? Thursday's class has killed
me!'

The hinterland of their life beyond their children laps at my
feet. No, I didn't bring Teddy, because it would have felt insensitive to do so. Isaac sees that, and I blame her for not doing so too.

Isaac hangs back a little from the group of boys by the
instructor.

The wall is not vast, although looking up at it, it gives the
impression of being so. The coloured grips project out brightly.
The instructor explains how to navigate a course of varying
difficulty. Isaac looks a little uncertain. Tom would be doing a
far better job than me. It's taking all my willpower not to shout
out, *Be careful*, or *Just do the easy yellow ones and stay low.*

Stay low. That's not what I should be teaching him; Julia the
social worker would no doubt be quick to tell me this.

Sarah, one of the other mothers, comes over. 'Rather them
than me. I've never had a head for heights!' She laughs lightly.

'No, me neither.'

What I can't say to her is how miraculous it is; all these children, tip-topped up with SMN, now firing messages into their lower motor neurons, their legs scaling the wall quick and sure. And yet how many of them are carrying the faulty gene as they do so; all set to sabotage a child they can't yet even conceive of?

'Don't look so serious, Anna, it's hardly Everest. Look at Harry's little brother, George – he's the nimblest of them all!'

Would Teddy have been so too? I transpose him onto George, who is scooting right up to the top. Is there any consolation in the thought that Teddy, too, would temperamentally choose to do that? Even now, if there were a hoist available, he would no doubt be lobbying to be winched to the highest possible point.

'Anna, has Isaac mentioned the hockey club to you?' Claire calls across to me. 'There's a new team for their age group – practices and matches are on Sunday morning. I'm taking Emily to the trials next Sunday. If Isaac wants to try out and if they both get in, maybe we can do a lift share?'

'I'll ask Isaac about it. Perhaps we could do that.'

My head is spinning and I'd like to bolt for my kitchen. How comfortable and easy in their skins they all are; how bright and breezy. Hockey sticks can fracture cheekbones; hockey balls in flight might strike the delicate scoop of the temple. The prospect is appalling. And yet what kind of mother am I? I worry about the things Teddy can't do, and now, increasingly, about the things Isaac can.

He's halfway up the wall now, and just below a promontory where another child has paused. If that child fell . . .

'Good boy! Well done. Keep going!'

In my palms, my nails make indents the shape of crescent moons.

Isaac

Harry's mum cuts the cake in thick, squidgy slices.

'Who'd like some?' she asks. She passes it round on paper plates.

'You are all exceptional mountaineers,' she says, laughing.

She's made some healthy brownies with sweet potato and beetroot and they're on a different plate, cut into small slices, for the mothers to eat. They're sitting around a separate table and there's a lot of chatting, about recipes and exercise classes and someone who you can go to and have your eyebrows shaped so that you look at least ten years younger.

Mummy is sitting at the table, but her chair isn't pulled in completely so her legs aren't properly under it. If I took a pair of compasses and drew a circle around the chairs, hers would be just a little bit outside of it.

She's not saying anything, but she seems to be listening, and she doesn't look bored or fed up, just as if what she is hearing is different from what she usually hears. She doesn't turn to her left or her right to talk to the mums who are the closest to her.

When I first started school, at the end of the term you had to sit with one of the teaching assistants and talk about what you had learned, and you told her the words and she wrote them down on a sheet, which went into a file all about you. You had to say what you had liked best, and what made you happy, and what you could now do and what you found difficult. I told her that the thing I found difficult was joining in; mostly in the playground at playtime, when a game had already started. It felt like trying to step onto a roundabout that was already spinning. 'Hello,' I'd say, 'my name is Isaac,' but that didn't help. The other children would whirl on by and I'd be left standing there, just saying *My name is Isaac* to the fresh air.

And that's what Mummy looks like now, with the sweet potato and beetroot brownie held carefully on her paper plate. She looks like she doesn't know how to join in, and like she doesn't have the right words either – *Hello, my name is Anna* probably also not the ones that will do it.

Tom

When we come out of the client meeting, it's already twilight. We stand on the pavement, confirming a few details about who will follow up what, and then we stand for an extended moment, me checking my watch and Eliza knotting her scarf around her throat, and it feels like we're waiting, both waiting for something, and reluctant to go our separate ways. It's two weeks since we had lunch on Saturday in the office; sitting against the filing cabinets, unpacking the Deliveroo boxes, a kind of hesitant intimacy emerging as we searched for cutlery and water glasses and laid out the food between us.

The words are out of my mouth before I've really considered them:

'Wasn't your degree in art history?' I know this because she told me over lunch. 'We're practically on the National Gallery's doorstep. Shall we go? Maybe you could show me some paintings? It would be a nice change from going through PowerPoints together.'

She smiles. 'I never turn down going to a gallery.'

'Okay. So pick your best three pictures. I'll be all ears.'

The early train will be pulling out of Marylebone; the early train that would mean I could have helped with supper and bathtime and Isaac's spelling homework, and instead I am turning towards Trafalgar Square, an anticipatory beat to my step. I walk up the pale steps to the National Gallery, and it's hard not to beam, not to feel this is a stolen moment, bright and precious as a carefully cut gemstone.

She chooses three paintings. First, van der Weyden's *The Magdalen Reading*. 'Not because of the piety in it, but because it speaks to me of the pleasure of being totally absorbed in a good book.' She points out the gold brocade of the Magdalen's underskirt.

Next she chooses Holbein's *A Lady with a Squirrel and a Starling*, 'because the white in it is so clever: the white fur, the white shawl, the white cambric at the woman's throat and wrist'. I find myself watching her as she looks at it intently. Is this how it begins: the learning of a face, the tilt of a cheekbone, the shape of a mouth?

Her third painting is Sassoferrato's *The Virgin in Prayer*. She turns to face me fully. 'I love the depth of the blue of her cloak, but more than that, that the Virgin looks kind and tender and as if she understands that it's actually very hard to be good.'

It is harder not to feel that we could be beginning a conversation that could weave through weeks, through years, through decades. Isn't that what all the hubbub at the beginning of a relationship is really about? An exercise in telling – tell me what you think, tell me what you like, tell me what made you. With Anna, it seems increasingly like an exercise in withholding.

'Each picture you have picked is a woman by herself.'

Eliza laughs. 'Unintentional, although I won't dwell on the significance.'

She blushes a little, and turns away from me, and then in what seems to be some kind of awkwardness, she changes the position of her arms, which have been folded across her body, and in doing so, she drops her bag, which has been pressed closely to her. Some of her things tumble out – her Oyster card, sunglasses case, a lipstick – and scatter across the floor. The noise is unexpected, and people's heads turn, and she ducks down to retrieve them, her fingers quick and then her hands suddenly full, the bag crimped tightly again, close to her ribcage. A strand of hair falls loose from the chignon it was contained in, and as she stands up, it is done before I have time to resist it, my hand reaching forward, my fingers tucking it behind her ear, and when she is at full height, my fingertips on her cheekbone for just a fraction of a second longer. Then a weighted moment when all I am aware of is her mouth, and mine, and the luminous space between us.

'Tom? Tom, is that you? Your voice is so like Edward's, I thought I couldn't be wrong. What a surprise to see you in here on a Tuesday afternoon.'

Tabitha. Tabitha swishing confidently towards me, her eyes taking in Eliza with cool precision. She extends her hand to her.

'Hello, I don't think we've met.'

'This is Eliza, my colleague; Eliza, this is my sister-in-law, Tabitha, my brother Edward's wife.' I try to pare away the strained note from my voice.

Tabitha raises one eyebrow almost imperceptibly. She lets hang, unspoken, the question of what we are doing here. She reverts to herself.

'I was going to whizz through the Goya exhibition so I could be on point if it comes up as a topic of conversation at Edward's tedious client dinner tonight, but there's such a queue and I can't be bothered to wait, so I'm picking one painting instead and I'm going to blag that it's a favourite I repeatedly come to look at. Any suggestions?' She looks pointedly at Eliza.

'Taste is such a personal thing, I wouldn't know where to begin.'

'I think I have in mind a moody and magnificent self-portrait. I'm due at the hotel shortly, so I better go and find it. We're staying at the Shard, which is compensation for what will be an unremittingly boring evening. Enjoy the rest of your visit. Nice work if you can get it.'

She moves off down the gallery.

Eliza looks back at the painting. 'I'm sorry if that was awkward. I mean, unexpected. You looked taken aback, and I'm sorry if it put you in a difficult position. Perhaps we're better off sticking to PowerPoints.'

I am momentarily lost for a response. I say, 'No, but I should go,' even though I don't know if I want to, or if I ought to, or if I have to. Eliza nods, and turns to look again at the Sassoferrato. She saves me the awkwardness of leaving the room at the same time.

I walk out into Trafalgar Square and I swear I can feel my heart in my chest; not thudding or beating or racing or pounding, but just there, very present, so that I am aware of its contours and weight.

It's followed by an image of Anna, carefully giving Teddy and Isaac their supper, and it makes me twist my head away from the thought, as if they are actually in front of me and it scorches my eyeballs to see.

Anna

The dog days of January are killing. Today is so grey, it feels like I've been shut in a saucepan, and the light is so poor it seems I have to blink and refocus to see my way properly through it. It has triggered a sharp need to get out of the house with Teddy.

At the park, Teddy is shoehorned into the swing intended for much younger children; that way I can push him and be secure in the knowledge that he will not fall out. There are only a couple of other children here; snow-suited and booted toddlers who are playing on a see-saw, their mothers holding them secure to the seat, their hands over theirs on the grip. So much effort and dedication expended on keeping them safe.

'Push me higher,' Teddy says, and I do so, just a little, watching his body rise and fall in a crescent.

I nod a mute greeting as one of the other mothers makes her way past me and back to the parking spaces. How remote everything seems; how blocked up with not saying.

'Come on, my little astronaut.' I bring the swing to a halt and kiss him fiercely on the cheek. 'I don't want you to get cold. That's enough swinging for one day. Let's go home and have lunch.'

After lunch, when he's sleeping, I sit at my computer and log onto the SMA support website. I click onto the Emotional Health page, and look at the Top Tips. *Go out with friends; don't give up work; stay positive; don't feel guilty; talk to other people in the same boat; use counselling.* I wouldn't know where to begin. And anyway, I've always felt it's not about me.

I click on the section that gives advice on starting school. The portage worker from the hospital team has phoned and said that the school has given notice that they are close to an actual start date. She has suggested I begin to write some of the preparatory information that will help make Teddy's first few days easier.

The website talks of the need to educate the school, teachers and carers, and to encourage pupils to talk with Teddy rather than about him. It recommends that I put together a book for the school from Teddy's perspective. I scroll down through the pages. I am urged to *Get SMArt*, and to coach Teddy in some responses: *'Why are you in a wheelchair?' 'Because my legs don't work'*; *'Can I still play with you?' 'Yes, I'd like that a lot.'*

It is helpful, and sensible, and grounding, and kind. It hits my skin like a nail bomb.

I take out my tin of coloured markers. At least I can cobble together a decent-looking pamphlet. I fold the paper in half and draw a quick, fluid outline of a child in a wheelchair. I add eyes to the front bumper so that it looks like Teddy's Wizzybug.

The questions that the book is supposed to address are suggested in bullet-pointed form. *I am . . . I need . . . I can . . . I cannot . . .* Why do I still find them so heartbreaking after all this time?

I put the lid back on the tin, and try not to cry. I bite my lip and think of all the films I've watched on YouTube that capture parents dedicatedly taking care of babies stricken with SMA Type 1, who find joy in their short and highly compromised lives. It's not that I am not dedicated or brave. It's just the hurdle I don't seem able to overcome is the grief for the life Teddy might have had if Tom and I hadn't carried SMA to him in the spiral of our conjoined DNA.

I look at the suggested questions again. I try to summon up my best self, rather than the version that feels like a small, crumpled piece of threadbare cloth. *I am . . . I am . . .* It shouldn't be so hard to focus. When Isaac comes home from school, I will ask him to help. He will think of things that will be lively and funny and will make other children laugh. Isaac is brilliant at focusing on the things Teddy can do. He's evidently not hopelessly stuck in a fury about the deletion mutation in the survival motor neurone 1 on chromosome 5.

Tom

Lunch with Edward always has a retrospective note. We never eat sushi, or ceviche, or tapas sitting in a bar in Soho. Instead, on the rare occasions we lunch together, it is always borscht, or steak and kidney with a suet crust, and puddings served with custard, all eaten in slightly too-dark restaurants where it's necessary to squint a little at the menu, and where elderly waiters appear from behind red leather buttoned doors.

'Anything up?' Edward arrives at the table where I am already seated. 'You sounded in a bit of a hurry to meet.'

I shrug and try to make a non-committal sound at the back of my throat. It comes out all wrong, and causes Edward to look at me quizzically.

'So yes, then.' He ruffles his napkin onto his lap. 'Something up, I mean. Evidently.'

Edward is always on to me, as if I am a code he can scramble on sight.

'Is it work or family? Don't tell me you've been made redundant and are about to start two months of gardening leave.'

I shake my head. I can feel my poise, my self-assurance, peeling away from me. We might as well be seven and nine, sitting again in Flanagan's meadow.

'No, no. I just thought it would be nice to have lunch together, and to catch up. I was thinking about you because I bumped into Tabitha a couple of days ago. Did she tell you?' I try to make it sound as casual as possible.

Edward is flicking through the wine list.

'She may have done, although I don't think so. Why, was it a notable encounter? Wait, have you summoned me to lunch to tell me, like a loyal, upstanding brother, that you saw Tabitha with another man?'

'No, of course not.'

'So what then . . . ah, wait . . . did she see *you*, then? You with someone else? There has to be indiscretion is this somewhere.' He laughs unconcernedly.

I swallow noticeably. 'As it happens, yes, she did see me with a colleague. Not being indiscreet, not that, obviously. Just someone I've been allocated to work with on a couple of projects.'

I'm gabbling; snatching for words to absolve me of what Edward is implying. Do I deserve absolution? I probably don't. The memory, resurgent, of lunch with Eliza in the office three Saturdays ago; an unspoken intimacy as we sat cross-legged on the carpet eating straight from the cartons. When she wanted to try something, stretching out my fork so that she could take it directly into her mouth, my hand cupped beneath it in case any food should spill, my fingertips almost, almost brushing her chin. Was that inappropriate intimacy? Likely yes. Perhaps this is what I should be asking Edward, like when we were children. *On a scale of one to ten, how bad is this?*

Edward is watching me carefully. 'And that anodyne but earnest response doesn't explain why you wanted to meet for lunch. I'm presuming you don't have any residual details to go through about Dad's estate. Surely to God we've completed all that now? I still can't believe you elected to keep your proportional share of the sheep.'

'It was mainly to help William so that he didn't have to buy me out. The boys will like the idea anyway, that something in the fields is actually theirs. Maintaining connections and all that . . .' I grind to a halt.

'Connections. Indeed; isn't that where this conversation started? Where, by the way, did you say you saw Tab?'

How adroit Edward is; how accomplished at steering the conversation in figures of eight. I am hesitant again. How polished and urbane he must be with his clients; how thoroughly he has shed all vestiges of our roots.

'Trafalgar Square. Well, not Trafalgar Square exactly. The National Gallery. She said she was mugging up on a painting before some client dinner with you.'

He laughs. 'All credit to her. She's Teflon. She often pops in to the National to look at a painting, and then over dinner cobbles together some schlock about how a painting viewed in this way becomes more acutely observed, more dearly loved. It always goes down well, suggesting a sensitive, intellectually emotional hinterland that of course she doesn't have and simultaneously allows a client to tell her at great length about his Italian holiday and about each and every fresco or Renaissance painting he looked at with his dull, dumpy little wife.'

The waiter takes our order, deferring to Edward. How does that still work? Is *younger, less wealthy brother* tattooed on my forehead?

'You, meanwhile,' Edward continues smoothly, 'were presumably not mugging up on paintings to impress a client, and I'm guessing art is beyond the remit of your project focus.'

'Yes, a meeting finished early, and we went to look at some paintings.'

'The "we" sounds pretty cosy.'

'It's not . . . there's not . . . I haven't . . .' I falter.

'*Yet* seems to be the word that's missing from the end of that sentence.' Edward's tone becomes brisker. Always he is intolerant of uncertainty and ambiguity. 'So sum it up for me, Tom: are you having an affair and you're worried that Tabitha has spotted you and will spill the beans to Anna; or are you not having an affair but you're worried that Tabitha will shop you because it looked as if you were, which means you'll have to take flak for something you've probably only contemplated. Only you, Tom.'

I am flailing. I'm not sure what direction I intended the conversation to take, but it wasn't this.

'It's not about me going to the gallery, or mostly it isn't. It's about Anna; Anna and me. Things are just really tricky between us at the moment. I'm not sure why, and I can't seem to do anything right. I feel I've lost my bearings with her; does that make me sound like a scout without a compass and a map?'

Edward pushes back on his chair.

'Probably even less efficient, to be frank, but it makes you sound like most of us. Marriage doesn't come with a sat nav, more's the pity. So, in this oh-so-casual-no-actual-reason lunch, what you are actually asking me is do I know if Tabitha is going to tell Anna, and if so, can I persuade her not to?' Edward laughs hollowly. 'I'm not even going to wait for you to nod. Your first mistake is to think I have any call over Tabitha's behaviour. She mostly does what she likes, although you may be surprised to learn she has a far too traditional, albeit cynical, respect for marriage to rock any unnecessary boats. You can take some comfort from that.'

Edward looks serious for a moment. 'Thing is, Tom, I can't really help you on this. Unfortunately I didn't think to marry a woman who would do what I ask, or one who pays much regard to what I think about anything. More fool me, possibly. If I were to mention this to Tabitha, and suggest a course of action, she'd still do whatever she wants. It's like when I told her I didn't think the girls would take care of a puppy, so she bought two. Remember all the rehoming hassle? In her latest news, one of her friend's husbands has got his mistress pregnant, and the wife

– Tab's friend – has made him agree that he'll never see the child. Tabitha describes it as a victory for wounded uxorial pride. I'm guessing that means she'd take Anna's part, whatever the circumstances.'

'But she didn't mention anything to you? Has she said she's spoken to Anna?'

Edward pauses for a moment and drums his fingers on the table.

'No. Now that I think about it, the only thing she said to me about the National Gallery was to do with a painting she'd been looking at. It was by . . . Salvator . . . Salvator Rosa, a self-portrait, and she was amused by a sign he was holding up. It said – and you'll have to give me a moment here – words to the effect of "Keep silent unless what you say is better than silence", which now, in the circumstances, is pretty bloody funny. I never underestimate Tab's ability to appear to be saying one thing while actually telling me something completely different. It would be just like her to be privately enjoying the joke. Even at her most disappointing, I am reminded why I love her.'

I look down at the table to try and avoid him reading my expression.

'Tom, I don't think I'm helping here, unless you feel better for getting it off your chest. Typical you, by the way – an almost-affair. Fact is, Tabitha finds Anna hard work; she says being with her makes her teeth hurt. On the strength of that, I'm guessing she's not going to be seeking out what would be a difficult conversation even if they were close.'

I feel truly miserable. Poor Anna.

Edward turns his palms upwards. 'Not much I can do to help, chap.'

When he leaves, after a lunch that then digresses into superficial chat about the markets and the exchange rate, and whether a company we both know of should be going public, he reaches across and pats me on the shoulder.

'On reflection, I hope I haven't made my wife sound like a total bitch. We chose our spouses with our eyes wide open. However it pans out, there's no point blaming anybody else. It's always the qualities we liked best that rear up and bite us. Truth is, my marriage is mostly oxygenated and eked out by turquoise boxes from Tiffany's. Anna was always feisty and spirited. If she's fighting with you now, that's only to be expected. She gives the impression of fighting everyone at once, with Teddy tucked safely in her slipstream. There was no way that wasn't going to result in some collateral damage.'

I'm not sure what I was trying to achieve by seeing Edward. It hasn't changed anything. I'm feeling like a heel about Anna – I haven't protected her from my family's harsh opinion – and I can't begin to make a call on what Tabitha may do. And then there is Eliza, and the more recent moment in the National which presses on my skin like a bruise.

I walk towards the tube station and reflect on what Edward has said. Most of all, it is his urbane cynicism that has surprised me, and the detached way in which he can talk about his wife and his marriage. And yet I can still see him marching towards me with the faulty walkie-talkie in his hand. That child is still there, protesting, but now also carrying a soft mitt of weary sadness, because Tabitha has become vaguely shocking to him, and the beauty that first captivated him has become something that chafes at his skin.

I get on the tube and become absorbed in the reflection in the window opposite of the faces of my co-passengers. Their bone structures blur in the mercilessness of the glass and become without definition in the darkness of the tunnel wall beyond. The train's onward motion compounds the impression, and I am mindful of the difficulty of remaining intact and authentic in life's forward trajectory. How did I become a man whose uppermost feeling is one of being unsure? How am I a man who seems to be folding in on himself?

Anna

Tabitha phoned, out of the blue and ostensibly with no reason. 'I'm just at a loose end. I thought I'd pop by and see you. January is a ghastly month, don't you think?'

Before she arrives, Paula is in the kitchen, winding up another meeting. It dawns on me that Tom mentioned he is seeing Edward for lunch today. Perhaps Edward has arranged this; I cast about wildly for a reason and wonder if perhaps he and Tabitha are separating, and this is part of a charm offensive, a careful exercise in laying blame.

Tabitha stands on the doorstep, and I gesture to the red car that is pulling away. 'That's good timing – I've just put Teddy down for a nap and that's the dietician who is leaving.' I'm not sure why I feel beholden to explain my morning, or why I account for myself. 'She really is the most appalling woman. A total bully.'

'I saw her as I pulled up. Ill-conceived hair colour, and dreadful footwear. What on earth was she thinking when she tried those on and decided they suited her?'

For a moment, I consider smiling. In a different life, might Tabitha and I have laughed, slightly mercilessly, a little reprehensibly, at some of the same things? Paula does wear dreadful shoes. It's not a one-off.

Tabitha follows me into the kitchen. Her own footwear is covetable: charcoal trainers with a fur trim.

'I haven't been here in an age.'

'Coffee?'

She nods, and glances around the room. 'This is the cleanest kitchen I've ever been in. Jesus, that tap's dazzling. I've sacked countless useless cleaners in my time. I wish I could teleport to my house whoever does this for you.'

I pass her the coffee and she stares hard as I do so. I curl my fingers into a ball, and tuck my hands behind me. She pauses.

'Oh wait, I get it, you do. You do it. While Tom's out striding around being the breadwinner, you're scrubbing the kitchen like a woman possessed.'

'I wouldn't say a woman possessed.' I keep my tone light. 'It just helps Teddy to stay healthy if the kitchen is . . .' I gesture to its order.

'And hopefully prevents any random acts of shittiness raining down upon you.'

'Depends what you define as random acts of shittiness, I expect.'

Tabitha reaches into her handbag and passes me a tube of cream. 'You can keep this. Apparently it contains most of the goodness of the entire ocean. It won't sort that out instantly, but it will get on top of it if you use it regularly.'

'Why are you here?' I suddenly have no appetite for circumflexion. 'You're never at a loose end; you're one of the most purposeful people I know. Have you got some kind of bombshell to drop? In my experience they mostly come from mouths and lips, not planes.'

She looks momentarily wrong-footed and uncertain. Her voice becomes a notch quieter.

'Why am I not surprised that you cut to the chase so directly and bluntly? It's just what I would do. I'm here, but it's without any glee, just in case you might attribute that to me. I saw Tom with a young woman at the National Gallery on Tuesday afternoon. I didn't see anything incriminating, but there was just a moment between them that suggested, to me anyway, that it wouldn't be out of the question. I'm guessing you two are hardly whiling your time away in galleries together. In fact I'm guessing you two are hardly doing anything together. Bear in mind there's always another woman who will; bonus points if she's younger, single and very pretty. I just thought I should tell you. If it were me, and if you saw Edward in the same circumstances, I would like to know. But then perhaps you'd rightly say that's typical of me; always inclined to see everything from my own perspective.'

Upstairs, with perfect timing, Teddy begins to cry. The snuffly wail he is making percolates down between us. She registers the sound.

'Would he totally freak out if I went upstairs? You might want to take a moment.'

I nod. Teddy will probably quite like it; Tabitha materialising in his room, mostly a vision in cashmere.

Her words feel as if they have come to me wearing ice-skating boots; their small, precise blades carving fine lines around the bowl of my skull. Eliza. It will be Eliza that he was with in the gallery. I know that with a certainty that winds me. And the Saturday when he supposedly went into the office, was that for something else too? He left the house like a man who was trying very hard not to whistle.

Tabitha comes back into the kitchen. 'Looks like my extending-a-morning-nap skills haven't entirely deserted me. Don't tell Edward or he'll be having my coil removed while I'm asleep. Teddy, meanwhile, is quite the charmer, even half asleep; he told me he liked my necklace and that my jumper was very soft.'

We both stand for a moment, silent, the awkwardness palpable between us. I take a deep breath.

'Thank you for telling me. I'm grateful for that, even though I am weary of coining out gratitude daily, both on my own and Teddy's behalf. I appear destined to spend my life saying thank you for things I don't want to hear.'

'You don't need to be grateful. What you do with what I've told you is for you to decide.'

'I'm particularly appreciative of your pragmatism and your seeming lack of pity. The thing I hate most in all of this – this, which you correctly identify as a random act of shittiness, which Teddy has to shoulder more than any of us – is being pitied. And especially Teddy being pitied; both of us being enveloped in other people's damp, shitty pity.'

'I don't pity you.' Tabitha smiles. 'Good heavens, Anna, not only are you far too prickly and confrontational, it would require far too much empathy and compassion on my part. I'm all about me, surely you know that.'

I manage to smile back at her. Kindness can come well disguised.

She checks her watch. 'I must be getting back to London. The girls will be home from school soon, and there's a programme I want to catch on the radio on the drive back. I listened to the trailer on the way up. It's about what happened to the family of the last Russian tsar. Apparently the women stuffed their dresses stiff with diamonds, ready for when they needed to bolt. Sounds quite the plan, although I presume the weight of the dresses ruled out making an actual dash. Imagine, though, having enough jewels with which to stuff a dress. Edward had better step up.'

She pauses for breath. Is it possible that she is feeling less composed than she appears? It's the closest to garbling that I've ever heard her. I cut her short.

'Thank you.' I say it with sincerity. 'This can't have been easy, however well your demeanour disguises it.'

Her face is hesitant momentarily. 'Edward doesn't know I'm here. It didn't seem his business, in the same way that it's not mine. Ah, that's Teddy again. Do you want to go to him?'

I nod, and she lets herself out of the front door.

I rub my palm in circles on Teddy's back and it soothes him into a doze. Tabitha's words are still skating around my head. It was hard to retain my composure while she conjured up images of diamond-stuffed dresses. I crumple down to the carpet and lean my head against the bed. Teddy's cheek is red where it is pressed warm against the pillow, and I reach and touch his lips lightly and feel his breath against my fingertips.

Of course something like this would happen. Did I really think we were so different, that our circumstances would rule it out? Tom has been looking at paintings in the National Gallery with Eliza; I know it will have been Eliza. The way he watched her when she walked away from the car after the office Christmas party. He has spent part of an afternoon with her, not at work, when he could have come home early. Come home to where I would have been grim-faced and taciturn and barely smiling when he came through the door. When did Tabitha say it was? Tuesday? I can't put an expression to him arriving home, or recall the first sentence he spoke. My attention would have been elsewhere. It is actually mostly elsewhere.

I stand up and look out of Teddy's bedroom window, where the winter sun gleams and skims low across the horizon. What causes a solar eclipse? Isn't it when a body passes between two things and thereby eclipses one of them entirely? I reach across and very gently take hold of Teddy's hand. Has Tom been swept away by the tsunami of my mothering?

I sit in the armchair and listen to the wheezy softness of Teddy's in-breath. I take off my wedding ring and roll it between my thumb and forefinger. I throw it up and catch it, repeatedly up and down, up and down. It's such a light, small thing, thinning slightly, delicately, where it sits against my palm. How can something so fragile anchor two people each to each? I put it back on my finger, and hold my left hand in the curl of my right, as if my fingers are broken and must be kept from further harm.

Tom

Lunch with Edward has given me indigestion, which feels fitting. I walk back into the office, rubbing my thumb against my lower ribs.

Did I tell Edward the extent of it? I touched Eliza's face, her cheekbone; was perhaps on the verge of kissing her when Tabitha called my name. I've stared at my hand several times since; it feels as if it should bear a smudge of disloyalty, of betrayal – some kind of stigmata. Also a blaze of light, because it felt like such a dazzling moment.

When I got home on Tuesday, I had an overpowering temptation to confess; watching Anna as she moved from the bathroom to the laundry with a huge bundle of washing in her arms. Then, at supper time, as she asked Isaac about what he needed for a school trip, the sudden realisation that she was paying me so little attention, it wouldn't matter if guilt was written all over my stricken face.

She has slept in Teddy's room the two nights since because his cough has come back, and although I offered to take a turn – coming to her in the early hours of the morning when I heard her moving about – she told me to go back to bed, and that she was fine. I stood in the doorway and watched her for a while; her body curled beneath the eiderdown that is usually thrown over the back of the couch. I stifled the temptation to go and sit beside her, in the almost dark of Teddy's room, where the silhouette of her face was visible but her features were not clear, and confess to her: *I did not kiss Eliza, but I wanted to.*

I begin to read a document on my screen but find I can't concentrate.

I have never kept a secret from Anna. Through all our years together, there is nothing I have not said. Perhaps this will be it; a small, hard, spiked secret, lodged just beneath my ribs like my indigestion, which will make itself felt each time I take a deep breath. The not-telling will become my punishment. And then there is also Eliza, and whether I need to square some kind of circle with her. I look up from my computer, and there she is, walking composedly into the office. She glances at me briefly, and makes her way to her desk. Her expression is unreadable. It is surely arrogant to think that I cause her any pain.

Anna

My mum sounded surprised. I have never asked her to come at
such short notice, never in fact asked her to come and look after
Teddy for a day. I was deliberately vague about what I needed
to do. I said, simply, that I needed to run an errand and that I
couldn't take Teddy because his teacher was coming in the
morning, and then the physio. I sorted out some jigsaw puzzles,
made a tureen of soup and a dish of rice pudding, and told Teddy
to be especially good.

Now, driving to Shropshire, the road spools before me and
allows me the space to think.

I've barely spoken to Tom since Tabitha came, although it
seems to have gone unnoticed. That in itself is a cause of pain.
I've slept in Teddy's room, although I was mindful of Tom, at
dawn, in the doorway, watching me for a while. I lay very still
and feigned sleep until he walked away. I felt as if I was spinning
and spinning in a galaxy of my own. I registered Teddy's breathing
and strained my ears to see if I could hear Tom's beyond it; his
breathing, in sleep, which has always been so steady and regular.
When Teddy was first diagnosed and I could not sleep for anxiety,
I would place my head on Tom's chest and try to synchronise
my breathing with his. In doing so, I felt absorbed into the weft
and weave of his skin, as if anything we faced would be immutably
together.

What has changed? I blink away tears. My love, my anxiety,
my obsession with Teddy has occluded everything from my view.

The friends I have gradually jettisoned because they do not say quite the right thing; either drenching me in sympathy and making soft cooing noises like turtle doves, or pretending that our lives aren't totally different and talking about prep school entrance exams when Teddy is battling with swallowing. There are no friends I have laughed with since Teddy was born; laughed frankly at an indignity, a mishap, an embarrassment. Everyone has tiptoed around me and then mostly tiptoed away.

I have chosen not to make friends with other women who have disabled children; have tenaciously avoided the singing groups, the swimming lessons that Julia has bombarded me with leaflets about. I recognise, now, with a small flush of shame, that I have been persistently hostile to the women in the same boat who have tried to be friendly. I have not wanted to be friends with them because that would be to say I am like them, and I am not. Or at least I think I am not; perhaps I should have tried a little harder to check.

I look at the sat nav. There are thirty miles further to drive. Around me, the Shropshire countryside looks scrubbed and raw in the February morning light. I am driving to the farm. It feels suddenly like a lodestar, and as if I will know what to do more clearly when I am there. Ruth will not be there as she is visiting a friend. Tabitha has driven to me, and now I am driving to Jenny, as if there is a thin skein of wool that links us to each other through the marrying of Ruth's boys.

The farm is where Tom makes the most sense to me; as if in that space, that context, he is more clearly illuminated and I can see him for what he is, understand how he became. What I want to do now – turning into the yard and seeing Jenny hurrying across it carrying an enormous hard-bristled brush – is to sit at Ruth's vast scrubbed-oak table and think about the distance that has opened up between us.

I am not angry about Eliza; that is surprising. How odd, that there is anger about many other things, but an absence about that. The insight, in his shoes, that I might be similarly tempted by a colleague who provides such a contrast. As I step towards Jenny, I see with crystal-clear clarity that since Teddy's diagnosis, I have systematically walled myself in, as literally as if I have taken bricks and mortar and begun building them in a neat circle around my feet. Teddy is walled in with me, and possibly Isaac too. What began as protectiveness has become an exclusion zone.

In the kitchen, Jenny looks puzzled; although also as if she is trying to disguise it.

'Is it okay if I make supper?' This said tentatively. 'This afternoon I work in the school office, so I try to make it in advance.'

'Of course, don't let me interrupt you.'

'Shepherd's pie,' she says, by way of explanation. She heaps potatoes onto the work surface, and begins to peel them with swift, smooth strokes. The skins loop onto the chopping board beneath. 'Shall I make us a coffee? Sorry, I forgot to ask.'

'Don't worry; don't bother about me. Is it okay if I just sit for a moment?'

'Of course. Whatever you need to do. Would you prefer me to be quiet and just let you be with your thoughts?'

'I'm sorry if I sound mysterious. I just need to get my head straight, and this weirdly seemed the best place to do it.'

She smiles. 'Thinking spaces are few and far between, aren't they? I usually stomp up to the old orchard and sit on a log. The boys never think of looking for me there, it's so overgrown and ramshackle. The problem is, I keep being distracted from whatever is bothering me and instead start imagining how I could transform it into a beautiful walled garden.'

'That sounds like a lovely idea.'

'It would be, I think. Raised beds would be easy to take care of. I'd give the boys one each and see how they did with it. No doubt they'd have me buying seeds for them and then be trying to sell me any veg they grew. Teddy and Isaac could have one too; that would be safer than flying a kite.' She pauses and bites her lip. 'I still feel bad about the kite, even though Teddy wasn't actually hurt. It just showed we weren't on the right page as a family, and that I haven't talked about Teddy's condition enough with my boys. I'm sorry. Sorry, actually, that I haven't talked enough with you about it. What started off as me worrying about saying the wrong thing seemed to fossilise into just saying nothing at all.'

'Don't be sorry. Please don't be sorry. I've just realised I mostly make people feel sorry, or bad, or uncomfortable about asking questions. It's quite the hat-trick, it seems.'

'Oh, but you don't—'

'You don't have to disagree. My mother said as much. She asked me, a while ago, when I became so difficult to help. She's right and I should have listened more carefully. You have been kind – unfailingly kind ever since Teddy's diagnosis – and I have kept you at arm's length; kept everyone at arm's length. I should be the one who is apologising.'

'I promise you there's no need.' She puts the potatoes on to boil, and starts to fry the lamb and the onion. 'Here, do you want to poke that about with a spoon?'

I do. 'And as for not telling your boys enough about Teddy's condition, maybe that's a good thing. It means they don't treat him with kid gloves; that when he is here it's the closest to a normal childhood that he gets. That's lovely for him, especially further down the line, if and when his mobility and strength is compromised further. This is a special place.'

'It is, although not without problems of its own.'

She wipes her hands on a tea towel and starts to take vegetables from the fridge.

'It's kind of you to let Ruth still live with you . . . to not mind about her living with you, I mean.'

'Not really. It's her home. I can't imagine what it would feel like to leave a place you'd lived in for sixty years. The boys love her, and she's great with them, and William said to me when we were first married, "There's God and then there's mothers," which told me all I needed to know.'

I move to the window and look out over the yard. 'It's as if the farm wove a spell on them in their childhood that still retains its power. It's compounded by the fact that nothing has changed; the teapot, the Persian rug, the big old ladles. Even the Christmas decorations are the same ones they put on the tree as boys. It must be as if they can step right back in here and find their childhood selves intact.'

Jenny laughs softly. 'Yes, I guess it gives them a kind of clarity of vision.'

'Not just them, I think. When I'm here, I feel I can see Tom more clearly. It's as if he's been preserved in aspic, down through the years. I can see where he began more directly than I can at home. Now, when I need to see him clearly, and when everything is muddied at home by the shape of our daily life.'

'Why do you need to see him more clearly now? If you don't mind me asking . . .' Jenny falters. 'I'm sorry . . . old habits die hard.'

'I don't mind you asking at all. I need to see him more clearly – see *us* more clearly – because Tabitha came to see me and told me she'd seen him in a gallery with a young woman, a colleague I think I've met. She clearly suspected them to be having an affair. I haven't suspected anything, but the truth of the matter is I haven't been looking. Mostly, from day to day, I blame Tom for a whole host of things. I expect it's a relief for him to be in the company of a woman who doesn't.'

'You don't do that.' Jenny pauses, the potato masher in her

hand. 'And I'm surprised if he is. Tom is loyal, that much I think I know.'

'How much do any of us know about anyone? That's what I realise, and also that blame is a complex, shape-shifting kind of thing. Tell me, does William still bring you tea every morning? I've always loved that image, from when you first lived in the cottage. It seemed such a wholesome, nurturing way for a married day to begin.'

'He does, but en route now to the one he takes to Ruth. He talks to her about the farm before going out into the yard. I don't mind; it's a kind of honouring. Selfishly, it's a good template for the boys to see, not that I have any illusions about them copying it.'

'But if you needed to talk to William, if ever something happened like this, how would you do it?'

'I'd write it down, I think, in a series of notes. That way I wouldn't get distracted, and it would be accurate, with no misre-memberings. I'd be too tempted just to sob, otherwise, because it would all seem terribly unfair. Me being here' – and now she gestures to the kitchen around her – 'a sort of backstop and catch-all for everything.'

'I think what I felt about fairness changed after Teddy's diagnosis. Everything, actually, changed. I've spent the last four years feeling totally besieged. I realise I've been a mother on the warpath to the exclusion of all else.'

Jenny crosses the kitchen and hugs me.

'Please don't be so hard on yourself. And it's good that you are talking. Can we make it a habit?' She looks up at the clock. 'Do you have time for a walk? I can lend you some wellies.'

I smile. 'Just a quick one, and yes please to the wellies. It'll do me good to stride out, to not be pushing a wheelchair or carrying Teddy. Then I'll go home and do what you suggest. I'll write it all down, and hopefully that will help Tom and me to talk.'

Tom

When I come home, I am weary. As I walk up the path, I can see Anna in the kitchen and the boys on the banquette, and Isaac is blowing a red plastic windmill for Teddy, and Anna is clapping in between washing saucepans. She momentarily disappears from view and I can't see her any more, and with that perception comes a strong sense of loss.

Teddy spots me pausing on the path. Isaac pushes him up onto his knees and Teddy lifts his arm and manages to wave the windmill like a flag. Anna reappears and I can lip-read what she is saying – 'Good boy, strong boy.' Teddy beams back at her. I am momentarily choked. Never for a minute has she mothered Teddy in any way other than for him to feel confident and happy.

Is it more reprehensible to consider leaving your wife for another woman if your child is disabled? When the damage inflicted on a child by divorce is primarily emotional, is it fair to assume that an able-bodied child copes any better? The questions disconcert me, ambushing me as they do on the doorstep. I am a man who never thought this would be something he would consider. Edward would tell me to stop being such a wetter and get on and have an affair; at least that way I would know whether Eliza is worth sacrificing it all for.

Anna looks tired; tired and something else. She looks at me purposefully as I hang up my coat and walk over to the boys.

'I'm doing fist bumps from now on. Only fist bumps.' This from Teddy. I oblige.

Isaac fills me in. 'Paula the dietician says it means you catch hardly any germs. That's why it's his new thing. She says if he only does fist bumps when he starts school after Easter then he'll be less likely to catch bugs so he won't have to have days off.'

I look across at Anna.

'Don't ask me; I wasn't here. My mum was, and she didn't mention it, and then Teddy told Isaac.'

'The ramps are ready at school,' Isaac confirms. 'The builders finished today. Mrs Jackson told me there will be a ribbon-cutting ceremony for Teddy; he'll cut it with the big craft scissors and then roll down the ramp for the first time. We'll get to clap.'

Teddy soft-punches the air. 'I'm properly going to school soon.'

I look again to Anna. 'Have they confirmed this?'

'My mum was here when the teacher came. I expect she shared it with her, but when I got back she was in a hurry to leave; she had a follow-up appointment about her hip and went as soon as I arrived. I'll phone the head tomorrow to check.'

It's only when I'm taking the rubbish out later, and I'm standing by the bins, a lazy frost beginning to scribble on the lids and the top of the bag scrunched into my fist, that it occurs to me: got back from where? Where has she been, and how strange it is that I feel unable to go back into the house and ask her where she spent her day. I am mindful of the dry-stone walls that loop their way through the farm; each one built from pieces of stone wedged neatly against another. Is this what Anna and I are building between us; each withholding, each not-telling an increase in the breadth of the flinty space?

I look back up at the house. Anna pauses in front of our bedroom window, taking down her hair. Teddy's room is in darkness. Isaac's light is on, and his blind is not drawn. He is holding an Airfix model in his upstretched hand, and making it swoop and sortie across the width of the glass pane.

It is my home. They are my family. Eliza recedes further and further away, as if I am looking at her down the wrong end of a telescope. The cold of the night seems to slap me forcefully on the cheek. How on earth can I jeopardise all this?

Across the road, a fox slinks brazenly beneath a parked car. It barks once, sharply, and ducks under a box hedge and away. I stand holding the dustbin bag until my knuckles are pinched blue.

Anna

I run the bath scaldingly hot. As I lower myself beneath the water, my skin blooms immediately pink. I submerge myself until there is only the oval of my face exposed to the air, and I feel my hair fan out around me like a child's drawing of the sun. I place the back of my hands beneath me, and lengthen my arms so that I push up my body to give me the sensation of floating. I close my eyes and allow myself to bob gently.

All evening I have not been able to look at Tom properly; busying myself with chores, and holding laundry to me like a protective shield. I have placed paper and a pencil on my bedside table. When he comes upstairs I will be waiting, and I will write what I feel.

What a tangle; what a terrible tangle we are in. I think of Ruth's knitting, and of Ruth's arms, extended, while the wool is rewound smooth. Can Tom and I be similarly reconfigured?

There have been so many words in my mouth since Teddy's diagnosis. So many words that are medical terms and mostly labels, and words that are logistical and that refer to appointments and meetings and job titles. There are words that involve the practical details of his care, which refer to equipment, to orthotics, and to evaluative tests. There are the scientific words I don't actually properly comprehend but which I pile on a small altar of hope and which have become my only discernible faith. But there are no words at my disposal – and I realise this with blinding clarity – no words that allow me, or help me, to say how all this has been for me. There are no sentences in my lexicon that have begun with *I feel* or *I am*. No words that have helped me to set aside my pride and say *Please can you help me with this*. No words that capture how it felt when the life I thought my child would have suddenly became something very different; and then, in the immediate immersion in the diagnosis and the flurry of changes, no available time to find the words for myself.

I went to a toddler group shortly after Teddy's diagnosis, when he had just got his first assisted seat. A mother who was sitting beside me in the circle frankly and kindly asked, 'What issues does your child have?' Her words were no doubt carefully chosen; she did not ask what was wrong with Teddy, or say, *What is the matter with him?* Perhaps she had more insight and personal experience than I gave her credit for at the time. But what I remember is my total inability to give a direct answer in return. The words were there in my mouth; I could, of course, have said accurately, *He has spinal muscular atrophy Type 2, which is a rare, genetically inherited condition that affects crawling and walking ability, arm, hand and neck movement, breathing and swallowing.* Or, blinding her with science, *It's a condition that results from a dele-tion mutation in the survival motor neurone 1 on chromosome 5.*

I said neither. Instead, I picked up Teddy and left the room. She followed me out of the hall; 'I'm sorry, I'm sorry,' she called, her own toddler stashed under her arm as I buckled Teddy's seat into the car. 'I didn't mean to upset you.' I never went back.

And then there is the meeting I had when Teddy was three, with a palliative care consultant. The notes he sent afterwards I have sealed in an envelope and put at the back of a drawer. If I cannot see them, they cannot exist as a possibility. The notes talk of interventional supportive care, and emergency resuscitation, and endotracheal intubation, and terminal dyspnoea. These are the words I could hardly bear to learn and that I hope never to have to use. On one of the websites, there's a photograph of a boy with SMA Type 2, and the dates beside him show that he died aged six. I scroll quickly over this page because it always makes me cry.

And all this – all of it – I have bundled and packed and crammed into my heart so that it is always heavy in my chest.

What is one of the Top Tips on the SMA website? *Ask for help and accept help.* My mother was only partly right; I failed at it from the outset rather than it being a recent accomplishment.

And Tom. I love Tom. How easy it became to forget that, to neglect that, to overlook it in the face of it all. I can't remember the last time I said it to him, or the last time I asked him about how he felt about any of it either.

I push myself upright, and sit for a moment as the water streams off me. I have been so determined in all aspects of Teddy's care, since the day the health visitor first had a hunch about his condition. My determination, I now realise, has been at great cost. It means I have never expressed how devastated I was. And what this means – and I see it clearly now – is that I have never got beyond the moment when the clinical geneticist calmly redrew my shattered family tree.

Tom

I'm sitting in front of the television. I'm not watching it; instead I'm listening to hear if Anna has gone to bed. The bath drains away. My cowardice makes me feel sick.

Tonight we should have been cock-a-hoop, celebrating Teddy's school start date. It's a triumph of persistence on Anna's part – so many battles, so much determination – and yet it seems to have rolled straight off her like a raindrop down a glass pane. When I came home, she was unstacking the dishwasher, and then folding washing and pairing the boys' socks. She had a complicated, thickly stitched silence about her that I could not unpick. I couldn't bring myself to ask her if she had seen or heard from Tabitha.

I switch off the television, and sit for a moment trying to calibrate my level of betrayal. In the hallway, I can see the ribbon of light that shines from beneath the bedroom door. I find myself taking a deep breath as I walk up the stairs.

She's sitting on the bed, cross-legged, with an A4 pad in front of her. She looks like a dancer, in her leggings, her black T-shirt, her wet hair pulled back from her face. She looks up at me as I come in.

'How did we get to this?' It is said abruptly and without preamble. 'I've been asking myself over and over, how did we get to this?'

I sit down on the edge of the bed. I am netted, wordless, in my wife's shimmering purposefulness.

'I'm going to write everything down, because somehow we

seem to have lost the ability to tell each other what we think, what we feel . . .'

'Anna . . .' I am suddenly afraid of what she is going to say.

'I'm going to write what I need to say, and then you can see it, and my words will stay fixed to the page, and there will be no misremembering of what I have said.'

How direct she is; her old self visible in the tilt of her chin.

She writes a few lines on the paper, then rips it from the pad, folds it in half and passes it to me. It is like an odd party game; but with no jollity or mirth. Instead, Anna looking at me, the paper held in her outstretched hand, bidding me to take it so that she can begin writing the next one.

'Don't say anything, don't say anything at all, until you've read them all.'

I open the first note.

Every morning when you leave, before the boys are awake, I scrub the kitchen, every bit of it, until my skin stings and is cracked between my fingers. I think that if I do this I will keep Teddy safe; I will keep him from getting an infection, from getting sick, from being hospitalised with complications, from his condition deteriorating. If I can't clean the kitchen – if you are here at the weekend, or if something unexpected happens – I cannot stop the not-doing-it clamouring at me all day. Sometimes my skin is so sore it bleeds. I think this is part of a contract to keep Teddy safe.

I look up at her, and at her hands, but she does not look back at me; instead she rips off the second note from the pad and continues to write.

I resent the people who help us with Teddy. Even if they are trying to be kind – and most of them are – I see it as interfering, as judging, and most of all as pity. I hate wading through their compassion; it feels like thick sinking sand. And I hate fencing their bossiness; their telling me what to do all the time. It means that for at least part of every day I am angry, and the anger spills out of me and mostly onto you.

I do not look up now. I smooth the second note out on my lap, and stretch my hand out to receive the third.

I have pushed away all of my friends, and my old work colleagues. I have pushed them away and I have punished them because I don't feel they understand. They are too sorry, too solicitous, too careful, too casual, or mostly too preoccupied, quite rightly, with what seem like the minor issues and hurdles in their own life. I never phone anyone just for a chat. Everything in my life feels too personal and too private to share.

The notes come thick and fast now, falling into my lap like a blanket of snow, the silence in the bedroom filled only by the smooth sweeps of the pencil on paper and the tearing from the spine of the pad.

I wonder sometimes why you come home at the end of a day, or after a trip, when your life outside of this house is so open, so free, so unconstrained. So not angry.

I am fearful of all that Teddy cannot do and of all that he may not increasingly be able to do, and of the responsibility and sensitivity this demands from Isaac every single day.

I worry. I worry all the time, and I am constantly on the alert. I think if I am responsible enough, vigilant enough, then nothing bad will happen. I am furious when you are casual, relaxed. I cannot step into that space and I resent you for being able to do so, so you become one of the people I am angry with too. When I kiss you, I am angry. I am angry with you for so much of the time, and I disguise it from you so all honesty has gone.

Other people, other women, mother children with life-limiting illnesses and manage it with courage and grace and joy. I don't. I am floundering, and I find that hard to admit even to myself.

It turns into a list now, the pad propped up on her knees, the back of her hand fiercely wiping tears from her eyes.

I don't think about Isaac enough. (She underlines this three times with dark scores of the pencil.)
I can no longer see where Teddy stops and where I begin.
If I allow myself to cry, I think I will not stop.
I think I have never reconciled myself to his diagnosis.

She stops writing, puts down the pencil and lifts her head to face me. When she speaks, her voice is suddenly calm and clear, and it is as if she is addressing me from a point long ago in our emotional history, when there was only a direct, bold connection between us.

'I can't talk to you any more. I can't tell you the things my heart feels because I am afraid if I give them oxygen they will tumble out and drown me, and so I am cold and uptight and put myself beyond your reach. And now I think there may be Eliza, who surely makes you feel happy rather than everything being fractious and vexed. I can understand if you would prefer to be with her; to begin again, freshly, with me and all my raddled emotion put aside. And that would be better, would be preferable to me, than if you stayed with me – with us – out of pity. I have so much unwanted pity in my life and I couldn't bear any more, especially coming from you. Staying with me because of Teddy would be the cruellest thing in the world. Either help me to find my way back to me, and then back to us, or please go.'

She wraps her arms around her legs, and presses her closed eyes to her knees.

I reach over to her so that she is contained by my embrace.

'I'm sorry, I'm sorry, I'm sorry,' is all I can say.

I weep with her for everything that has become muddled and tarnished and lost, and for all she has told me in this frantic, unexpected flurry of notes, which have tumbled into my lap in a soft free-fall of grief.

Isaac

It's a funny morning. Not funny like a joke, or when something is funny to look at. It's funny as if things have slightly slip-slided out of place, and as if Mummy and Daddy are treading carefully around everything that is in the kitchen. The fact that Daddy is even there is a surprise. His usual train will have left for London ages ago. When I come downstairs whistling a tune because whistling is a thing I've just learned to do properly, the sound of it seems very wrong in the kitchen, and as loud as the foghorn of an enormous ocean liner. Daddy is making breakfast; that is to say, he has put out the boxes of cereal on the side for me to choose from, whereas Mummy knows which one is my favourite. Mummy is sitting at the table. She looks like she's broken her arms. Not actually broken them – that's a relief – but she's holding them folded across her as if there is a problem with her elbows, and her palms are carefully cupped around them as if not to cause further damage.

The mop isn't out. The bucket's not been swilled and upended to help it dry. The counter tops aren't still damp from wiping and there's no smell of bleach coming up from the plughole. The kitchen hasn't been cleaned – not that it looks dirty, but it hasn't got the new-pin feel that it has every school morning. Daddy is by the kettle and he's making Mummy tea; and then he's by the stove taking a boiled egg out from a saucepan. He balances it carefully on a tablespoon and it looks like a smooth white eye.

There aren't many words being said. Daddy puts the tea in

front of Mummy, and slices some toast and puts it next to the egg in its cup. It's not exactly boiled egg and soldiers, but it's close, very close. The slice of toast is just cut directly in half. Mummy makes boiled egg and soldiers whenever I am sick. She does not look ill; perhaps just a bit pale.

'Mummy, are you poorly?' I stop next to her, by the table, before taking a spoon from the drawer.

'No, no, I'm fine.' Her voice is softer than usual. Daddy is fussing around her, and as he passes her the milk for her tea, his hand has the smallest of trembles. After she has taken it from him, he cups his hands together, and moves his fingers as if he is washing them with invisible soap. Then he sits down next to her, takes her hand in his, and kisses it very softly, right where her knuckles meet her fingers.

'What's happening at school today?' He asks this in a hearty voice that doesn't match his flutterings around Mummy.

There's a secret in the kitchen, that's what I know as I start walking to school. A secret, a not-telling, a not-in-front-of-the-children, a something that is sad and gentle all at the same time. Sorrowful would be the word. My Mummy and Daddy are sorrowful this morning. And Mummy is not spitting feathers, not spitting at all. She is as quiet and as still as I can ever remember.

Tom

On the late train in to work, I'm still in the moment. There, on the bed, the notes in my lap, Anna's face held in my hands. 'I haven't been unfaithful, but I have thought about it. I'm sorry. If you'll please let me, I want to find the way back to us.'

I held her while she fell asleep, and it felt as if last night merged with the very first night we knew about Teddy, and only now was I comforting her, only now understanding how she felt.

In the charcoal dawn I thought back through the years, trying to pinpoint where each thing began: the dinner parties with friends when she sat in silence all the way home; the evenings after hospital appointments when she said, 'I'd prefer not to talk about it, you know what it's like.' But I didn't, actually, and I don't, and I see that now. Instead I have become one of the people for whom appearances must be kept up.

As the first throes of daylight appeared on the horizon, I realised that if someone were to ask me why my marriage had reached this point, I would say that it was not about having a disabled child, or at least only in part. What has happened is that our roles have polarised, and led us far apart. It can happen, I surmise, in marriages where there is a tribe of completely healthy children; the conscientious ploughing of furrows and then the lifting of heads to see, with mild surprise, a pathway of completely opposing directions.

Anna. My Anna. I have let her slip from my hold; I have not been there for her even though I thought I was. I remember a cricket ball I carried in my school blazer pocket between the ages of nine and fourteen. The cricket teacher told us that whenever we had a moment, we should practise throwing and catching, tumble the ball in our hands and feel the seam with our fingertips. The ball deteriorated so rapidly; the red of the polish scuffing away to black baldness; the cream stitches on the seam fraying a little; the gold of the logo fading to an indecipherable smudge. Marriage is like that. What was once most precious carried casually in your pocket; knocked about a little, taken mostly for granted. Treated with insufficient care. I am guilty of all that.

And then there is Eliza, who rose before me like an iridescent possibility. How could my battered and bruised marriage possibly compete with that; my flawed marriage that is burdened by both Anna's shortcomings and mine?

I think of Eliza, and of what I should say to her; whether least said is soonest mended or whether an apology is due. I look around the train carriage at my fellow commuters, and imagine each one of them trying to maintain the emotional tapestries of their lives. Roads not taken, adventures not had; the overarching, compelling sanctity and moral imperiousness of family and home.

When I arrive in the office, I am quick to realise that my own deliberations have been adroitly and tactfully out-stepped. Perhaps they were also based on a false assumption. Eliza greets me in the meeting room. 'How are Anna and the boys? You haven't spoken much about them recently. I hope they're well. Teddy not risking life and limb, I hope?' Her tone is direct and bright, and underpinned, somehow, by a new impersonality.

'He's starting school, the date's finally been fixed. I think it will be great for Anna, too. I hadn't quite realised how much she's been taking the strain.'

'Good that you have now, then, and that you can focus on being a supportive husband. Shall we get started on this? I don't want to stay late because I'm going out to dinner tonight with an old friend from university.'

There is a silent acknowledgement between us of what she is actually saying. I realise what she has inferred from my awkward, hasty exit from the National Gallery. I nod, and she gives me a beautiful smile.

At lunchtime, I leave the office and go to Hyde Park, and sit on a bench next to the Serpentine. I allow myself, very briefly, the indulgence of mourning the loss of the possibility of Eliza, and at the same time I give thanks that she has gently, and with astute grace, helped restore me to my wife.

Isaac

The posters on the trees and the fence posts call it a snowdrop walk.

It stretches along a path through a field, and then alongside a vast house where there are snowdrops beneath all the trees. It finishes at a tiny stone church where the snowdrops are clumped between the graveyard headstones, and there is tea and cake for sale under a canopy. Women who mostly look like Granny are slicing cake onto paper plates, and putting the money into a Quality Street tin.

We are walking, the four of us. Teddy, obviously, is not actually walking; he is in Daddy's arms. Through the clouds there is some gentle spring sunshine, and so Teddy and Daddy make a very wide shadow, and I jump in and out of it as we make our way through the field. Mummy is holding my hand, and also sometimes Teddy's foot where it lies on Daddy's chest, and she has just heard what she says is the first skylark of the year. We have stood looking upwards, trying to spot it against the clouds, but we still cannot see it, even though we watch the clouds race until we are almost dizzy, and our eyes spin with the looking.

The walk is not just full of snowdrops, it's full of plans. As we walk along, Mummy and Daddy seem to be hatching a new plan with every few steps we take. When Teddy starts school, Mummy is going to go back to work for two days a week. She says everything will likely have changed and that she has nothing to wear, but she laughs just a little bit as she says it, and I think she does not properly mind. Teddy is also going to start hippo-therapy at the same time as I go to hockey. Hippotherapy has made us laugh a lot because it sounds as if it's got something to do with hippopotamuses, but sadly it doesn't; it's a kind of physiotherapy that involves horse riding and will help stretch Teddy's muscles. Daddy is going to take him each Sunday morning. Before, Mummy didn't want Teddy to do it because she thought he might fall off and hurt himself. Now she's changed her mind, and Teddy says he will make an excellent cowboy. He's planning on wearing a sheriff's badge for his first lesson.

Mummy and Daddy are going away for a long weekend too, in Bath. Me and Teddy are going to stay at the farm, and Toby has phoned and said they have an injured seagull in a straw-lined apple box in the barn. He says it pecks like fury and likes eating chips. I like the thought that it has flown so far from the sea to get mended, and that when its wing is fixed it will make its way home. Auntie Jenny is coming to our house soon to learn a little bit more about what Teddy needs at the start and end of the day. Mummy says it won't be my job to be helpful, but instead to play with my cousins and run like the wind. She says Auntie Jenny will have to make sure Teddy is sensible. 'And that'll be a full-time job,' she adds, gently tweaking his ankle.

Another weekend soon, we are going as a family to visit Crosby to see *Another Place*. Mummy has given me a bag to collect hats and scarves, all set to dress the figures when they are out of the water. In the bottom of the bag I have put the small wax man that I carved in the autumn, and I am planning on pushing it into the damp sand and letting him stand with them awhile.

I jump; jump high, so that I am almost as tall as the hedgerow, which is sprouting into green.

I'm not sure why all this should make me feel so happy, but happy I am. I stand on my tiptoes so that I can reach Daddy's chest and give Teddy a big fat kiss on his leg.

Anna

It is a bright, sun-drenched morning in very early April. It's the first day of the new school term, and I have walked with Isaac and Teddy to school. Teddy has fist-bumped half the playground before the bell has rung. He drives his Wizzybug up the ramp, and turns round and sticks his thumb merrily up to me. Isaac is standing just beyond him. He waves and gives me a nod and I blow them both a kiss in return. One of the other mothers who also has a child starting has asked me if I would like to come for coffee before pick-up time tomorrow. I said yes. We both have boys in the reception class. That is commonality enough.

I don't drive home. Instead, I drive to the Ridgeway and park near a bridle path that will allow me to walk through the woods to the church that we came to when we did the snowdrop walk as a family.

We did not go into the church then – the boys were too busy eating cake and looking at the masses of snowdrops – but it intrigued me; its ancient flint-and-stone neatness set in a verdant scoop of land. The sign outside said it was built in 1020. Now, on this morning, I am drawn to it, and I set off up the hill, through trees that are bursting vividly into the brightest of greens. The ground is carpeted thick with bluebells and I think I have never seen a morning more alive with spring. I pause at the top of the hill and listen to the birdsong spilling between the trees, and I smile at the unruly life force that is tumbling around me.

At the entrance to the church there is a sign asking walkers to remove muddy boots. Mine are clean because the ground is dry, but unexpectedly it feels like an appropriate act of humility, so I find myself pushing the door open in my socks.

When I flip on the light switch, it is hard not to exclaim out loud. It is like stepping into a small jewellery casket. The ceiling is turquoise, with white and gold ornamentation. To my left is a stained-glass window through which light is streaming. I walk towards the apse and the altar, which are contained in a semi-circular recess. The dome is frescoed with a scattering of gold stars and the silence is soft around me. I step towards the altar, and notice two icons to my right. The first is a statue of a Madonna holding a child. The way that she is cradling him – tenderly, carefully – reminds me of the dream I used to have repeatedly but which no longer wakes me. The plaster of the Madonna's head is chipped along her hairline – the child's head too – and also on the edges of her blue and coral cloak. Her expression, though, is contemporary and vivid. She looks down at the child with intense, fierce protectiveness. The second icon is contained in a simple wooden frame, with a background of gold leaf that makes the image glow. The child is wearing white robes that resemble contemporary pyjamas. He lifts his face to his mother's, and presses his cheek to hers.

I will not pray. I cannot do that. This is not a prayer, but it is a rapprochement, a ceasefire, a divesting of pain.

St Botolph, I read in a leaflet, is the namesake of this church and the patron saint of travellers. I stand by the altar, mindful of taking small daily steps back to myself. It has taken me almost four years to accept that Teddy will not have the life I would have chosen for him.

I look at the chipped Madonna and resist the temptation to reach out and touch her; instead I bow my head briefly, mindful of what mothering entails.

I think for a moment of all those who have gathered here;

centuries and centuries of people making their way into the small cocooned space, bringing with them their collective heartaches and sorrows. Mine are not particularly different. I understand that now, and will use it to the good.

There will still be all of Teddy's difficulties to deal with. Some of my hopes for him will be dashed, others will be exceeded. Perhaps in the future there will be a scientist who can magic SMN. There will still be the people and the scrutiny I wish weren't part of our lives. But I will no longer be walled in, and Tom will be with me. Sometimes both nothing and everything can change.

I sit for a while longer in the calm, quiet space, feeling myself steeped in a common, century-spanning humanity. All will be well. I feel it in my heart.

I walk softly in my socks to the door, and to the birdsong outside.

Acknowledgements

Every book that reaches a reader's hands is the fruit of a team effort. Huge thanks are due to the brilliant trio who have worked with me on this one. Emma Herdman, Senior Editor at Hodder, Abby Parsons, Editorial Assistant at Hodder, and Becky Ritchie, my agent at A M Heath, are creative, determined, whip-smart, and a joy to work with. Heartfelt thanks.

Thank you also to the wider team at Hodder & Stoughton, especially Karen Geary, Naomi Berwin and Sarah Christie. I am very much the beneficiary of their combined talents.

Thank you to Linda Longshaw, whose early reading helped to crystallise Anna as a character, and to Dr Corinne Hayes, for advice on paediatric protocols and procedures. Any inaccuracies or embellishments are my own.

Another Place, which fascinates Isaac, is Antony Gormley's.

I am grateful to the many SMA support sites which formed the basis of the research for this book. They are, above all, a testament to formidable children, parents, medics, and scientists.

A Q&A with
Kay Langdale

What inspired you to write about a marriage put under strain by the realities of caring for a child with a life-limiting illness?

It seemed to me to be the perfect hot-house for dialling up all the pressures placed on any contemporary marriage: the juggling of roles, the polarisation of tasks, the need to be a filter between the world and your infant child, which is the same for every parent. It allowed me to explore what are frequently gender issues within a marriage and also some of the key drivers of motherhood. All mothers are protective, all mothers occasionally feel somewhat besieged, and Anna's situation allowed me to push this further.

You write from the perspective of different characters in your books. Why do you choose to do that?

In the case of this book, I chose to write from multiple perspectives after writing the first draft in the third person. That version felt too removed and detached to me, as if in somehow using the third person the story lost a degree of emotional rawness and openness; I felt somehow that we couldn't get under Anna's skin and understand how pincered she is by the desire to do absolutely everything she can for Teddy, which stems from her capability and competence, and her absolute inability to ask for help, which stems from her pride. Using the first person also helped me to explore what Tom feels more immediately; the push–pull between his loyalty to his family and his attraction to Eliza, and the fact that he feels so pushed away by Anna. The boys' voices also helped to build the picture of the whole family dynamic. It became clear to me as I wrote them that what Anna intuits is correct; Teddy is in fact far more robust than Isaac. In giving Isaac a voice, it allowed his watchfulness, and his empathy, to inform the whole novel.

Why do you think Anna finds it so hard to ask for help?

I think Anna finds it so hard to ask for help for a number of reasons. Firstly, prior to Teddy's diagnosis she's a woman who has aced the challenges in her life. She has a good job which she has juggled successfully with parenting Isaac. She has a good marriage, and feels in control of her life. The fact that she no longer feels this to be the case is huge for her. I think there is genuine difficulty too; she's an intelligent woman and realises that she is in the position of having to sift and evaluate all the information that is given to her. By definition this means that she has to challenge some of it, which becomes a rebuttal of help or advice. I think she also feels that her default setting has to be strong because Teddy is not; and that because Teddy is vulnerable she must be invincible. I think it's a classic case of mothers feeling that they have to 'set' themselves – like a navigational course – in direct relation to what their children need. For most mothers, this lessens in relation to a child's growing independence but my intuition is that with a child who has a life-threatening illness, this subtle, gradual recalibration is disrupted.

How do you find writing from the perspective of a child?

I love writing from children's perspectives – it's been a dominant motif in all of my books. All of my central child figures are watchful. I think children are generally so observant and so mindful of the adult world, which is frequently unreliable, mystifying or censorious. I think children frequently see through to the heart of things because their emotional vision is not so cluttered or preconceived, and that's why their perspective is so interesting to write. Isaac sees Anna's vulnerability when others do not.

Writing about a child with such a serious illness requires a lot of research – how did you go about doing this?

I did lots of research while writing this book. I was very mindful that whilst it is not intended to be a novel about the intricacies of caring for a child with a life-limiting illness (there are many brilliant non-fiction accounts which do that), it was important for it to be factually correct and to honour the truth of that experience. Therefore, I spent a lot of time on websites which deal with the issues, practicalities and therapies available to a child with SMA type 2. Like Anna, I also watched lots of YouTube videos posted by parents describing their experiences. I researched university and hospital projects which are currently trying to find a cure for SMA because I knew that was exactly what Anna would do, and that she would have this knowledge at her fingertips. I spoke with a paediatrician about diagnosis protocols and procedures. What was uppermost in my mind was that the novel should be factually correct about SMA, even though the actual focus and theme of the book is the emotional fallout of the diagnosis.

Do you think, given the right circumstances, Tom would have engaged in a relationship with Eliza, or do you think he fundamentally would never have betrayed Anna?

I think that's a tricky question, although there was never a version of the book where Tom did leave Anna, which I guess is conclusive.

The starting point for the novel was how two people could find their way back to each other once their relationship was cracked by circumstance. In order for this to be feasible, Tom had to have enough loyalty and decency to make staying with Anna a credible narrative for him. However, when Eliza, Tom and the boys are playing the straw game at the party, Anna is suddenly mindful of a different family shape for them, and I wanted the reader to be aware of that too. One of the questions at the heart of the novel is whether society judges someone more harshly if they leave a marriage when a child has a life-limiting illness, even though we know the impact of divorce is primarily emotional. My intention is always to come to the page without judgement, allowing the reader to decide for themselves.

Kay Langdale is the author of seven novels: The Way Back to Us, The Comfort of Others, Away From You, Choose Me, Her Giant Octopus Moment, What the Heart Knows *(Rowohlt, Germany) and* Redemption *(Transita; published as* If Not Love *by Thomas Dunne Books.)*

Visit Kay's website at www.kaylangdale.com. Follow her on Twitter: @KayLangdale.